TO THE STARS

A POWERFUL PROHIBITION NOVEL

RENEE EDWARDS

❀ Created with Vellum

To Jason, who believed

MAP OF DOMAMUNDI

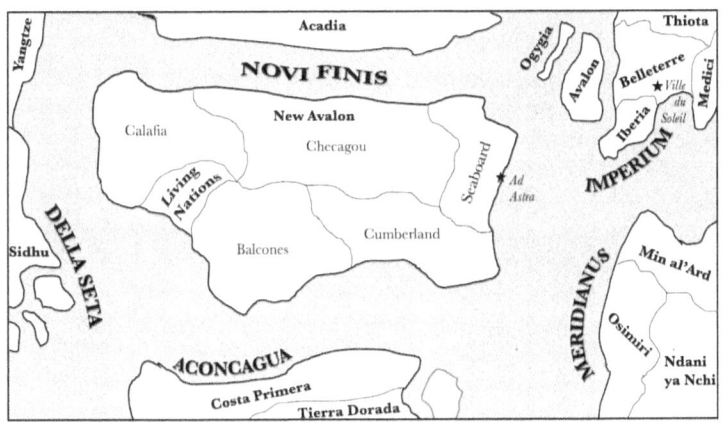

Love is not love
    Which alters when it alteration finds,
    Or bends with the remover to remove.
    O no! it is an ever-fixed mark
    That looks on tempests and is never shaken;
    It is the star to every wand'ring bark,
    Whose worth's unknown, although his height be taken.

              — WILLIAM SHAKESPEARE, "SONNET 116"

CHAPTER 1

CECILY

*E*veryone called Ad Astra the City that Never Sleeps, and for once, Cecily wished they had it wrong.

As the auto moved through the familiar avenues, the energy was palpable. Restaurants and bars were still packed, though it was nearing midnight. Evening performances were ending, and crowds spilled out of theaters and onto the sidewalks, fur coats hanging open despite the cold to display silks and sparkling jewels of every color and description. Normally, she would be out there among them, but tonight was not a normal night. Not by a long shot.

With a sigh, she gazed longingly at the passing skyscrapers, which stood proud and shining against the dark sky. It looked peaceful up there. Quiet. A part of her longed to leap from the auto, select a building at random, and hop in the elevator. Then she would press the button for the highest floor and ride all the way up. Even if the city lights blotted out the constellations she'd always loved, perhaps she'd find some sanctuary there. She could hide herself away from prying eyes, with only the birds for company.

Instead, when Sims pulled up to a stoplight, Cecily slid lower in the plush leather back seat. Even with the privacy granted by the smoked glass of the windows, she felt exposed. The ocean journey had been uneventful, but now that she was back in the city, it was only a matter of time before the vultures descended. She had felt so confident when she'd left to study abroad, like she was finally taking charge of her life once and for all. Now here she was, slinking back with her tail between her legs and a scandal nipping at her heels. It was humiliating and exhausting, and all she wanted to do was make it home so she could crawl into bed and forget about everything for a while.

But as they turned the corner onto the Grand Boulevard, that beautiful reverie was quashed by the mass of photographers and reporters camped out on the manicured lawn in front of Dearborn House. Cecily sighed.

"Do you want me to go around the back, miss?" Sims asked, his tone sympathetic.

The notion of putting off the confrontation just a bit longer was tempting. She'd have a chance to eat, sleep, and even take a bath before the onslaught. But she'd already spent days plagued by the dread of this moment, and the thought of one more night of that, especially now that the prospect was literally staring her down, seemed unbearable. She sighed.

"No, Sims. I think it might be best to meet the enemy head-on."

"Yes, miss." Sims pulled the auto off the street and into the curved driveway before coming to a stop in front of the house. He parked, got out, and immediately came around to open Cecily's door. As he did so, the illustrious members of the press closed ranks around the car, jostling each other for a better view. Cecily took a deep breath and plastered on her most charming smile. She drew strength from the familiarity of the gesture, almost a ritual at this point—donning her armor. Girding herself for battle.

Then her door was open, and she was stepping out onto the pavement.

A barrage of camera flashes met her exit. Her palms tingled in response, but she pointedly ignored them. The reflex was still manageable; if she could only get inside, away from all the prying eyes, she would be able to keep it in check. So she pulled her new coat

—peacock-blue wool with a fox-fur collar that artfully framed her face—tighter to block the icy wind coming off the harbor.

"Hello, boys," she drawled, looking up at the throng from under the brim of her hat. "Long time, no see."

"Miss Dearborn, over here!"

"Cecily, why did you come home on such short notice?"

"Smile for the birdie, sweetheart!"

The pungent smoke of flashbulbs filled the air as the lights continued to burst in her face. This was one thing she had not missed at all while she was overseas.

"Cecily," called a reporter at the front of the scrum. Glancing over, she saw it was Stewart Mills—an old timer on the society beat, but all things considered, a decent enough sort. "Is there any truth to the assertions that your homecoming is connected to the fire that destroyed a portion of the University of Belleterre's historic library last month?"

Cecily clicked her tongue. "Stewart, darling, isn't there some actual news in this city that needs covering? A bank robbery, perhaps? A politician stepping out on the missus?" She lifted her chin, gazing down her nose at him. "Why don't you go out and get a real scoop and stop wasting your time with the likes of me, hmm?"

He didn't respond, merely gave her a wary look as the others in the crowd began shouting her name again. Thankfully, Sims had gotten her bags from the trunk, and now he took her elbow and began steering her through the mass of humanity toward the house. She continued to wave and banter but never stopped moving, and before long, she was in the foyer with the door closing behind her. She let out a sigh of relief that echoed against the marble.

"Are you all right, miss?" Sims said.

"Yes, Sims," she said. "I'm fine. Thank you ever so much for the assist."

Sims nodded. "Well then, I'll see about getting your bags squared away."

"No need, Sims," an authoritative voice rang out from the stairs. "I'll take care of it. Just leave it there by the umbrella stand."

Sims deposited the bag on the floor as Pearson, the Dearborns' long-time butler, reached the foyer.

"I am sorry about that band of scavengers, Miss Cecily," he said as he helped her with her coat. "We contacted the authorities, but they said the street is a public area, and the press has a right to be there, however infuriating they may be."

"It's all right," Cecily said. "The city has to get its gossip from somewhere after all."

"A gossip's mouth is the devil's postbag," Pearson grumbled as he took her hat, and Cecily felt a surge of warmth at the familiar curmudgeonly devotion. "In any case, there's coffee and nibbles waiting in the study, if you're hungry."

"Oh, bless you," she said, giving herself a quick check in the mirror and smoothing down her finger waves. "I haven't had a thing all day. I'm famished."

"Mr. and Mrs. Dearborn said they would be up directly," he said. "They just arrived home from a fundraiser."

"Well," she said, forcing some levity into her voice, "best not keep them waiting. We all know patience is not their strong suit."

She began her trek to the study, a room that had seen many a dressing-down in its time.

"Oh, and Miss Cecily?" Pearson called out.

She paused and turned back, curious what else there might be to discuss.

Pearson smiled, a little sadly, with more sympathy and under-standing than was probably considered proper for his station. "Welcome home."

Tears threatened behind Cecily's eyes, but she pushed them away, a habit she'd perfected from long practice. She focused instead on being detached. Self-possessed. Those were the things that had helped her survive this long. Before she retreated into herself entirely, though, she conceded, just a little, to the welcome kindness. Stepping forward, she placed a hand on the butler's arm and gave it a gentle squeeze. "Thank you, Pearson."

He nodded once.

Taking a deep breath, she turned once more toward the study. As she crossed the threshold, the sounds of the house faded away; the thick Persian carpet and upholstered walls of this room tended to swallow them up. It always made Cecily feel like the rest of the world had ceased to exist, as if this room were a pocket world unto itself. She was fairly sure her father had done that on purpose. Because to him, it was.

Just as Pearson had said, there was a spread of tea and sandwiches on the table in front of the divan. She sat down and poured herself a cup—no milk, two sugars. Her stomach rumbled, and she devoured one of the delicate smoked salmon finger sandwiches. When she picked up another, though, she found herself reluctant to eat it. The worst of her hunger sated, her attention had shifted to her apprehension at the upcoming conversation with her parents. This was not a new worry; it had been her constant companion during the days-long voyage from Belleterre. It was, she knew, part of her punishment. She could have been home in half the time coming by airship, but the ocean journey gave her the maximum opportunity to stew.

Just then, she heard voices in the hall, the volume increasing as the speakers came closer. She dropped the uneaten sandwich back onto the platter and got to her feet. As the study door opened, she joined her hands in front of her demurely, exuding the kind of poise that had earned her top marks in deportment.

Her father stormed in first, a tall, broad bull of a man, still wearing his dinner jacket, though he'd dispensed with the tie. His hair was fashionably slicked back from his ruddy face, but he had refused to go so far as getting rid of his trademark handlebar mustache, no matter how many of his set were going clean-shaven these days. Cecily suspected this was a never-ending source of irritation to her mother and felt a grim niggle of satisfaction.

"Cecily Anne," her father said brusquely as he crossed to his desk, where he opened an elegant teak box to retrieve a cigar.

As he trimmed and lit it, his wife glided into the room, still giving Pearson instructions over her shoulder. Melanie Bedford Dearborn was one of the great beauties of her generation, lithe and graceful with the thick dark hair and green eyes that Cecily had inherited. Now well into middle age, she looked ten years younger and was, as always, turned out in impeccable style. She was a vision in her beaded gown, her chiffon scarf drifting behind her like gossamer.

When she saw Cecily, though, the vision wavered. Her mouth settled into a grim line, and she gave her only daughter an assessing look, head to delicate silk pumps. Not for the first time, Cecily's mother found her wanting.

"For pity's sake, Cecily." She closed the door and walked to the sideboard to fix herself a drink. "Stand up straight."

Cecily suppressed a sigh. Her posture was perfect, honed by years of obligatory ballet lessons, but she knew arguing was pointless. This was more or less what she'd been expecting.

"How was the voyage?" her father said finally, puffing away.

"Fine," Cecily said. "Calm seas all the way through. The northern lights on the second night were especially impressive."

Mr. Dearborn made a thoughtful noise and nodded. "I always have enjoyed that particular part of sea travel in the winter."

Across the room, Mrs. Dearborn banged the crystal decanter back onto the bar tray. "Oh, stop it, both of you. There's no point in making small talk when we all realize what's happened."

Mr. Dearborn sighed, and Cecily dropped her eyes to the floor. Mrs. Dearborn turned her fierce gaze to her daughter. "When we decided to let you go abroad, the agreement was that you would work on getting these… episodes under control. Do you remember that?"

"Yes, Mother."

"And yet," Mrs. Dearborn continued, "we find ourselves embroiled in a crisis bigger than anything that happened before you left." She sipped her drink. "Care to explain yourself?"

Cecily cleared her throat and looked up, glancing back and forth between her parents. "I was making progress. Truly. The Belleterrans are on the cutting edge of research, and there have been some significant developments lately in the origins of special abilities. Before I left, I was reading up on theories of how the human body can interact with and manipulate ambient electricity at the atomic level."

Mr. Dearborn's eyes lit with interest. Whatever distance existed between them, he did share some of her interest in the mechanics of the physical world. He'd built his fortune on them, after all. "Manipulate? Does that mean there's a way to collect and store that energy..."

His voice trailed off as Mrs. Dearborn leveled him with a devastating glare. He busied himself with brushing away a bit of cigar ash that had fallen onto his cummerbund, and she returned her attention to Cecily.

"None of that matters," Mrs. Dearborn said. "If you're still unable to control your... your..."

"Magic," Cecily said quietly. "My magic."

Mrs. Dearborn recoiled at the word. She went out of her way to never say it, as if the very mention of magic were forbidden. It wasn't, though. At least not yet.

Nobody had thought the magical ban would go through when it was first proposed in New Avalon's legislature. The sponsors had come from the fringes of the political parties and been considered something of a laughingstock. But the naysayers had underestimated the lurking fear of magic and those with magical abilities in this new age. In times past, magic had simply been a regular part of life, with practitioners regulating themselves and keeping any threats and imbalances in check. Over time, though, the rise of science and development of new technologies—wondrous and wholly mundane—had made magic seem old-fashioned and irrelevant.

But rather than fading into obsolescence, the old ways acquired a different kind of strength—that of sowing fear and suspicion across the country. New Avalonians who hadn't been raised with exposure to magic only knew there were people out there with power that was beyond their comprehension, power that felt like superstition and secrecy in the face of their orderly, reliable lives. And they couldn't let that stand. Not in their land of equality and progress.

And so, the Embargo had come to pass.

The Embargo had forbidden the practice of magic throughout New Avalon. Conjurors, or practitioners who had no natural magical ability but gained some degree of power through practice and study, were vilified—fired from their jobs, cast out of communities, their books burned and left in ashy heaps in the streets. Adepts, while also barred from practicing magic, had a slightly easier time of it, in the court of public opinion at least. Adepts had been born with their magical talents; it wasn't as if they'd had a choice. Merely *having* an ability was not the problem—using it was.

But in the Dearborns' political and social circles, that wasn't good enough. When Cecily had started manifesting powers that allowed her to channel electricity at age twelve, her parents had demanded she do whatever she could to suppress her power. If word of it had gotten out... Well, it was just not the thing for a respectable family like theirs. What would people think?

High school had been a torment. Only the promise of leaving for university had kept Cecily going at some points, so she'd been devastated when her mother insisted she "take some time to consider her options" after graduation. Cecily had known what that really meant: staying home, staying out of trouble, and landing a husband. She had lasted six months before desperation drove her to concoct an escape plan. She could go to Belleterre, where the Embargo did not reach, to learn what she could about magic in general and her own powers specifically, so that she could keep them under control. So that fear of them would not dictate her life. It was the only argument that could have swayed her mother, and she had nearly wept with relief when it worked. But her studies had not gone according to anybody's plans.

As the two women stared at each other, each stubbornly refusing to break the silence, Mr. Dearborn cleared his throat.

"Cecily, what your mother is trying to say—"

"What I *am* saying," Mrs. Dearborn cut in, "is that this situation needs to be dealt with once and for all. The incident in Belleterre would always have been a disaster, but the timing is particularly inopportune for us, with the vote on the infrastructure bill coming up."

As one of the nation's foremost industrialists, Mr. Dearborn traveled in rarefied circles, hobnobbing with other members of society's elite in private clubs around the city. Against this opulent backdrop, factions routinely emerged based not on personal feeling, but mutual interest. Among the most selective and secretive of these, which counted Cecily's father as a member, was the Reason and Prosperity Coalition. The group of businessmen and politicians was dedicated to promoting what they called a "traditional" agenda for New Avalon—one that, among other things, had been a driving force behind the Embargo's passage. Led by the bombastic Colonel Emerson Teasley, the billionaires and Members of the National Congress who made up the Coalition plotted among themselves to ensure that the country grew in the way that best fit their vision and lined their pockets. An RPC-backed infrastructure bill that would steer millions into Dearborn Consolidated's coffers was up for a vote before the Congress within the next week. The papers were reporting strong resistance from the opposition.

"I'll say again that I think you're worrying for nothing," Mr. Dearborn said, his words tipped with irritation. "Sutterfield and Turner-Hoff have both assured me that the deal is in the ba—"

"Sutterfield and Turner-Hoff are idiots," Mrs. Dearborn said over him. "I've always told you Vandermark was a better bellwether for these sorts of things."

Mr. Dearborn harrumphed. Thaddeus Vandermark was the MNC representing Ad Astra. He'd also been a close friend of Mrs. Dearborn's in her school years. These two qualities left him open to constant disparagement from Mr. Dearborn. He liked to proclaim that Vandermark was a "toady," the absolute worst epithet in his arsenal because it implied that the man used flattery and cunning to get his way rather than good old honest aggression. For her part, Cecily didn't find Vandermark any more sycophantic than the other men her father palled around with, but it was true that he was shrewd when it came to turning a situation to his advantage. Mr. Dearborn probably would have appreciated that more if their goals had aligned consistently, but they didn't. So Vandermark remained persona non grata in her father's graces.

"In any case," Mrs. Dearborn said, taking a cigarette from the case on the mantle and lighting it, "it was bad enough that your brother has hared off on a fool's errand at such a critical time. We don't need any of that." She gestured vaguely toward the scene on the lawn.

"Yes, where is Herbert, anyway?" Cecily asked.

"He's in Costa Primera at the moment," her father said, a touch defensively. "Exploring new business opportunities."

Even in her state of heightened anxiety, Cecily could barely suppress a snort. If he was exploring anything down there, it was the bottom of a liquor bottle or the quickest way to divest pretty girls on the beach of their bathing clothes.

Mrs. Dearborn took a long drag on her cigarette. "The point is, Cecily, we have given you ample opportunity to sort yourself out, and it has come to nothing. Worse than nothing, actually. So we have enlisted some outside assistance."

"Outside assistance?" Cecily asked. "What do you mean?" It was entirely out of character for her mother to bring a stranger into unpleasant family business.

"We've hired a consultant," her father said. "A specialist for cases such as yours."

Cecily felt the color drain from her face. She'd heard of these "specialists", who claimed they could purge adepts of the compulsion to do magic. They maintained that natural magic resulted from an imbalance within the body and that pulling that imbalance back into alignment, or harmony, rendered the potential for magic dormant. In theory, this would allow adepts to lead respectable, productive lives. The reality, however, was that harmonic therapy was quackery at best and malicious cruelty at worst—ice water baths, drug-induced catatonia, in some cases even trephination, in which a hole was drilled in the skull to expose the brain directly to oxygen.

"Father, no," Cecily said, a tinge of desperation in her voice. "Please, I—"

"Oh, spare us the histrionics, Cecily," her mother said. "We've indulged you for far too long. It's time to get this… situation settled once and for all. Every girl in your deb year is married or engaged at the very least." A look of something that might have been genuine concern flitted over her face, but it was gone before Cecily could be sure. "You're not a child anymore, and we will not indulge your whims any longer."

"Mother, I—"

"Enough." Mrs. Dearborn kept her voice quietly controlled, and that made it all the more cutting. "This is what it means to be a grown-up. We all have to make sacrifices for the good of the family."

Cecily stood wordlessly, staring at the carpet and trying not to cry. All was quiet in the room until Mrs. Dearborn stumped out her half-finished cigarette in the ashtray on Mr. Dearborn's desk.

"I, for one, am going to bed," she said. "You should get some rest, too, Cecily. Dr. Fairchild will be here first thing in the morning."

Cecily tried to swallow around the lump in her throat.

"Come along, Arthur," Mrs. Dearborn said over her shoulder as she breezed out of the room.

Slowly, Mr. Dearborn extinguished his cigar in the same ashtray his wife had just used and followed her to the door. He cast one last look, of apology or possibly regret, at Cecily before stepping into the hallway and easing the door shut behind him.

Then Cecily was alone.

CHAPTER 2

DANIEL

Daniel was late.

Being late was bad, as he'd only been back at Dearborn House for a week and had not yet built up the level of camaraderie he needed to smooth over such an infraction. Pearson was a decent and fair-minded boss, but he'd already approached the limits of that decency by hiring Daniel in the first place. As they both knew, that decision had been influenced more by the memory of Daniel's father, the former and widely beloved groundskeeper at Dearborn House, than it had by anything related to Daniel himself. The butler was not liable to let any transgression, even a small one, slide.

Daniel tugged the starched collar of his underfootman's livery as he bounded down the house's back stairs two at a time. There was no one in residency just then except the family, which meant the morning would be less frenzied than if they'd had guests. Even so, Mrs. Dearborn was exacting in her expectations of the household, which meant all hands on deck.

When he pushed open the door, the kitchen was in full swing, with the cook shouting instructions at the underfootmen who were readying breakfast to be taken up to the dining room and scullery maids bustling about to take care of various tasks. Daniel hoped that amid all the hubbub, no one would notice him sneaking in, but it was in vain.

"Mr. Sullivan!" Cook bellowed from the stove. "Good of you to join us!"

Daniel flashed her a disarming smile. "Well, you know, I had planned on maybe working in a round of golf today, but breakfast service is a good time, too."

She gave him a supremely unimpressed look before turning back to the soup she'd already gotten started for lunch, which was precisely what he'd been hoping for. He was still getting used to this version of himself, and frankly, he suspected he was laying the jovial, carefree persona on a bit thick, but nobody seemed to notice. The newer staff didn't know any better, and to the employees who had been there in his father's time, this Daniel tracked closely with the one they remembered. They didn't realize how much had changed since then.

Loath to attract any more notice, he hurried over to join the other underfootmen at the line of silver trays weighted down with mutton, bacon, kippers, pastries, fruit, and a host of other foods that could keep a working-class family fed for a week—and probably would, once the leftovers came back downstairs. He hoisted a tray, only to look up and see Pearson staring pointedly down at his pocket watch.

"Your day begins at eight, Mr. Sullivan," he said. "Not eight fifteen, not eight ten, not eight oh one. Eight o'clock *on the dot.*"

"Yes, sir," Daniel said, tossing a stray lock of hair out of his eyes. "Sorry, sir. Won't happen again." He tried another smile, but Pearson wasn't falling for it.

He arched an eyebrow as he put the watch back into his trouser pocket. "See that it doesn't. Now make yourself presentable and get upstairs."

Sighing, Daniel set his tray back on the table and smoothed his hair into place. Then he lifted the tray again and followed the other footmen to the dining room.

The curtains had been thrown back from the windows, and the winter sunlight gleamed on the rich wood paneling. The table was dressed in immaculate linens, and Gerald, the first footman, had already laid out the china, crystal, and silver. Daniel and the others set the food out along the table's length, making sure each dish was ready for serving. The family members typically came down individually to eat between eight-thirty and ten, and they expected the food to be ready for them.

Just as the men were finishing up, Mrs. Dearborn glided in, looking careless and beautiful, as always. Daniel wasn't sure how she did that. He knew she and Mr. Dearborn had been out late the night before, but she looked as fresh as a daisy and ready to make the domestic staff's life a living hell. Daniel wondered sometimes if she recognized him from his time at the house as a boy, but that would require her seeing the servants as individuals, which she did not.

"And do make sure the committee is composed of our preferred candidates," she was saying to Emily, her social secretary, as George pulled out her chair and draped the waiting napkin over her lap. "Last time, the director went off-script, and it was a *disaster*. You know I expect better."

"Yes, ma'am," Emily said, jotting notes into her ever-present notepad. Emily had worked for Mrs. Dearborn for years and mastered the skill of keeping her face carefully blank, but when she caught sight of Daniel, she did widen her eyes in a subtle but eloquent expression of spleen. Daniel gave her a quick sympathetic smile, then ducked his head and slipped out the door, grateful it wasn't his turn to stay in the dining room to wait on the family.

Not that his next duty was much better. It was helping Mr. Dearborn's valet, Tompkins, prepare Mr. Dearborn's clothes for the day. They brushed his jacket, shined his shoes, and laid out his shirt and trousers, all as the master of the house's snores reverberated through the door to his bedroom. If the younger Mr. Dearborn, the infamous Herbert, had been in town, Daniel would have assisted his valet as well. Herbert, though, had been off in parts unknown since Daniel had started working at Dearborn House—and good riddance.

Next, Daniel went downstairs to join Gerald, who was preparing the special-occasion silver for an afternoon tea scheduled later in the week. Gerald was a bit of an odd duck, though Daniel supposed he might be, too, if his sole purpose in life was looking after another family's cutlery. They spent an hour retrieving and rearranging various bowls, platters, and ladles until Gerald wandered off, muttering under his breath about candlesticks and freeing Daniel up to go back to the kitchen to check in.

Daniel had been at these sorts of tasks for days now, and they still left him feeling oddly disconnected from reality. It was almost as if they were being carried out by someone in another time, another life —a cross between a bad dream and a haunting. When he'd left this house behind all those years ago, he'd never intended to come back. He'd expressed that sentiment frequently, in fact, with quite a lot of colorful language. And he definitely hadn't pictured himself *in service*.

But then Cecily Dearborn had come home.

He hadn't thought much of the news when he'd first heard it, aside from the dull, distant pang he often felt when he came across Cecily's name. Then the whispers had started—of accidents, of abilities. At first, he'd thought they were the same baseless speculations that popped up from time to time around most prominent citizens of New Avalon; hells, it wasn't even the first time he'd heard them about Cecily. But it soon became clear that the rumors carried new weight in Daniel's world. It was suddenly crucial that someone from that world was insinuated into Dearborn House to keep tabs on what was happening, and with his connection to the family, and Cecily in particular, Daniel was the obvious choice.

That was how it had been pitched to him, anyway. Technically, he'd had a choice in the matter, but he was fairly certain everyone involved knew it was a sham. He'd been given far too much over the years to back out when he was needed. Thinking on it as he strode through the halls of Dearborn House, he sighed. Having a sense of honor was a real son of a bitch sometimes.

He was almost to the kitchen when he heard Pearson call his name. He turned to find the butler walking toward him.

"Mr. Dearborn is having a visitor this morning," he said. "He's requested ice for drinks in the study."

Daniel's eyes flicked to the grandfather clock at the end of the hallway, which showed the time as not quite ten.

"They're having cocktails at this time of day?" he blurted, then winced internally. He was usually better than this. The tendency of his mouth to get ahead of his judgment was an affliction he thought he'd finally mastered, but he every so often, his control slipped. He could only hope Pearson wouldn't take it as an impertinence. Luckily, Pearson seemed as bemused by their employer's idiosyncrasies as Daniel was.

"I'm only the messenger," he said. "Be quick about it, though. His guest should be arriving any time now."

"What type of guest?" Daniel said as he fell into step next to the butler.

"A physician," Pearson said. "Some sort of specialist or other. Fairhope, I think? No, Fairchild."

"Do I need to stay to serve?" Daniel said.

Pearson frowned. "I don't think so. I got the impression from Mr. Dearborn that the conversation required... discretion."

Daniel's brow wrinkled at that. A meeting with a mysterious doctor the day after the prodigal daughter had returned from overseas? It was possible the timing was just a coincidence, but somehow, Daniel doubted it. Pearson turned off into a side hallway with a nod, leaving Daniel to his errand.

In the kitchen, Daniel retrieved one of the silver ice buckets from the pantry, went to the refrigerator, and began emptying ice trays into it. He was still nervous around this contraption. The old way of getting ice—using a hammer and pick to chip it off an enormous block set into a cooling box—had been a pain, but the convenience of these new machines didn't come free. He'd heard stories of the unstable cooling gases igniting, causing multiple injuries and at least one death among the kitchen staffs of the city's most expensive homes.

And what did they need ice for today anyway? It was well below freezing outside. They all knew, however, that Mr. Dearborn always got what he wanted. So if he'd asked for ice, then by the heavens, he would have ice. With a sigh, Daniel slid the refilled trays back into the refrigerator, wrapped the ice bucket in a towel to stave off melting, and headed to the study.

It was the first time he'd been in this room since coming back to the house. He'd never liked it much as a kid; it had felt more like a museum than a room in somebody's home. It seemed smaller now, less intimidating, but still not particularly pleasant. He'd always preferred the library on the opposite side of the house. Neither of the elder Dearborns were especially big readers, so that room hadn't received as much attention and updating as the others. While hardly shabby—*nothing* in this place was shabby—it was a bit less pretentious. Quieter. More peaceful. A good place to curl up alongside Cecily on a rainy afternoon to read…

Coming back to himself, he shook his head. What was wrong with him? Was he getting nostalgic? For *Dearborn House*? The absurdity of it boggled the mind. He wasn't sure how long he could keep this up.

Just as he was getting the ice bucket settled onto the bar cabinet, he was drawn out of his abstraction by a dull creak somewhere behind him. He spun around, wondering if someone had followed him into the room without him noticing, but everything was still and empty. He frowned. The house was getting on in years, having passed through multiple generations of Dearborns, and it occasionally made the odd groans and grumbles that came with old buildings. This had sounded different, however. More like the weight of a body stepping on the heavily carpeted floor.

He was debating whether to investigate or just chalk it up to an overactive imagination when the decision was made for him by another sound—voices out in the hallway. Mr. Dearborn's specialist had arrived, which meant it was time for Daniel to make himself scarce.

As he slipped out the door, he saw Pearson escorting the man toward the study. He was tall, with thinning blond hair swept back from a pinched face. His suit was expensive and well-tailored but understated, veering away from anything that could be considered flashy or gauche. Daniel knew the look of him. He was the type who had gone to expensive schools and then expensive colleges, never having to strive very hard for any of it. He would have played polo or rowed crew until his age caught up with him, and now he was settled into portly middle-age. He would call people things like "old boy," if he deemed them worthy of his notice.

Daniel hated him immediately. Or the idea of him at least. The luxury, the privilege. The doctor was the embodiment of this entire house—this entire life—walking around in bespoke loafers, and spending so much time in close proximity to that life after being away was truly making Daniel feel ill. Wrapped up in these thoughts, he took the corner a bit faster than he might have otherwise and collided with someone coming from the other direction.

The person's hands came up to catch Daniel's shoulders for balance, and he instinctively reached out to steady them, his own hands coming to rest on a narrow waist.

"I'm so sorry—" he began, just as the other person said, "Oh, please do excuse me."

Taking a step back, Daniel found himself face-to-face with Cecily Dearborn.

He'd been anticipating this moment for the past few days—for the past few years, if he were honest—but he found he still wasn't ready for it. Seeing her up close like this again felt so familiar, so *normal*, yet also like standing too close to a stranger. They'd been the best of friends once. But she had become a distant figure over the years, in all the ways that counted.

He'd watched her grow up from afar, tracking her exploits through photos in the papers. Both Dearborn siblings were fixtures in the society pages. While Herbert was the more likely of the two to wade into fountains, crash brand-new autos, or end up in gin-soaked screaming matches with paramours, Cecily was featured often, too. She always seemed to be holding court in fancy hotel bars and sweeping out of nightclubs in evening finery. She was witty. She was aloof. Some columnist or other, trying to be clever, had even bestowed a nickname upon her: the Snowflake—complex, beautiful, and cold. And the label had stuck.

It was hard to remember, sometimes, what they'd ever had in common.

Today, though, she seemed more like the girl he'd known. She wore a simple hunter-green dress with long sleeves and a drop waist. Her leather shoes were elegant, yet practical—a sight better than those ridiculous satin evening slippers, which were little better than socks— and her bobbed hair curled in soft waves around her face, free of any sparkling clips or bands. Even dressed in what passed for casual attire among her set, she was stunning. Like her mother, she looked beautiful in every circumstance; unlike her mother, she seemed tired this morning, with dark circles under her eyes.

Suddenly realizing his hands were still at her waist, he snatched them away. Thankfully, she hadn't seemed to notice, distracted by social niceties.

"I must apologize," she said. "I suppose I was woolgathering rather than—oh!" Her eyes went wide. "Daniel? Daniel, is that you?!"

Daniel sighed and squared his shoulders.

"Miss Dearborn," he said with a respectful nod.

"Oh, don't Miss Dearborn me. You used to call me Cece, for heaven's sake."

Daniel smoothed down the front of his uniform. "That was a long time ago."

Some of the light faded from her eyes, replaced by uncertainty.

"What are you doing here?" she asked in a more restrained tone, then flushed. "I'm sorry. That sounded terrible. What I meant was, how is it that you've come to be here again?"

"Well, I needed a job," Daniel said. "And Pearson was a good friend to my father all those years ago, so..."

"Oh, yes, of course," Cecily said. "How is your father?"

"He passed," Daniel said. "Not long after... well, once he didn't work here anymore."

Cecily looked stricken. Seemingly without thinking, she reached out and squeezed his hand.

"I'm so sorry, Daniel."

Warning bells blared in Daniel's head. It had been less than five minutes, and here he was—painfully, viscerally reminded of what it was like being pulled into her orbit. In all of his imaginings, he hadn't seen this moment playing out quite this way. He thought he'd see her for the first time in a formal setting. She might notice him, perhaps give him a nod of recognition, but otherwise carry on with whatever it was posh people carried on with—planning galas or collecting stamps or something. He hadn't expected her to look at him as if it hadn't been a decade since they'd last met, with those ridiculous, long lashed eyes that had always made him believe in things.

This wasn't what he'd signed up for. He needed to get away from her. Fast.

"Yes, well. It's been years ago now. But thank you." He set about extricating his hand as delicately as possible.

"Could we—" Cecily began, but Daniel was already saying, "If there's nothing else, Miss Dearborn, I should probably get back to work."

He stepped back to incline his head deferentially and cringed inside as her face fell even further.

She clasped her hands in front of her. "No, no, don't let me keep you," she said, voice cooling into politeness. "It's good to see you again, Daniel."

Daniel gave her a final nod, then turned and all but ran back to the kitchen.

CHAPTER 3

CECILY

Cecily watched Daniel go, trying to make sense of the emotions roiling inside her. She'd been delighted when she recognized him. He'd been so important to her once, and in that first moment, something warm that she hadn't felt in years stirred in her chest. But the way he'd looked at her, as if she were a stranger, or worse, someone deserving of his scorn...

Turning once more toward her father's study, she pushed away those thoughts. This was the absolute last thing she needed at the moment. It was time to see Dr. Fairchild.

She crossed the remaining distance slowly and paused with her hand on the knob. *I can do this,* she told herself. Heavens knew she'd been through worse. She just needed to remain objective. Gather information and evaluate. Not jump to conclusions.

Squaring her shoulders, she pushed open the door and strode into the library.

She was so busy trying to emulate her mother's easy poise for this encounter that it took her a moment to realize the room was empty. Her steps slowed, then stopped, leaving her standing next to the coffee table as she took in the divan and armchairs, the fireplace, and the east-facing windows with their view of the street. No Dr. Fairchild. Her father was absent, as well.

That was odd. This was where her parents had said they would be meeting, and Pearson had confirmed it when he told her that the doctor had arrived.

Where could they be? Perhaps Dr. Fairchild needed to use the washroom? But what about her father?

Cecily's eyes settled on the liquor bottles arrayed on the sideboard and decided that wherever he was, she was going to use his fortuitous absence to get herself a drink. Yes, it was ten o'clock in the morning, but she'd sometimes had wine with breakfast in Belleterre, and this was essentially the same thing, right?

With quick steps, she crossed the room and picked up one of the crystal tumblers. She paused for a moment, taking in the bucket of ice someone had brought up. It was silly, having it out on a frigid day like this, a classic example of her father doing something just to show that he could. Usually, she appreciated a chilled drink, but out of principle, she poured herself a few fingers of her father's best scotch, neat.

She knocked half of it back in one gulp and coughed against the burn. She'd been hoping for a jolt of liquid courage, but as the fire of the alcohol mellowed into something softer and warmer, she found it was having the opposite effect. She wanted to disappear inside that softness, pull it around her like a blanket and forget about doctors and scandals and powers. Forget about awkward conversations and Daniel scrambling to get away from her.

It had never been like that when they were children. Daniel had been her closest ally—her refuge. The first day they'd met, she'd been running from Herbert, who was in one of his towering rages over some inadvertent transgression on her part. On that day, he'd somehow insinuated himself between her and all of her usual hiding places inside the house, so she'd slipped through the conservatory and out into the gardens. It had been a beautiful spring afternoon. The sun was warm on her face and the scent of plants heavy in the air, but she only had a moment to appreciate it before she heard Herbert's footsteps behind her. She put on a burst of speed and plunged down the gravel path toward the fountain at the edge of the grounds. If she could only make it to the fountain and the wooded area beyond that marked the edge of the property, she would be safe. He was never able to find her back there.

Her breath was loud in her ears as she ran, but she could still hear her brother gaining on her, his heavy tread accompanied by the occasional heated and highly detailed threat of what she was in for. With a sinking feeling in her gut, she realized she wasn't going to make it to safety. If she didn't think of something quickly, he was going to catch her.

Just then, she rounded a corner and spotted the hedge that ran along the brick wall enclosing the roses. Without stopping to worry about the scolding she would receive for dirtying her clothes, she dove behind it, setting her back to the wall and tugging her legs up so Herbert wouldn't be able to see her feet as passed. Seconds later, he went thundering by and disappeared down the path without any hitch in his step. He hadn't noticed her.

Cecily pressed her forehead to her knees, trying to get her panting under control. The trouble was it wasn't just the exertion that had gotten to her; it was what her mother called her "fretfulness." Sometimes, Cecily became so overcome with fear or worry that she couldn't do much of anything—even breathe. Mrs. Dearborn had no patience for it. She always ordered Cecily to pull herself together, which only made things worse. Eventually, she'd dragged Cecily to a doctor, who'd taught her how to count the seconds of her inhales and exhales, and that was what she tried to do now. *In-two-three-four. Out-two-three-four. In-two—*

Something touched her hand. Worried that Herbert had found her after all, she jerked her head up, yanking her hand back and getting ready to bolt. But it wasn't Herbert. It was a skinny boy, about her age or maybe a little older, with unruly dark curls falling over his forehead. He wore grubby overalls and had blue eyes that shone even in the shadows. He held some kind of book in one hand and had reached to touch her with the other, but now it hovered in the air between them.

"Are you all right?"

"My, my, brother…" she tried, still fighting to catch her breath. "He…" Her voice hitched on a gasp.

The boy shifted so he was sitting next to her and took her hand in his. He sat there with her as she slowly got herself under control. Once she was calm again, she worried he would ask her questions she didn't want to answer or drag her back up to the house. But he didn't.

"I'm Daniel," he said. "Want to see some of my drawings?"

So they sat there and looked through his sketchbook. As they turned the pages, Cecily felt some of the dark heaviness she carried around inside her chest all the time lighten a little. Daniel didn't seem to care, or even notice, that Cecily was shy and clumsy at making conversation, the way the other children she knew did. He was happy to explain his drawings and tell her stories and make her laugh.

When the light began to fade, she reluctantly made her way back to the house, but only after she had promised to return to the garden the next day. Predictably, her mother had taken one look at her dress and declared her a menace before sending her to wash up for dinner; in those days before Cecily's powers had manifested, Mrs. Dearborn had been far more indifferent to Cecily's behavior — to her very existence, really—until it came to grooming, which was sacrosanct in the household. But when she arrived at the table, nobody asked what she'd been doing all afternoon. Herbert didn't look at her twice, his fury from earlier forgotten. It was just like any other night, as if the afternoon had never happened. Except for one thing— now she had Daniel.

Until she didn't. Until he'd disappeared. That had been bad enough, but then she'd gotten her powers, and everything had become more complicated and difficult and impossible to control.

She was shaking her head and turning toward the divan, raising the glass to her mouth for a second sip, when she saw it. A shoe. A very expensive men's shoe, poking out from behind her father's desk. A shoe which was presumably attached to someone lying on the library floor, where nobody had any business lying.

Very slowly, Cecily set her glass down on a nearby end table and walked toward the shoe. As she rounded the corner of the desk, she found that there was indeed someone sprawled there—a large blond man, presumably the esteemed Dr. Fairchild. Instinctively, she dropped to the floor next to him and rolled him over so she could figure out how to help, but when she got a good look at his face, her hands flew to her mouth in horror.

Dr. Fairchild was dead. Very obviously, very gruesomely dead. The skin of his neck was black, with angry patches of red peeking through. Charred streaks disappeared under his collar and ran up his chin, stopping just under his bottom lip. His mouth was open in a silent scream, and his eyes bulged. While the skin around them was untouched, the blood vessels had burst under the strain of whatever had happened, turning the whites a ghoulish red.

Cecily's mind reeled. Someone had clearly attacked him, but who? How had they managed to get into the house? How had they gotten out without someone seeing them? And why did he have what looked very much like electrical burns?

Cecily felt her stomach go terribly, sickeningly cold. The old, familiar sense of panic that she'd spent years learning to master clawed its way up her throat, and she squeezed her eyes shut, desperate to keep it at bay. *Stop it*, she commanded, the order directed at both her brain and her body. *Stay calm. Figure this out.*

She grasped frantically for the reassuring constancy of the scientific method. She just needed to treat this like the experiments she performed at university. Observe. Hypothesize. Sort through the information until it made sense.

But she couldn't. There were too many variables, too many unknowns. She tried to breathe deeply, to settle her racing thoughts, but it seemed like no matter what she did, she couldn't get enough air. She needed help. Yes, that was it. If there was someone else in this with her, she would be okay. They could untangle this mess together.

But who was going to help her? Her parents? They already thought she was a danger and an embarrassment. Even if they believed she'd found Dr. Fairchild in this state, which was far from certain, they would still lay this at her feet. He was there because of her, after all.

And however unseemly the stories attached to her might have been seemed in the past, this was murder. *Murder*. That meant law enforcement. Interrogations. Charges. And she had no defense. She had been alone in the room with Dr. Fairchild. He bore the marks of her power. It was her word against what they could see with their own eyes. She had nothing. Her worst fear had come for her, and she had *nothing*.

Despair rushed in, overpowering, and the fretfulness took her.

CHAPTER 4

DANIEL

Daniel berated himself all the way to the kitchen. What a disaster. He was admittedly not as skilled at socializing as Oliver, but by the heavens, he should have been able to have a simple conversation. It was going to be hard to observe Cecily if she was hiding from him because he'd been such a creep.

As he reached the final bend in the hallway, he detected the low rumble of Mr. Dearborn's voice. A few steps later, he noticed the door to the phone room was open. Calling it a room was really gilding the lily; it had been a storage closet in his younger days. The transformation had been a result of the Dearborn insistence of having the best of everything, as quickly and ostentatiously as possible. There had been telephones in the house for years, but those phones had only connected the family to the rest of New Avalon. Once transoceanic lines had been established, Mr. Dearborn had demanded one. Never mind that he'd had them installed in his many offices; the house obviously needed one, as well. But even the man's substantial hubris couldn't overcome the limits of technology. In their residential neighborhood, which lacked the infrastructure of the business district, a special terminal near the street was required. And so the phone room, with its plush chair and stained glass door, was born.

To be fair, it seemed to get a good bit of use. Just days ago, Daniel had heard Mr. Dearborn bellowing down the line at Herbert, who had taken a break from being an embarrassment in Ad Astra to be an embarrassment in Costa Primera. Daniel was genuinely grateful not to have been on the receiving end of the tirade. Mr. Dearborn may have gone full papa bear if anyone else had a contrary word to say about Herbert, but he himself had plenty.

Today, the bit of the conversation Daniel heard as he passed— something about transfers, possibly with a bank in Avalon?—was far less interesting, but still somewhat urgent, based on the tone of Mr. Dearborn's voice. Something about it niggled at Daniel. He turned the impression over in his head as he walked, and after a moment, it clicked. Why was Mr. Dearborn down here when he was supposed to be upstairs with the doctor? True, important business calls must be part and parcel for the head of a multinational corporation, but the timing seemed questionable. Someone needed his attention *right then?*

As Daniel entered the kitchen, where breakfast dishes were returning and lunch service preparations had already begun, seemingly unrelated details began connecting in his mind. The phone call. The creak in the study. Cecily walking toward that room, alone. Something was wrong. Very, very wrong. Grabbing a tray of glasses to make himself look busy, Daniel swept back out of the kitchen and retraced his steps to the second floor.

As he approached the entrance to the study, he slowed his pace, searching the hallway for anything suspicious. Satisfied that nothing outside the room was amiss, he eased up to the door, knocking softly. "I have those hors d'oeuvres you requested, sir," he called, hoping to elicit some kind of response.

None came. There was only a low, rhythmic sound coming from inside the room that he couldn't quite identify.

Whatever the sound was, it didn't bode well, but Daniel had come too far to turn back now. Steeling himself, he twisted the knob and eased the door open. As soon as he crossed the threshold, he recognized the sound—one that was sickeningly familiar, though he hadn't heard it in years.

The sound of Cecily hyperventilating.

Swearing under his breath, he pulled the door shut behind him and deposited the tray he was holding on a nearby table. Then he rounded the desk to find Dr. Fairchild's ruined body, eyes still fixed on the ceiling, and Cecily perched on the floor next to it. She was rocking slightly and had both hands pressed to her mouth. The sound of her ragged breathing seeped out from between her fingers.

Daniel swore again. He'd been anticipating something bad, but this exceeded all expectations. What had happened? Had she attacked Dr. Fairchild? Lost control of her powers? She had seemed distressed in the hallway, but not angry or overwrought.

And he hadn't come back upstairs on a whim. There had been definite signs that something strange was going on. Something not of Cecily's making.

He needed to get her out of there immediately.

Slowly, so as not to startle her, he knelt on the floor next to Cecily. He cleared his throat. "Miss Dearborn," he said and immediately felt like a dolt. They were far past pleasantries when she was in this state. They didn't have the time for it.

"Cecily," he said with a bit more force.

She didn't look at him, but when he scooted closer, she didn't flinch away. Did she recognize him, or was she so far gone his voice wasn't registering? "I know this is a terrible shock, but you're all right." He paused, correcting course. "You're going to be all right. The thing is, I need you to breathe. Can you do that for me?"

She dropped her hands, and her lips moved, forming a word that looked like *no*. She continued to stare and rock, but he took that as a good sign. He reached out and took both of her hands in his, trying to lean farther into her line of sight.

"I used to help you when we were kids. Do you remember that? We would inhale together—" He took a big lungful of air. "And exhale." He blew it out. "And eventually, you wouldn't be upset anymore." Cecily took a breath, and if he wasn't mistaken, it was a bit longer than the one before it. She took another, then another, each one progressively longer, which was a relief, but he knew they couldn't sit there like that forever. Someone could walk in on them at any second.

"Cecily, we have to leave, right now. If anyone finds you like this, it's going to be very bad. Do you follow?"

Her eyes flicked to this, and the anguish he saw in them told him she followed perfectly. And he understood now that he was in way over his head. He would have faced an army to protect her based on that look. Except, it wasn't an army he had to worry about—it was the authorities and all the narrowminded people who would be calling for blood over this because they were afraid.

"Come on." He pulled Cecily to her feet.

She was still letting out little shuddering breaths now and then, but her steps were steady enough. He held up a hand as they reached the door, signaling for her to wait while he checked the hall. Everything looked clear, so he led her out into the hallway, but as they approached the servants' stairs, he heard voices. He threw his arm out, pressing Cecily to the wall and waited for what seemed like an eternity, heart loud in his ears, to see if they would be discovered before they'd even made it off the floor. Eventually, though, the maid and footman who were carrying fresh linens upstairs passed right by them, oblivious to their presence. Daniel let out a relieved breath and tugged Cecily into the stairwell.

As they descended, he turned over the essential facts of the situation in his mind. If there was any silver lining here, it was that Cecily hadn't screamed when she'd found the body. But then, she wouldn't, would she? She never did. She buried all the bad things—her hurt, her fear, her sorrow—deep, deep inside herself so they couldn't touch her.

Did they know that, whoever did this? Presumably, they had timed the murder so that Cecily would be found with the body—and she would have, if Daniel hadn't gotten there first. Screaming would have drawn people to the library, ensuring the discovery of the crime. But would a scream have cast doubt on her guilt? In his experience, someone who'd just committed a crime would not have done anything to summon help to a scene that was so obviously incriminating.

So perhaps the killer had planned for her silent anguish rather than hysterics. They might have been counting on her being discovered insensible with fear, the man at her feet presumably a victim of her unhinged power, just like the unfortunate library in Belleterre. But how would they have known? Only a handful of individuals were aware of these episodes of Cecily's, and she hadn't chosen to confide in any of them. Cecily never showed that side of herself to anyone willingly.

She showed it to you, a small voice inside his head whispered, and he pushed the thought away.

Sticking to the passages used primarily by the staff, they reached the ground floor of the mansion without incident. Daniel felt the vise of tension around his chest ease ever so slightly as they reached the hallway that led to the garage. Not much farther to go now. If their luck could hold just a bit longer, they would be out of the most immediate danger, and he could stop for a minute and come up with something approximating a real plan.

The garage, a large, high-ceilinged space that had only recently been modified to accommodate autos rather than horses, was dim, still, and cold when Daniel opened the door and maneuvered the two of them inside. He took the keys to the least-flashy of the Dearborn's many vehicles from the set of hooks on the wall and led Cecily to the gunmetal-gray sedan near the front of the garage. He deposited her in the passenger seat, then hurried to unlatch and throw back the wide garage doors that opened toward the street. Once he finished, he ran back to the car and started it, wincing at the roar that broke the morning quiet. He eased out onto the driveway, threw the car into park, then hopped out to resecure the doors. It was only a matter of time before someone in the house realized something was wrong, but he didn't want to speed things along by leaving the garage wide open for any passersby to see.

He swung back into the driver's seat, and finally, they were on their way. Daniel threw a quick glance over his shoulder just before turning onto the street and steering away from Dearborn House. Nobody was running frantically out of the house yet, which he figured was the best he could hope for. Now, he just needed to put some distance between them and that miserable place he was now leaving behind for the second time in his life.

He was so wrapped up in his musings that it surprised him when Cecily spoke.

"What will happen to him?" she asked in a strained voice.

"I'm sorry?" Daniel said.

"What will happen to him? Dr. Fairchild. When they... When someone else finds him?"

Daniel had admittedly given little thought to whatever was going to happen once they'd left the house, but even if he hadn't, Cecily asking about the doctor before addressing any of her own troubles would not have been his first prediction.

"They'll call the authorities, I'm sure," Daniel said. "Then the inspectors will come out to investigate. There will be an autopsy on the body, to collect evidence and determine a cause of death."

Cecily let out a strangled laugh. "I doubt they'll need an autopsy for that. It seemed pretty obvious to me."

The slightly manic tone of her voice then was better than her blank unresponsiveness in the study, but only just. From the corner of his eye, he saw she was trembling with shock and cold. When they pulled up to an intersection, he took a moment to shrug out of his livery coat and hold it out to her. She just stared at it for a moment, as if it were some mysterious object she couldn't quite identify, but eventually, she took it and slipped it on, curling her hands into the too-long sleeves, then wrapping her arms around herself.

"Our first order of business now is to get you somewhere safe," he said. "We can worry about the rest later."

"Before that, there's something I should tell you," she said, then paused as if she was summoning her courage. She took a deep breath. "I'm an adept. I didn't come into my magic until after you'd left, but it's true. And my power is manipulating electricity."

"I know," Daniel said.

She stared at him for a very long moment.

"*You know?*" she burst out finally, her indignation seeming to snap her out of her fugue state.

"Yes," he said calmly. "It's why I was in the house in the first place. My... associates heard murmurings of what happened in Ville du Soleil and wanted to keep an eye on you. So I became a footman."

"You were *spying* on me?" Her tone shifted toward icy even as her cheeks flushed with anger.

"Monitoring," he corrected. "And a good thing I was, too, or what would have happened to you today?"

That seemed to take some of the wind out of her sails. She still looked as if she wanted to argue, but instead, she shifted in her seat and glared out the window.

"I didn't kill that man," she said quietly.

"I know that, too," he replied, realizing as he said it that he actually did. Whatever doubts or uncertainty he'd had before were gone now. She was innocent. He would have bet his life on it.

The silence stretched between them until she spoke again.

"So, who are these associates, exactly?" Her eyes widened. "You're not Shining Light, are you?"

Daniel gave a startled laugh. "Oh, hells no. Nothing like that." Shining Light was a militant organization who, once the Embargo passed, had begun a campaign to "reclaim New Avalon in the name of all magic users, adepts, and conjurors alike, who will crush the heretics beneath their bootheels and lead true believers and disciples of magic into a bright new future." They had claimed responsibility for a variety of bombings and assassination attempts and were considered extremist zealots by just about everyone, even those sympathetic to practitioners.

Daniel despised them. But that wasn't the point right now. He considered his words carefully, not sure how much to share with her.

"We're friends to practitioners. Dedicated to resisting and rolling back the Embargo, but the right way."

She raised her eyebrows. "And they had you monitoring me?"

"Yes."

"Why?"

"There have been low-level rumors for years that you had abilities, but we'd largely dismissed them." That had been in no small part because he'd assured everyone that she had no natural magic, but he wasn't going to tell her that. It was galling enough that he'd been so far off the mark. "Then the whisper networks around town lit up after the fire happened and everyone discovered you were coming home. Suddenly, the rumors seemed a lot more plausible." He gave her a sideways glance. "Were you responsible for the fire?"

There was another long moment of silence.

"I was," she said finally, voice barely audible over the engine.

"What happened?" he asked, careful to keep his tone gentle.

Cecily sighed. "A group of us had gathered in the library to study. We were discussing some papers we had just read on magical physiology, and the debate got fairly heated. I wasn't angry, exactly—just frustrated because I felt like Robert wasn't listening to me. It didn't matter. It was enough."

She uncrossed her arms and began toying with a loose thread on her skirt. "My hands sparked. That part of the library is centuries old, built almost entirely of wood and filled with paper. It went up like a candle. The fire service got it under control before it spread too much, but the damage was done. The dean of the university had a nice, long chat with my father on the phone, and after negotiating a substantial donation to the school, they agreed nothing would be reported to the Belleterran authorities, but it would be best for me to finish up my studies in New Avalon." She slumped in her seat, leaning her head against the window. "Not that that's ever going to happen now."

Daniel cleared his throat, wanting to reassure her but not sure how.

"Well, let's not get ahead of ourselves. Like I said, safety is our top priority. We can deal with salvaging your academic career later."

Cecily gave him a weak smile and nodded, then she lapsed back into silence, watching the city go by outside.

They weren't far from their destination now. This was a very different part of the city than the one they'd just left. More crowded, far more working-class, maybe a little rough around the edges, but also friendly and vibrant. The streets were largely empty today because of the cold, but curtains had been thrown back to let in the sun, putting cheerful living rooms on display. The booths and counters inside diners were full of people getting on with their day. Daniel had lived in neighborhoods like this his whole life. He felt at ease here. Like he belonged, as much as he belonged anywhere.

The auto, however, stood out like a sore thumb. It would draw far too much attention if he left it parked on a curb; he'd already noticed a few heads turning to follow its path. So at the first opportunity, he veered into an alley and wound his way between the buildings until he found a spot that seemed sufficiently clandestine. Then he cut the ignition and glanced around to make sure nobody had spotted them.

"Come on," he said to Cecily as he opened the door and swung out of the car. Even blocked by the buildings, the wind was like a knife. Daniel cursed himself inwardly for the chivalrous gesture of giving up his coat, but there wasn't anything to be done about it now. It wasn't like he could ask for it back. Not if he wanted to maintain an ounce of self-respect.

They walked a block or two down the alley, past wooden fences that had all faded to a uniform dull gray, then Daniel waved Cecily through a gate into a bare but well-kept backyard. He led her up the back steps and opened the rear door with a key from a ring in his pocket.

It was warm inside, which was something, but otherwise, the interior was unremarkable. It was a rooming house, indistinguishable from the dozens that dotted the city, except that this one was usually somewhat or even completely unoccupied. The landlady received rent for the entire building every month like clockwork, so she'd apparently decided it was no concern of hers whether or not anybody was actually in the rooms. She had proven herself to be discreet, and the arrangement worked well whenever someone needed a place to lay low.

Like now.

Daniel and Cecily moved up the worn wooden stairs to the second floor, then down a central hallway. Daniel stopped at the last door on the right and opened it with a different key. He ushered Cecily into the room with a sweep of his arm and stepped in behind her.

He looked around the small space, taking it in with Cecily's eyes. The room was simple—rough floorboards and whitewashed walls that had seen better days—but it was tidy, and there were homey touches here and there. A wrought-iron bed was topped by a colorful quilt that almost hid the fact that the mattress sagged, and a worn armchair with a needlepoint throw pillow sat on a rag rug in front of a small fireplace. A cross-stitch sampler hung on the wall over a washstand with a chipped bowl and pitcher. There was a door to a tiny closet next to the radiator, and a window with net curtains overlooked the street.

"I know it's not fancy," he said, feeling a reflexive need to defend the place to her. "But you'll be safe here."

Cecily's chin came up a bit. "I lived in a flat very much like this when I was in Belleterre. Most students did. I don't require anything fancy."

Daniel wasn't sure what to say to that, so he just nodded.

She sat in the armchair and picked up the pillow, wrapping her arms around it. "What are you going to do?"

"Well, first I'm going to take the car back," he said. "Things are going to be messy enough without throwing a charge of grand theft auto into the mix."

"Won't it look suspicious, though?" Cecily asked. "You showing back up with the car after I've apparently fled a crime scene?"

"Oh, definitely," Daniel said. "I'll leave it a street or two over for someone to find. Might even send a message over to let them know where to look, if I'm feeling generous."

"You're not worried they'll connect it to you?"

Daniel shook his head. "There's no guarantee anyone knows I'm the one who took it. And even if they do, it won't matter. There's no reason for me to be going back there anymore."

"Isn't there a way for them to find you? Can't they just use the address that they have for you?"

"Well, they do have *an* address," Daniel replied. "But it's not *my* address."

Understanding dawned in Cecily's eyes. "Ah…" Her gaze drifted around the room once more before settling back on Daniel. She swallowed. "What am I going to do?"

"Stay here," Daniel said. "Try to get some rest. There's a bathroom at the end of the hall, but other than that, I don't think you should leave the room until I get back."

Cecily's brow furrowed. "So I should just… sit?"

Watching her face, Daniel softened a bit. If she'd seemed tired before, now she was clearly exhausted, but she just as clearly did not want to stay in the boarding house. He remembered what that was like: feeling so forsaken and powerless that he was desperate to do something, anything, to keep the emptiness from swallowing him whole. He'd sworn then that he would never let himself be that powerless again, and he'd succeeded. Now, maybe, that's what would allow him to help Cecily.

"Let me talk to my people," he said. "They—we have resources that can help. We'll make a plan. We'll figure this out. But we don't want to go in blind. Understand?"

Cecily looked as if she might argue, but then she pressed her lips into a tight line and nodded.

"I'll be back as soon as I can," he said, trying to reassure her. "Trust me."

As he closed and locked the door behind him, he thought he might have heard a whispered "I do trust you," but he couldn't have said for certain.

CHAPTER 5

CECILY

Cecily did venture to the bathroom at one point in the afternoon, but it was as much out of boredom as anything. Waiting was a tedious business. There was a small collection of books on the lower shelf of the nightstand in her room, but when she tried paging through them, she found she couldn't focus. In the end, she spent most of the day curled up in the armchair under the quilt she'd dragged off the bed, staring at the patch of sky she could see through her window.

This was hardly the first time Daniel had rescued her. More than once, when she'd been mired in a tedious social call or cotillion practice or any of the myriad of agonizing things proper young ladies were required to do, she'd seen Daniel's tousled curls pop up over the windowsill, a grin plastered across his face, and within minutes, someone had come into the room with a matter that needed Mrs. Dearborn's immediate attention. Then Cecily was free to sneak down the backstairs and disappear into the garden or hide in the library with the one person who never made her feel awkward or nervous or sad. And, somehow, after all these years, he'd done it again. There was a symmetry there that pleased her, but it was overshadowed by her uncertainty as to how he'd done it and why he'd had to. Who had gone to such lengths to set her up? What was Daniel really up to, that he had been on hand to help her at all? These were the points she came back to again and again over the course of the long afternoon.

Darkness fell, and Cecily turned on the desk lamp, but still, Daniel did not return. More time passed, and she had to turn up the radiator to combat the falling temperatures outside. She began to alternate between worrying that Daniel had been caught and was never coming back or that he had decided this whole situation was too much trouble and was never coming back. Around eight o'clock, though, there was a knock on the door.

Cecily was up and across the room in seconds, but she hesitated before slipping the deadbolt. "Hello?" she said tentatively.

"It's me," Daniel answered.

She felt weak with relief.

As soon as the door was unlocked, Daniel slipped in, pulling it shut behind him, and slid the deadbolt. The first thing she noticed was that he had changed clothes. Gone was the formal, starched livery uniform. Instead, he wore dark-gray wool trousers and a leather coat in one of the newer styles that stopped at the hips rather than the knees, along with a tweed flat cap. Even without being able to see what was under the coat, Cecily could tell he felt more like himself in these clothes. They suited him, and he moved with more confidence.

She pushed away her musings as he held a bundle of cloth out to her. "I brought you a coat. And some food."

Cecily shook out the garment and held it in front of her. It was an unremarkable brown, and the cut was at least a decade out of fashion, but the fabric was of high quality, and it looked to be roughly her size. She pulled it on, twisting a bit and stretching her arms to test the fit. It would do. That settled, Daniel handed her a small parcel wrapped in paper. She opened it to find a ham-and-cheese sandwich, which she began devouring in large, unladylike bites.

"Oh!" Daniel burst out, startling her. "I brought you something else, too." He began patting his packets, eventually pulling out a smaller bundle of soft gray fabric. He opened it and lifted out a gold object that gleamed in the lamplight.

"What is that?" Cecily asked, dusting the sandwich crumbs off her hands, and he passed it to her. The object was a small oval locket on a chain. Looking at it more closely, she saw that it was engraved with ivy and what appeared to be a capital letter *J*. It looked old.

"It's a charm," he said. "One of the girls at the club, Ebony, made it for you. She can exert influence on people's thoughts, and she infused the necklace with a little of her power. It will keep people from noticing you."

Cecily's eyes widened. This was nothing she'd ever encountered before—both natural magic *and* conjuring, the kind that required extensive study. In her experience, the combination of the two forms was rare. "Really? It will hide me?"

"Well," Daniel said, "to a certain extent. It's not powerful enough to work on someone who is actively searching, but it will encourage casual onlookers to let their attention just kind of drift past you. So if anyone should ask them about it later, they won't have any recollection of seeing you at all."

Cecily looked at the locket again, both intrigued and a little frightened by such a contrivance. Still, she could use pretty much all the help she could get, so she set about clasping the chain behind her neck.

It was only after she finished that something else Daniel had said fully registered. "Wait. Did you say something about a club just now? What kind of club?"

Daniel gave her a half smile that made her chest flutter in a way she refused to examine more closely. "You'll see."

He led her down the stairs and into the alley, where a different auto awaited them. Once they were settled inside, Daniel pulled out onto the thoroughfare, whistling absently to himself. Cecily knew they must be retracing at least part of their route from earlier, but it all felt different at night. The streets seemed more forbidding now—and lonelier—while the lights shining through curtained windows promised comfort and refuge. Those snug homes seemed downright alien to Cecily just then; safety and security felt like things that were now entirely out of her reach. She swallowed a lump in her throat as they continued on.

Before long, Daniel slowed. They were approaching a building that was larger and taller than the others on the block. Other than its size, though, the building was rather nondescript. It was made of brick that had seen better days, with a tilting water tank on the roof alongside a billboard that was so worn and faded that Cecily couldn't tell what it was supposed to be hawking. She would have guessed the place was abandoned, but Daniel pulled the auto into a dark lot behind it and killed the engine. As he handed her out onto the packed dirt, she gazed up at the building, wondering for the hundredth time what she'd gotten herself into.

"Come on." Daniel jerked his head toward the building, and then, to Cecily's great surprise, he took her hand to pull her along. For a few steps, she just stared down at the place where her fingers disappeared into his grip. Granted, he had done that while hurrying her out of the house earlier, but that was understandable in the heat of the moment. This was… Well, what *was* this?

A gust of frigid air swept past them, and Cecily decided it didn't really matter what it was. She tightened her own hand around Daniel's and hurried after him.

He led her into the alley behind the brick building, and she began her to wonder if he had something against using actual sidewalks. Around to the far side, he stopped in front of a wide metal door. Hunching against the cold, he reached up and knocked three times with his knuckle.

A second later, a slot opened in the door. "Password," a deep voice said.

"Victor, come on," Daniel said. "You can see it's me. Just let us in."

"Password," the voice repeated in the same unruffled tone.

Daniel sighed. "Oracle."

The slot snapped shut. A moment later, Cecily heard the sound of a bolt turning, and the door swung open.

The hallway in front of them was gloomy, lit only by a few caged light bulbs set into the concrete walls. A tall, bald dark-skinned man in evening clothes stepped aside to let them pass. As soon as they were inside, he closed the door and rebolted it with a solid clunk.

"Are we seriously going to do that every time?" Daniel asked, scowling.

Victor shrugged. "The boss lady said everyone needs the password. If she gives the order, I intend to follow it."

Daniel's face relaxed a bit. "Fair enough. Are you doing okay? Want me to have someone bring you a drink of something."

Victor shook his head. "I'm good. Just planning on getting some reading done." With that, he settled himself onto a tall stool positioned under one of the feeble lights and picked up a book.

Catching a glimpse of the cover, Cecily saw that it was by one of her favorite poets, in the original Belleterran. Impressive.

Daniel led her down the hallway to another door, but instead of knocking, he grabbed the handle of this one and swung it wide.

Cecily gasped. A wide, high-ceilinged space, much larger than she would have guessed from outside, opened up before her. Chandeliers hung at intervals around the room, casting light that wasn't much brighter than that in the hallway but felt far more intimate and inviting. A beautifully inlaid wooden floor spread out from the door, and to each side, elegant ramps curved up toward raised platforms that hosted a bar on the right side and an expansive poker table on the left, both flanked by potted palms. Farther in, the walls were papered in deep red and gold, interspersed with golden arches that framed private little dining nooks, and the bulk of the open floor was peppered with matching leather banquettes and tables, where fashionable couples and small groups sat nursing their drinks. At the front of the room, an elaborate gold proscenium arch framed a stage where a troupe of acrobats in sparkling outfits twirled and spun. In the center of the activity, a dancer in turquoise satin trimmed with tulle and lace that looked like sea foam waved her arms gracefully as shining ropes twined around her in complicated patterns. With a start, Cecily realized the ropes were made of water.

"This is a charm school," she said, a statement rather than a question.

Daniel smiled. "It is indeed. The Hierophant—widely considered the best in the city, according to those in the know."

Cecily had heard about these places, of course, once they'd started popping up—hidden spaces where anyone with money to spend could indulge in a taste of forbidden magic. She'd made sure to steer clear of them, knowing she would have been in a world of hurt if she'd been caught up in one of the periodic raids by the authorities. In Belleterre, where magic was practiced openly, with none of the risk or stigma it carried in New Avalon, the notion of such establishments had almost seemed quaint, like kids plotting mischief in a secret clubhouse, away from interfering adult eyes. Now, though... Now, it felt like a lifeline. A place where people might not simply assume she was a monster.

Daniel led her up the ramp to the bar and pulled out a stool for her. She settled on the edge, legs crossed at the ankles, as he claimed the stool to her right. Her gaze drifted over the crowded tables, and she bit her lip.

"There's an awful lot of people here." Her hand drifted up to touch the locket at her throat.

Daniel glanced at her, then at the busy dining area. When he turned back to her, his face softened. "It's fine. Everyone's watching the show, and the house lights won't be up for a while. We'll be okay as long as we stay back here." He gave her a reassuring smile, and she managed to give him a small one in return just as the bartender made his way down to them.

"Daniel," he said brightly, in a Cumberland accent as thick and sweet as honey. "Wasn't sure you'd make it tonight."

"You know me," Daniel said. "Social butterfly, can't help myself."

The bartender snorted.

"Is the boss lady available?" Daniel asked.

"She's with clients, but she should be done in a little bit." The bartender picked up a glass and flipped it into the air before catching it with a flourish. "What can I get you in the meantime?"

"We're here for business, Aaron. Not pleasure."

Aaron tutted. "All work and no play makes Danny a dull boy," he said before turning his attention to Cecily. "What can I get for you, sweetheart? A sidecar to take you away from all your troubles? A bee's knees that will have you dancing until the wee hours of the morning?

Just say the word, and the finest cocktail known to humanity will be yours."

"A club soda with lime would be lovely, thank you," Cecily said.

Daniel snorted a laugh, and Aaron sighed mournfully.

"All this talent, gone to waste," he said, shaking his head. "Club soda with lime coming right up."

"I also enjoy a good club soda," a voice said from behind Cecily.

Cecily turned toward the voice, and her first thought was that she was looking at one of the brightest people she'd ever seen. He was tall and lean, dressed in a white pinstripe suit that practically glowed in the dim light of the bar, accented by a black tie, shiny watch chain, and carnation in his buttonhole. His hair had the look of burnished copper, though Cecily suspected it would be true gold in the sunlight. He held a wooden walking stick that had been polished to gleaming and was topped with an elaborate golden handle.

The bright man settled on the empty barstool to her left, smiling and folding his hands atop his cane. He nodded toward the drink Aaron was setting down atop a napkin on the bar. "I find the bubbles invigorating."

Aaron scowled at him. "You are not helping."

"Deepest apologies," the newcomer said with zero sincerity. "Daniel, are you going to introduce me to this ravishing creature?"

"Cecily," Daniel replied, looking exasperated, "this is Oliver Fullerton. Oliver, this is Cecily."

"*Enchantè.*" Oliver took her hand and brought it to his lips, looking up at her through his unreasonably long eyelashes. As he brushed a kiss over her knuckles, the corner of her mouth quirked up, partially against her better judgment.

As someone who understood the power of cultivating charm, she appreciated his, but she knew far better than to actually fall for it.

"Did you need anything?" Aaron asked flatly. "Or are you just here to kill my business?"

"That's merely a bonus," Oliver said. "I was sent to retrieve these two. Madame Esmeralda is waiting."

Aaron nodded, sobering.

Daniel slid off his stool and laid a hand on Cecily's arm. "Come on. This is who we're here to see."

Cecily felt a sudden rush of trepidation, but no one else seemed agitated or ill at ease. Daniel was still giving her that gentle, comforting look, and that gave her the strength to push her anxiety down and get to her feet.

"Rain check on the drink?" she asked Aaron, and he grinned.

"Anytime, sweetheart," he said with a wink, and he flicked a pristine white towel over his shoulder as he moved to greet a new customer.

Oliver led them around one of the potted palms and opened a door that Cecily hadn't even noticed. He ushered them through, and they walked down another dark hallway, this one narrower than the first, with papered walls hung with paintings and soft carpet that cushioned their footsteps. Cecily had assumed that Oliver's cane was an affectation, but now she saw he limped slightly as he walked. Almost as if he could sense her thoughts, he began talking again, redirecting her attention.

"These portraits are antiques, you know." He gestured at the wall. "The subjects were the bigwigs of Ad Astra back when the city was new. Many people walking down this hallway have said they felt like the portraits were watching them."

"Hmm," Cecily said, because it seemed like the kind of thing that required some acknowledgment.

"Of course, they were probably right," Oliver continued. "There's a secret passage on the other side of that wall with peepholes that let you see into this corridor"

Cecily was about to give a perfunctory nod when his words fully registered.

"Wait, what?"

"And here we are," he said as they approached a heavy wooden door at the end of the hall. In the top panel, a swirling pattern with the words *Madame Esmeralda* was painted in gold. Cecily felt a sinking sensation, as if she somehow knew she would not come away from whatever was behind that door the same.

"This is where I leave you, unfortunately." Oliver gave Cecily a little bow. "*Au revoir, ma belle.* It has been a pleasure."

Cecily couldn't help but roll her eyes as he moved off down the adjoining hallway, and from the corner of her eye, she saw Daniel smile. Then he knocked on the door, and a moment later a low, musical feminine voice called, "Come in."

Daniel opened the door and gestured Cecily into a space that felt even stranger and more otherworldly than anything else she had encountered that night. The walls were swathed in deep-blue velvet embroidered with gold and silver stars. The domed ceiling was draped in silks of similar blues and purples that gathered at the pinnacle, where a golden moon of hammered metal dangled on a chain, surrounded by lit candles. Below the chandelier was a table covered in a cloth that matched the ceiling. The table was spread with a variety of objects, including a deck of cards, a plaster hand, and a pair of dice in a gold dish. In the center was a clear glass globe with a green-gold chunk of crystal suspended within it. And seated at the table was one of the most striking women Cecily had ever seen.

She had the type of clear, pale skin people referred to as "porcelain," and while her eyes and lips were painted, her face was truly dominated by her sharp cheekbones and dramatic brows. A purple-and-gold paisley turban sat atop gleaming auburn curls that spilled down her back, and she wore several gold necklaces over her velvet robes. There were rings on most of her fingers, and her nails were painted a deep red.

"Daniel," she said pleasantly. "Is this her?"

"It is," Daniel said.

"Welcome, my dear." Madame Esmeralda gestured to the empty chair across from her. "Please have a seat so we can get to know each other."

Cecily flicked a glance at Daniel, who nodded, then stepped forward and sank into the chair, crossing her hands in her lap.

"Daniel has told me a lot about you," the fortune teller said.

Cecily, unsure what to say, since Daniel had told her nothing about this woman, just nodded.

"It seems you've found yourself in a bit of a predicament."

Cecily couldn't entirely hold back a surprised huff at the under-statement.

Madame Esmeralda smiled. "Yes, well, we're going to see about that. Don't you fret."

Cecily shifted uncomfortably at the sound of her mother's language in this woman's mouth, but Madame Esmeralda didn't seem to notice.

"Tell me, Cecily," she continued, "have you ever had your fortune told before?"

"No," Cecily said, relieved that her voice came out strong and steady. In her world, fortunetelling was something that happened in back rooms at parties, a titillating misdeed like smoking reefer and necking, and she'd given it a wide berth for the same reasons she'd avoided charm schools.

"Would you do me the honor?" Esmeralda asked. She held out her hands to Cecily, palms up.

Cecily looked at them uncertainly, then flicked another glance to Daniel.

Again, he nodded, his eyes serious.

"All right." Cecily reached her own hands out to settle them onto the fortune teller's. "Is this where we stare into the crystal ball?"

Madame Esmeralda laughed softly. "No. In fact, for this particular exercise, we need to close our eyes." The woman let her own eyes slip shut, her long, dark eyelashes splayed across her cheeks. "Go ahead. I think you'll find this quite illuminating."

After a final moment of hesitation, Cecily closed her eyes as well.

"Just relax," Madame Esmeralda's voice said in the darkness behind Cecily's eyelids. "Breathe. Allow your mind to drift. Feel your consciousness expand and take in your surroundings."

Cecily took a deep breath and waited. She felt startlingly vulner-able like this, on display with none of her defenses in place, but she did her best to follow Madame Esmeralda's instructions. At first, all she could see were the spots behind her eyelids, but slowly, something else appeared, coalescing like mist.

It is nighttime, and she is standing on a street much like the one outside the Hierophant, but something about it seems out of place. It takes her a minute, but then she catches it: the air is warm. She can feel it through the fabric of the thin dress she wears. There are people moving around her, but she can't tell who they are or what they are doing. Her full attention is on what looks like a warehouse in front of her. As she watches, a door opens, and several shadowy figures spill out. She knows, somehow, that they are armed and that they wish her ill. But instead of running away like a normal person, she smiles. She raises her hands, and blue electricity crackles over and around her fingers. She feels the energy building, and normally, she would be terrified, worried that it is about to overwhelm her, but here, she only feels determined. And just when it seems like it might be too much, she unleashes all that power at the figures moving toward her in a great roaring whoosh, throwing up a wall to block their path as exhilaration rushes through her...

Cecily's eyes popped open, and she gasped.

CHAPTER 6

CECILY

Madame Esmeralda sat back in her chair, her eyes on Cecily. "I thought so," she said, a note of triumph in her voice.

Cecily fought to catch her breath. "What... What was that?" she panted.

"Daniel," the fortune teller said, not looking away from her, "I suspect Cecily and I are going to have quite a bit to talk about. Will you have someone bring us some tea?"

"Yes, ma'am." Daniel moved for the door.

Cecily cast a frantic glance at him, and he gave her another reassuring smile, but this time, it did nothing to reassure her. She watched as he slipped out the door, then she swallowed and turned back to Madame Esmeralda.

"Come, my dear," the older woman said. "Let's go somewhere more comfortable."

With that, she rose and walked to the side wall, where she swept aside a panel of velvet to reveal another door.

Was there no end to this place? It felt like a maze. At the rate they were going, Cecily half expected the next room to transport them to a foreign palace or a colony on the moon, but it turned out to be rather ordinary. In the far corner, a radiator rattled away near a window covered in heavy paisley curtains. Nearby, a hodgepodge of worn velvet furniture and a mahogany coffee table atop a burgundy rug formed a comfortable seating area. Floor lamps cast warm light over walls decorated with invitations, ticket stubs, and photos of local performers, many of them signed. On the near side, a folding screen stood next to a rack filled with jewel-toned dresses and wraps. Next to that was a vanity with a large trifold mirror and a variety of boxes and jars. Madame Esmeralda's dressing room, then.

"Please have a seat," she said to Cecily, gesturing to the armchairs.

Cecily, who was beginning to feel this entire night was going to be an endless parade of standing up and sitting down, perched on the edge of a chair as the fortune teller moved to the vanity. Stopping in front of the mirror, she reached up to remove her turban—and took the curls with it. Cecily couldn't suppress a small *eep* of surprise, and Madame Esmeralda glanced at her in concern, but then she smiled.

"Oh, sorry, I ought to have warned you." She ran a hand over her own sandy-blond hair, pinned-up and mussed from the wig. "I'm so used to it, I just forget sometimes."

"No, it's fine," Cecily said faintly, as Madame Esmeralda placed the wig on a mannequin head and disappeared behind the screen.

"Make yourself comfortable," she called. "The tea should be here before long."

A moment later, she came out from behind the screen. She had exchanged her velvet robe for a silk one that was less elaborate but somehow just as exotic, decorated with birds in flight and trimmed in vivid pink. Settling onto a stool at the vanity table, she began removing her jewelry, placing each piece into a tray filled with other baubles. Once that was finished, she dipped a cloth into a jar of cold cream and began cleaning the paint from her face. Cecily couldn't help but marvel at the woman's calm self-assurance—not a façade, like Cecily's own, but true, unshakeable confidence. It felt like something far beyond Cecily's reach.

"I must say," the woman said as smoothed the cloth over her eyelids, "you have done very well taking all this in stride, Cecily. Sorry, may I call you Cecily? I supposed I should have asked before."

Cecily nodded. "That's fine, Madame Esmeralda." At the mirror, Madame Esmeralda laughed brightly.

"Oh, no, please don't. Madame Esmeralda is just my stage persona. You can call me Esme."

"All right... Esme."

Moving on from her makeup, Esme began unpinning and combing out her hair, only to sweep it back up into a neat plait that circled her head like a crown. Just as she was finishing up, there was a soft knock at a door across the room from the one they'd used to enter.

"Ah, that should be the tea." Esme got to her feet to open the door. When she did, a pretty, petite girl with warm-tan skin and dark hair came in with a tray of tea things, which she set on the low table in front of Cecily's chair.

"Oh, you're a lifesaver, Claudia," Esme said. "Did we get any of the chocolate madeleines, by any chance? Alphonse knows I have a weakness for them."

"Sorry, ma'am," she said. "Oliver got the last of them. Lemon was all that was left."

Esme gave an exasperated sigh. "Oliver," she said, shaking her head, but Cecily could detect a note of affection in her tone. "He'll be hearing about that later. The lemon will have to do."

"Can I get you anything else?" Claudia asked, hands folded in front of her.

"No, I think we're fine. Thank you, Claudia."

The girl nodded, throwing a wary glance in Cecily's direction before she let herself out. Esme settled herself in the wingback chair across from Cecily and began pouring out for both of them.

"How do you take it?" she asked.

"No cream, two sugars," Cecily said.

Esme chuckled. "Strong and sweet, a girl after my own heart."

As they both sat back and sipped their tea, a silence descended. It was not a comfortable silence. Cecily had dozens of questions, but she couldn't seem to actually ask any of them. Meanwhile, Esme watched her intently over the rim of her cup. She seemed to be expecting something, but Cecily wasn't sure what.

She picked up the little cake Esme had placed on her saucer and nibbled on it, just for something to do. It was delicious, but it did little to soothe her nerves. She was out of her depth here. She was used to being looked at and to people having certain opinions and expectations of her, but something about this was different. It seemed like Esme wasn't merely looking, but *seeing*. It was unnerving. Nobody ever really saw Cecily.

Except for Daniel. Daniel may have been absent from her life for a decade, she did still trust him. And he had brought her here to this strangely beguiling woman, so presumably, Cecily could trust her, too.

Also, Cecily was the Snowflake. The Snowflake didn't get intimidated. The Snowflake took care of herself. She straightened her spine.

"Daniel tells me you're a friend to practitioners," she said with the cool, detached tone she typically employed over tea, honed on companions who, however erroneously, fancied themselves just as formidable as this one. She did not acknowledge that Esme was clearly more than just a friend to magic users; she didn't have to.

Esme smiled. "I am. We all are here. We don't subscribe to the notion that magic is to be feared."

Cecily nodded. "So, what is it that you do?"

"We try to make the world a safe place for magic again," she said. "To push back against the injustice of the Embargo and help practitioners lead free lives of their choosing."

"How?"

"We use a variety of methods," Esme said. "Some are as simple as providing shelter and employment to adepts who might not have them otherwise. We also have contacts with people in high places, whose access allows them to steer public policy in our favor. And we've helped practitioners escape New Avalon and start fresh overseas." She gave Cecily a sympathetic smile. "Though it seems you've already tried that, and it didn't take."

"Why did you have Daniel spying on me?" Cecily asked, determined to keep her wits about her no matter how kind this woman seemed.

Esme's face remained placid. "After we heard what happened in Belleterre, it seemed expedient to find out more about you. An adept in one of the wealthiest and most influential families in New Avalon? With close ties to the RPC? You can see how that might be of interest to us."

"You were planning on using me," Cecily said, letting her voice go just a bit colder. "How does my now being a fugitive affect your strategy? Am I still the asset you expected?"

Esme cocked her head, and a handful of emotions passed over her face—there was calculation there and maybe something like approval. "Listen," she said finally. "We're going to help you no matter what, for Daniel's sake if nothing else."

Cecily shifted in her seat, at a loss of how to respond to that pronouncement.

"But is there a way that you could reciprocate? Yes, I think there is."

"And what way is that?"

Esme leaned forward to place her cup on the table, then settled back into the chair, tucking her bare feet up underneath her. "Where do you think magic comes from, Cecily?"

Cecily followed her example and put her tea down before answering. "Well, a lot of the most current research suggests there is a genetic component, though the mechanism is still largely a mystery, since powers don't consistently run in families—"

Esme held up a hand, cutting her off. "But why do you think the genes do what they do?"

"Well, they're the product of evolution—they allow our species to adapt to the environment so we can survive."

Esme shook her head. "Evolution has nothing to do with it. At least not the way you mean." She shifted in her seat. "Tell me, how old were you, when your powers first manifested?"

"I was twelve," Cecily said.

Esme nodded. "I had my first vision when I was sixteen." She smiled at Cecily's look of surprise. "I know—fairly old as these things go, but that's how it happens sometimes. Visions are relatively rare among adepts, and that may have something to do with it. Our conjurors have been trying to pinpoint a connection, but they hadn't made much progress even before the Embargo."

"*Your* conjurors?" Cecily asked. Historically, adepts and conjurors did not get along. While they shared an affinity for magic, adepts typically harbored distrust for conjurors, whom they saw as interlopers.

But Esme just nodded. "We don't traffic in the old grievances. I know a bit of what you were studying in Belleterre, and that type of scientific research is valuable. But learning about magic through a practitioner's specific lens can be enlightening as well, which makes the knowledge conjurors have invaluable. I'm getting off track, though—we were discussing visions.

"Even compared to other powers, visions can be… difficult. If your body can suddenly produce flame or turn invisible, the first step is obviously to learn how to control those things. With visions, it's less clear. My first vision was exhilarating, and it was terrifying. I didn't know if what I saw was the past or the future or something utterly fantastic. I wasn't even sure I was still sane. I certainly didn't know what to do about it. But over time, I learned about other adepts with my gift, and I had further visions that helped me place that first one in context. I began to understand what I'd seen. And do you know what it was?"

Cecily shook her head.

"It was a war."

"A war?" Cecily asked. "What kind of war? One that's already happened? Or one that's coming?"

"I suppose you could say it's both," Esme said. "People like to think that the world we live in is singular. That it is all-encompassing and finite. They are wrong. There are worlds beyond our world and a world beyond even those. It is a world inhabited by beings of great power. Their lives are long, and their capacity for wisdom is practically infinite, but so is their penchant for pride. One group of them decided they knew what was best for their kind, and then, for all of creation. They believed they could use their sovereignty to instill a harmonious order across the cosmos. But they were rigid in their thinking; they couldn't tolerate dissent or disagreement. And so sides formed. The unyielding thinkers began calling themselves the Ascended Ones, and the beings they saw as their enemies became the Open Ones. The name was meant as an insult, implying that anyone who didn't subscribe to their beliefs lacked discipline, but the opposition took it on as a badge of honor. And the fight between them began.

"That fight has lasted longer than a human mind can even conceive. According to the stories, the Ascended Ones constructed a magnificent weapon, one they were sure was going to turn the tide for them once and for all. But they were wrong, and when the Open Ones destroyed it, fragments of it were scattered across galaxies and planets, even entire universes. Ever since, both sides have tried to reclaim those fragments and the power they hold." Esme reached into her robe and pulled out a crystal pendant on a long chain.

Cecily dimly registered that it contained a chunk of green stone, just like the crystal ball on the table in the other room.

"This is one of them—just a tiny one, a sliver. Our planet is seeded with thousands like it. Their power has infused the soil, the water, even the air. Even our bodies. That power is the source of our magic, Cecily. And because we possess that magic, that war between those ancient beings is our war, too. We have our own part to play in who will ultimately control the destiny of all that is."

When Esme had begun speaking, Cecily had listened intently, but as the story progressed, her focus had shifted to maintaining a look of polite interest as she revisited every lecture her mother had ever given about making a graceful exit. Because Esme might have been interesting and charismatic, but she was also obviously cracked. What she'd said about injustice and agency had resonated with Cecily. But ancient mystical beings? An eons-long war that somehow involved the humble citizens of her planet, her country, the very city of her birth? It was like a story out of the pulps, although it might even be a reach for them.

"Will you assume your part, Cecily?" Esme asked, seemingly oblivious to Cecily's turmoil. "Will you help us?"

"Why me?" Cecily asked quietly. As insane as the whole thing sounded, she had to know what it was that Esme saw. This was, after all, possibly the first time in her life someone had truly valued what she could do,

"You're very powerful," Esme said. "I don't know precisely how to judge that power, based on our very brief acquaintance, and I doubt you do, either, since you've been forced to suppress it. But I suspect you know it's there. And I think you could do wondrous things with it. You could blaze a path of righteous fury through the world."

Cecily ran her hands down her thighs, smoothing her skirt and taking a moment to collect herself. She had a sense that this was an important moment, but her feelings were all over the place, leaving her muddled. There was exhaustion, because it really had been a very long day. Frustration, because on top of her very long day, she was now having to deal with this… whatever it was. Gratitude, because everyone here had been so generous and kind to her. And guilt, because she didn't think she was able to respond in kind. She simply could not wrap her mind around what Esme was saying. It was just a bridge too far.

"I appreciate everything you've done for me," she said slowly, eyes on her lap. "Truly. But I don't think I'm the one you're looking for."

"You don't?" Esme asked.

"No," Cecily said. "I just want to clear my name so my life can get back to normal." Her old life may have been stifling and grim, but it was still better than the all-consuming terror that had descended upon her as she sat next to Dr. Fairchild's body.

"I see," Esme said. "Well, I'm sorry to hear that." While she had been telling her story, her face had been lively, animated, but now she was calm and composed. Cecily recognized that look because she'd spent years perfecting it herself—she'd slipped into it here just a few minutes ago. Only Esme's eyes gave away any of her inner workings. They were shadowed in a way they hadn't been before.

"In any case," she said, swinging her legs out of the chair and sliding her feet into a pair of silk slippers that had been stashed under the coffee table, "you need to get some rest. Let's find Daniel and have him take you back to the boarding house. We'll figure out what to do next in the morning." She got to her feet and held out a hand to Cecily, helping her rise as well. "I'm sure everything will look a little more manageable after a good night's sleep." She looped her arm through Cecily's, steering them toward the door Claudia had used, and Cecily suddenly found herself close to tears.

"Esme," she said, realizing only after she'd done it that she didn't know what to say next or, indeed, why she'd spoken at all.

Esme stopped walking. "Yes?" she said, eyes scanning Cecily's face.

Several things bubbled up in Cecily's brain, but she couldn't seem to make them come out of her mouth. "Thank you," she finally managed, hardly more than a whisper.

Esme smiled and patted her arm. "Come on. There's no telling what trouble our Daniel is getting up to." And she led Cecily out to the stairs.

CHAPTER 7

DANIEL

Daniel stood in the hallway, gazing at the door he'd just pulled shut behind him. It wasn't that he was worried about Cecily's safety—he trusted Esme implicitly. It was just that... he hadn't liked leaving Cecily. Something inside him was even now protesting that he should be at her side, watching out for her.

Oh, yes, a contrary voice piped up in his brain. *Because that worked out so well for you before.*

Daniel sighed and shook his head, then turned and made his way to the stairs that would take him to the one place where he felt he could let his guard down.

The second floor of the Hierophant was dominated by a long open space that roughly matched the footprint of the main dining room below. It was far less grand than the public rooms—unpainted brick walls and bare floorboards rather than gilt and velvet—and had, over time, become a sort of catch-all storage space for a wide variety of odds and ends. Surplus lumber from old stage sets was stacked along one wall, next to a jumble of battered furniture and a few faded table-cloths. There was an outdated wireless that still sort of worked if the wind was right, a broken accordion that Esme kept saying she was going to have repaired, and some boxes of leftover programs from the last New Year's celebration.

Also, Daniel.

The back corner of the room was sectioned off with folding screens, and that corner contained all of Daniel's worldly possessions. Beside a narrow metal cot, a rolling wardrobe rack and crooked dresser provided storage for his clothes. A small desk and chair sat in front of one screen. On the other screened side of the nook, a small bookcase had been pushed close to a sink mounted on the brick wall. The top of the bookcase boasted a kettle and hot plate, which Daniel used to make coffee. One shelf held a jumble of cups and other mismatched dishes and cutlery. The other two held a few things to actually read but were dominated by his collection of sketchbooks. Posters featuring his favorite acts from around the city and his favorite artists from the museum were tacked up on the walls. It was everything he felt he needed in life, except a bathroom and shower, which were in the dressing rooms just a quick trip away, down the backstairs.

When Daniel had first arrived at the Hierophant, Esme had been at a loss for where to put him, so she'd led him up here, promising it was just for the night. That had been ten years ago. She'd tried to make good on her promise as soon as she could, but Daniel had found he didn't want to leave. Over time, it had become a bit of a running joke, how they would never be rid of him, but he didn't mind. He felt safe up here. He felt calm.

He was planning to stay for as long as they would let him.

Normally, once he'd made it upstairs, the first thing he did was take off his coat and shoes to get comfortable, but his coat was downstairs with Victor, and he was going to be heading out again soon, so there was no point in taking off his boots. Instead, he contented himself with popping into his nook to grab a sketchbook off the desk, then heading to the collection of castoff furniture that had been wedged in among the clutter and dubbed the Lounge, since various friends and club folk tended to gather there to socialize at all hours, including, sadly, when Daniel was trying to sleep.

He slumped onto the worn upholstery of one of the sofas and stared at the cover of the sketchbook for a moment. Then he flipped it open, turning to a page featuring one of his most recent sketches. It was a lavish garden in full bloom. The foreground was dominated by a manicured lawn bisected by a meandering gravel path that led to a small gazebo off in the distance. Hydrangea bushes with daylilies and ornamental grasses clustered at their bases lined the path. To the right, a hedge of roses ran alongside the brick wall that separated a fishpond from the rest of the garden. In the hedge's shadow sat two children, a boy in ragged overalls and a girl in a dress that was too fine for her to be crawling around in the dirt. A careful observer might be able to tell that the children were holding hands. Daniel curled his own hand in his lap, remembering.

He was so immersed in the past that he didn't notice anyone coming into the room until Oliver was practically on top of him.

"There you are," Oliver said, rounding the trunk they used as a coffee table.

As he sank into a nearby chair, his shadow fell across the pages of the open book, and Daniel instinctively snapped it shut. Oliver raised an eyebrow at him. His art wasn't a secret to anyone around the club —least of all to Oliver—and normally, he wouldn't have been so jumpy. But he was feeling off today. Unsteady. Raw.

He settled the book on his lap and schooled his features into blankness. "Here I am," he said, trying to keep his voice light.

Oliver clearly wasn't buying it, but rather than commenting directly, he stretched his legs out in front of him. "So, that was Cecily."

"Yes, that was Cecily." Daniel allowed himself to sink back slightly into the sofa, but he knew better than to let his guard down entirely. Oliver was, of course, already picking up plenty of tells regarding Daniel's mood, but Daniel didn't need to make it any easier for him.

Oliver pursed his lips thoughtfully. "She's quite exquisite. Lucky for her, she seems to take after her Bradford side. Just imagine having to navigate the world looking like old Arthur with a bob." He shuddered.

Daniel narrowed his eyes. "What are you even talking about? You already knew what she looked like from her pictures."

"Yes, well, she's different in person," Oliver said. "There is a certain sense of *joie de vivre* about her."

Daniel snorted. "I wouldn't say she's *joie*-ing much *vivre* at the moment."

Oliver sobered a bit. "How is she doing? Really?"

Daniel sighed. "About as well as can be expected, I suppose."

Oliver nodded, then reached into his pocket for his cigarette case and lighter. "How did she seem when you left her?" he asked as he lit a cigarette.

"Confused," Daniel said. "Unsettled. Overwhelmed. Esme shared a vision with her."

Oliver rolled his eyes. "I wish she wouldn't do that right off the bat. It's the kind of thing you need to work up to."

Daniel shrugged. "She's your mother."

Oliver sniffed. "I don't see how that's relevant."

"I mean," Daniel said, "it's pretty well-established that a flair for the dramatic runs in the family."

Oliver sighed extravagantly. "I will not dignify that with a response."

"You were certainly laying it on thick there with the flattery," Daniel said. "Do you even know any Belleterran beyond the flirty bits?"

Oliver shrugged. "It amused her, and that amused me."

"Well, I guess it's a good sign that she *can* be amused at this point," Daniel conceded.

Oliver shifted in his seat and narrowed his gaze. "So that's how she is. How are you?"

And that was the question, wasn't it? How *was* he? That morning, he'd been driven by urgency and necessity—get her out, get her safe, make a plan. He hadn't had time to worry about things like his feelings. It wasn't until she'd answered the door that evening that it had really hit him—she was truly there with him again, this girl who had been his dearest friend and caused his greatest pain This girl who needed him. There had been a point when he had needed her, too—but she hadn't come then. And he wasn't sure if he'd ever be over that.

How was he? Hells if he knew.

"It's not really about me, is it?" he muttered just to say something, to steer Oliver away from this dangerous topic, but the look on Oliver's face suggested he'd picked up on at least some of the turmoil in Daniel's mind.

"You said you could handle this," he said. "You said you had it under control."

"I can," Daniel said. "I do."

Oliver looked as if he wanted to say more, but then a voice trilled out, "I heard the murderess was on the premises! Is it true?" and Paloma breezed into the room.

The flush was high on her cheeks, the way it usually was after a performance. While she had thrown a robe on over her costume—the blue one with the fancy trim—she still wore her stage makeup with her hair scraped back from her face into its elaborate twist. She was barefoot, revealing toes that had been painted with the same crimson nail varnish as her fingers. Daniel would have guessed that the floorboards were freezing, but the cold never seemed to bother Paloma much. Or the heat, for that matter. She made herself comfortable more or less wherever she went.

"She's not a murderess, Paloma," Daniel said, his voice coming out harsher than the comment probably merited.

She looked down her elegant nose at him as she got closer. "Oh, don't be such fuddy-duddy, Daniel. It was a joke."

She dropped onto the couch next to Oliver and reached out to pluck the cigarette from his fingers. She took a long drag, beaming at him in the face of his scowl.

"I've seen the books here, you know," he said. "I'm aware that you are more than capable of buying your own smokes."

"Yours are better." She passed the cigarette back, glancing around. "But seriously, where is she?"

"She's with Esme right now," Daniel grumbled. "Thank the gods. You would have made a terrible first impression."

Paloma rolled her eyes and stretched. "Please. Like I care what some uppity social climber thinks of me."

"She's not a social climber," Oliver said, and Daniel felt a surge of warmth, but then Oliver continued. "There's nowhere for her to climb. She's pretty much in the uppermost of the upper echelon."

"She's also a fugitive from justice," Daniel said, glaring at them. "Who happens to be innocent. Probably shouldn't overlook that detail."

"Oh, boo-hoo," Paloma said. "Poor little rich girl. With her daddy's money and fleets of lawyers, there's no way she'd get more than a slap on the wrist, even if she'd hacked that doctor to pieces with an ax. I don't know why you even bothered bringing her here."

Daniel scowled. "It's not like that."

Paloma raised an eyebrow. "Oh, yeah? How is it, then?"

Daniel was saved from having to respond by Aaron bustling in the door with a cardboard box in his arms and Ebony at his heels. They made a somewhat comical pairing just then. Ebony wore a sunflower-yellow fringed dress and feathered headband, vivid pops of color against her dark skin, while Aaron was swaddled against the cold in his serviceable coat and hat, a thick but otherwise unremarkable scarf around his neck. An unsuspecting observer would never have guessed they were twins.

"What's that?" Oliver asked, lifting his chin in the box's direction.

"Popped out to get some dinner in between shows," Aaron said.

"You know," Oliver mused, "there is an entire kitchen full of food downstairs."

"Yes," Aaron replied, pulling a carton out of the box. "But the only prepared food in that kitchen at this time of night is Belleterran haute cuisine, which may be posh, but is also lacking in the seasoning department." He opened the carton and inhaled the spicy steam, a look of bliss on his face. "Now that's more like it."

As he unloaded more cartons, Ebony disappeared into Daniel's nook and came back with silverware. There was a flurry of activity as food and utensils were distributed, and soon, Aaron, Ebony, and

Paloma were digging into their servings of stew and rice. Daniel and Oliver exchanged a glance.

"You didn't bring us any?" Oliver asked.

"Some of us are actually working tonight," Aaron said around a mouthful of food.

Daniel made an affronted sound, just as Oliver protested, "I've been working!"

"No, you haven't," Aaron said. "You've been hobnobbing and making sure everyone sees you looking all suave in your new suit, especially that young banker you've had your eye on. The one who played college football or something?"

Oliver scoffed. "As if I would need a new suit to get his attention. He's half-caught already. And it was basketball."

"What about me?" Daniel asked, returning to the matter at hand.

"Yeah," said Paloma. "He spent the day shuttling a wanted felon around the city." Daniel glared at her, and she sighed. "Fine—*alleged* felon."

Aaron paused, the spoon halfway to his mouth. "Huh. I forgot."

Daniel gave him a flat look. "You saw us together less than an hour ago."

"Okay, fair point." Aaron held out the carton to Daniel. "Want some?"

Daniel considered it but, after a moment, he shook his head. "Thanks, but I'll pass."

Aaron nodded sagely. "Thought it might be a bit much for that Ogygian palate of yours."

"Aaron, don't be rude," Ebony said, dabbing at her mouth with a napkin that had been lifted from Daniel's nook along with the silverware. "It's not Daniel's fault he has no taste buds to speak of."

Daniel smirked at her.

Oliver chuckled. "How are our card players tonight, Eb?"

"Flush and overconfident, just the way I like 'em," she replied.

Suddenly, a head topped with a shock of prematurely silver hair popped around the door —Leo, the club's band leader and Esme's right-hand man.

"Paloma," he called, "Dennis has some questions about the lighting setup he wanted to ask you before the second show gets started."

"I went over that with him this afternoon!" she fired back, dropping her spoon into her carton of stew. "Twice!"

Leo shrugged. "I'm just the messenger," he said and disappeared back into the hall.

Paloma sighed and got to her feet, taking her food with her and muttering under her breath as she made her way to the door.

"Be nice," Oliver said as she passed him.

"And don't forget to bring back my spoon!" Daniel shouted after her. The sound of descending footsteps drifted into the room from the hall, but a moment later, they were followed by a set that increased in volume and then a creak on the landing.

"Well, that was fast—oh!" Oliver called out, but when they all glanced at the door, it wasn't Paloma who was standing there.

It was Esme and Cecily.

Without thinking, Daniel got to his feet, taking the two of them in. Their very presence there was a bit of a red flag, as Esme rarely ventured upstairs with the others. Esme had her arm around Cecily, and on the surface, she looked calm and composed. However, Daniel knew from experience that this particular brand of poise was carefully cultivated. Cecily, meanwhile, looked small somehow, even though she and Esme were around the same height. Something had not gone to plan.

"I hope we're not interrupting," Esme said. "I didn't realize there would be such a crowd up here."

Daniel felt color rising in his face as Oliver, Aaron, and Ebony glanced back and forth between him and the door with wide eyes.

"No," Daniel said. "Not interrupting at all. We were just... just, uh..."

"Just finishing up," Oliver said, levering himself to his feet. "Come on, Aaron. I'll help you get the bar ready for the next performance."

"Bar's ready," Aaron said. "And I'm eating." Oliver stared daggers down at him, and he sighed. "All right fine, but don't touch my glassware." He got up, scowling, and made his way toward the door with Oliver on his heels.

They slipped past Esme and Cecily, followed by Ebony, who gave the women a little smile as she passed. Then it was just the three of them.

"Daniel," Esme said, "I think it's time for you to see Cecily back to the boarding house. It's been a long day, and she needs her rest."

"Of course," Daniel said, abandoning his sketchbook on the sofa.

Esme gave Cecily's shoulders a squeeze, then let go as he approached them.

Daniel paused in the doorway for an awkward moment before gesturing toward the stairs. "After you."

Without a word, Cecily turned and headed back the way they'd come.

Daniel fell in behind her, feeling Esme's gaze all the way down. He took the lead when they reached the bottom, passing through the dining room, now empty but for employees cleaning up for the next round of guests. Back at the front door, they reclaimed their coats from Victor, and when they stepped out into the cold, he took Cecily's elbow to guide her over the brittle brown grass toward the car. He tried to convince himself that it wasn't significant that it hadn't been her hand this time, that he wasn't bracing himself for something, but it didn't work. For her part, Cecily didn't even seem to notice. She remained worryingly silent, only speaking as he pulled out into the deserted street to return to the boarding house.

"You didn't tell me what to expect before we went in there."

His initial relief at hearing her voice dissipated a bit as her words registered. So she was going to call him to the carpet on this.

"I didn't," he admitted.

"Why?"

His hands tightened on the wheel. He couldn't answer that honestly. Couldn't tell her that he took her through the main entrance instead of the more sedate back door because he wanted her to have the full experience of seeing the club for the first time. All the splendor, the celebration of what magic could do, everything they'd all worked so hard for. He couldn't tell her that he, foolishly and selfishly, wanted to impress her. He wanted her to see the life he had built and realize that there were people who wouldn't judge and reject her because of who she was. It would have been agony to say all that before she had come out of her meeting with Esme looking like that, so now…

"It's something you need to see to understand," he said finally.

"The people who work there," Cecily continued after a beat. "Are they all adepts… like me?"

"Not all of them," Daniel said. "But most everyone you met. You know now that Esme has visions. Paloma obviously manipulates water. Aaron can subtly influence people's emotions. It's why the drinks are so good; he can slip in a touch of enchantment along with alcohol. His sister, Ebony, runs the card table, and her power is similar to his, except she works with thoughts, not feelings."

"She's the one who made my necklace," Cecily said, and Daniel nodded. "What about Oliver?"

"Oliver can read people," Daniel said.

"Read them?"

"Yes. He can sense their emotional state, tell how they respond to different situations. It comes in very handy when you need a confidence man."

Cecily seemed to mull that over for a moment, and he wondered if she would ask him more about Oliver, but when she spoke again, she changed course.

"Do you…" She licked her lips. "Do you have any natural magic?"

All things considered, Daniel was surprised it had taken her this long to ask.

He shook his head. "Not a drop."

He'd always had mixed feelings about that fact. On the one hand, it was difficult not to wish he could do some of the marvelous things his friends could, but he knew all too well at this point that such gifts were sometimes more trouble than they were worth. Cecily nodded, looking perhaps a little relieved that one thing had remained constant in the middle of all the chaos. When her voice came again, it was even softer than before.

"Did Esme tell you what she wanted to talk to me about?"

"No," Daniel said, which was true, though he'd had a good idea.

Cecily toyed with a loose thread on the sleeve of her coat. "She asked me to help her... you... the group."

Daniel took a long, slow breath. "And what did you say?"

"I told her she had the wrong girl. That I appreciated her help, but I wanted to go back to my normal life."

From the corner of his eye, he could see her watching him, looking to see if he was... What? Disappointed? His jaw clenched. If he was, he had only himself to blame. He knew what the world she came from was like. He knew what it did to people. However terribly Cecily's family treated her, however much she wanted to be different than the rest of girls from "good" families, the hold that life had on her was strong. She was defined by her birth just as surely as he was, and he would do well to remember that.

"Well," he said gruffly. "You gotta do what you gotta do."

She looked as if she wanted to say more, but just then, they pulled up behind the boarding house. Daniel cut the engine and went around to the passenger door. He handed Cecily down to the rutted ground, making a point not to meet her eyes. He could feel her watching him as they entered the boarding house, but they made their way up to her room without a word.

On the landing, Daniel gave Cecily the key. "I'll be over to collect you sometime tomorrow. Try to be ready by around nine."

Cecily nodded, staring at the key in her hand. Again, he was struck by how small she looked, different from both the imaginative young girl he'd adored and the glamorous, confident creature he'd come to resent. But he hardened his heart to the sense of protectiveness that stirred up within him. He was a professional, and he knew now that this was just business. He would see this assignment through, then they would go their separate ways.

"Get some rest," he said curtly and turned to go, but Cecily called out, "Wait!"

Daniel stopped, waiting for her to continue. Under his gaze, her face flushed, as if now that she had his attention, she didn't know what to say. She finally settled on "I'll… see you in the morning."

Daniel nodded, then turned quickly and left. He tried to pretend he didn't listen for the door closing behind her all the way down the stairs, only hearing it when he reached the entry. And he also tried to pretend he didn't notice her face at the window, watching him as drove away.

He failed.

CHAPTER 8

CECILY

Again, the shadowy figures spill out of the warehouse. Again, she just smiles. She raises her hands, the blue electricity crackling around them. And just when it seems like it might be too much, she unleashes all that power, exhilaration rushing through her...

Cecily snapped awake. She'd barely slept, plagued by the events of the day before, and once she had drifted off, echoes of Esme's visions had snuck into her dreams. Slowly, she became aware of the room around her. It was still dim, but sunlight was sneaking in around the cracks in the curtains. A glance at the clock told her it was eight thirty.

Oh, and someone was knocking on the door.

Still groggy, she threw off the covers and made her way across the room on stocking feet. She was about to turn the lock when she thought of Daniel's instruction to be cautious and let out a tentative "Hello?"

"It's me," Daniel said.

Cecily let her forehead fall against the door, a combination of relief and apprehension flowing through her. She was glad it was him, obviously, but their final exchange the night before had left her off balance. She could tell she'd misstepped, but she wasn't sure how. It left her feeling rattled. Vulnerable. Because, if she didn't know what it was that had upset him, how could she keep from doing it again?

Also, even though she was still fully dressed aside from her shoes —her clothes from the day before had also served as her pajamas— something about Daniel seeing her straight from bed seemed almost indecent.

Pull yourself together, Dearborn, she thought. This was ridiculous. They had more pressing matters at hand. Taking a deep breath, she schooled her expression and opened the door—but just a crack.

"Esme sent me to get you," Daniel said. "She wants you at the club."

"Now?" Cecily asked.

Daniel nodded, his mouth a grim line. "Now."

Whump.

The sound of newspapers landing on the table resounded through the room, the inch-high letters of the top page's headline declaring:

MAGIC AND MURDER AT MOGUL'S MANSION
ENERGY HEIRESS IGNITES INVESTIGATION

"Applesauce," Oliver muttered, which Cecily thought wildly undersold the situation.

The two of them and Daniel were standing in Esme's office. Esme had also joined them, as had Leo, whom Daniel had described as Esme's "special friend," and Oliver, who was apparently Esme's *son*. The ride to the Hierophant hadn't been any less awkward than the initial encounter with Daniel at the boarding house, but that awkwardness had been forced aside in favor of this entirely different source of tension and distress. Daniel reached out to lift the paper from the top of the stack and began to read.

The highest ranks of Ad Astra society were rocked on Tuesday by the revelation that respected physician and harmonic therapist Dr. Ernest Fairchild was discovered dead in the home of energy baron AG Dearborn.

While evidence remains under examination, Ad Astra Law Enforcement supervising inspector Michael O'Connell confirmed that foul play is suspected in the case. Furthermore, sources close to the situation have revealed that debutante Cecily Dearborn, who only recently returned to Ad Astra, fleeing scandal after an extended stay in Belleterre, was reported missing shortly after Dr. Fairchild's body was discovered, suggesting she could be a primary suspect in the crime.

"Certain details pertaining to Dr. Fairchild's death indicate that an adept was involved," an anonymous source told the Chronicle. *"Rumors have circulated among Ad Astra's elite for years that Cecily possessed magic and that her parents were desperate to keep it quiet, considering Mr. Dearborn's close dealings with Colonel Teasley and the rest of the Reason and Prosperity Coalition. It is an open secret that her hasty departure from Ville du Soleil resulted from the damage she caused to the university library with her power. Clearly, the girl is unbalanced and should be considered dangerous."*

When approached for comment, both Mr. Dearborn and his wife, socialite and philanthropist Melanie Bedford Dearborn, declined to speak to reporters, but Mr. Dearborn later released a statement regarding the matter:

"Mrs. Dearborn and I are, of course, devastated by the loss of our esteemed friend Dr. Fairchild under our very roof. Our thoughts and prayers are with his loved ones in their grief. We are also deeply concerned about the whereabouts of our beloved daughter, Cecily, who has already been maligned by baseless accusations regarding her connection to Dr. Fairchild's death. We believe that the parties responsible for Dr. Fairchild's untimely demise are also behind Cecily's disappearance, and we are cooperating fully with the authorities to see those parties brought to justice and our darling daughter returned to us. We ask the public for privacy at this difficult time."

Cecily was surprised by the lump that swelled in her throat in response to the statement. She knew it wasn't really an emotional and heartfelt plea. In her mind's eye, she could see her parents dictating it to some secretary or other, strategizing over the significance of every word. But on some deep level, it was what she wanted to hear, and so her traitorous heart had reacted regardless. With effort, she swallowed and turned her attention back to the room.

"Well..." Daniel sighed, dropping the paper back onto the table. "I suppose it was too much to hope the whole thing would stay quiet." He glanced at Cecily. "I honestly thought your mother would have been able to keep the whole mess hushed up for a little longer by sheer force of will."

Cecily pursed her lips. "She probably did, too."

Oliver drummed his fingers on the table, his face pensive. "I'm curious about these 'unnamed sources.' Who would have been close enough to what was happening to give out those kinds of details? Are we looking at servants?"

Cecily eyed him warily. He seemed different this morning—less refined, more plainspoken. She felt like that should have put her more at ease in his presence, but somehow, it was just the opposite. Something about him was setting her on edge.

"I don't think so," Daniel was saying, shaking his head. "The Dearborns tend to inspire fear in the staff, but they also pay well. That combination keeps everybody pretty tight-lipped. My guess is that the information isn't coming from inside the house."

"Someone close to the family, then? A friend, a business associate?" Oliver asked.

"Can you think of someone with a grudge against you, Cecily?" Esme said. "Someone who would want to cause you harm?"

Cecily considered the question, but she had to shake her head. Not that she thought she was widely beloved—quite the reverse, in fact. She was well-known, famous even, but she couldn't think of anyone who was close enough to her to bear her that kind of ill will.

Despite having a laissez-faire approach to parenting through most of Cecily's childhood, Mrs. Dearborn had developed an iron grip on her social calendar as she'd gotten older, determined to keep any suspicion that Cecily was anything other than a normal, respectable girl from taking root. The short list of acceptable companions had only gotten shorter after a handful of incidents that had required deft social maneuvering and not a small amount of hush money to cover up, including the impromptu fireworks display a twelve-year-old Cecily had initiated for a Freedom Day celebration with MNC Vandermark's niece in attendance. Then there was the time when she was fifteen and Tommy Featherstone had gotten handsy in the back-seat of his father's auto. Cecily's father had been forced to come up with some ridiculous pretext for giving Tommy a "scholarship", to make up for the night he'd spent in the hospital after Cecily fought him off. Situations like these had taught her to keep everyone at a safe distance. Plus, she'd been on the other side of the ocean for almost a year. Multiple people in her set had stirred up trouble recently and seemed far more likely to become embroiled in a major controversy than she would.

"Whoever it is," Oliver continued, rolling his cane from one hand to the other absentmindedly, "they didn't just want the doctor elimi-nated—they wanted the public to know about it and to know that it was magic. But they could have set that up any number of ways. Why did they..."

His eyes brightened. "Oh. *Oh!* That is *good*. Exactly the kind of break we've been looking for!"

Cecily felt a flash of anger at this sudden burst of jubilation. "I beg your pardon?"

Daniel took a step in her direction.

"Oliver," he said, a note of warning in his voice.

"Hmm?" Oliver responded, still clearly lost in his train of thought.

"I believe Daniel is trying to communicate his disapproval of this ghoulish delight you seem to be taking in the murder currently being laid at Cecily's feet," Esme said dryly.

Oliver stared at her for a moment before the penny dropped. "Oh. Right. Obviously I didn't mean 'good' from Cecily's perspective. And definitely not from Dr. Fairchild's—"

79

"What precisely did you mean, Oliver?" Leo asked, apparently used to handling this type of redirection.

"What if this isn't about Cecily at all?" Oliver said. "What if the killer is trying to drive a wedge between the RPC and Papa Dearborn?"

"Okay," Daniel said slowly. "And why would they want to do that?"

"To divide the ranks!" Oliver replied. "The RPC is powerful because whatever disagreements they may have behind the scenes, they always act in lockstep when it counts. But what if there was a very public falling out? One that they couldn't sweep under the rug? There's a lot of money at stake in that infrastructure bill, and they won't let Dearborn near those contracts now. Plus, his stock is going to take a nosedive, if it hasn't already. He'll be out a fortune, and he's going to lose face in the deal. Hardly a way to ensure his loyalty. And that's just the finances— the rest of RPC is going to be scrambling to distance themselves from the unseemly business of magic. They will have to address the allegations against Cecily in a way that protects their own standing and prospects. That divide could be the catalyst that causes the whole faction to collapse in on itself. It's an insidious bit of political maneuvering."

He looked perversely impressed at this prospect. Nobody else seemed quite sure how to respond.

"Who would even try such a thing?" Esme said after a beat. "Shining Light? Someone else entirely?"

"Don't know!" Oliver said, still strangely cheerful. "Honestly, I don't think it matters. Whoever it is, this is could be our in! We've been looking for a lead that helps us figure out what's going on in the RPC's inner circle. Maybe this is it!"

"But if the goal is to sow discord between Dearborn and the rest of the coalition," Daniel said, "that means whoever's doing this is on the outside, acting against the RPC's interests. What insight is that going to give us into the RPC's inner workings?"

"If we can figure out what the killer stands to gain by targeting them," Oliver said, "we can reverse engineer what's at heart of their agenda. Their actual agenda, not just the political veneer."

Cecily's head felt light. He was talking about the situation as if it were just a grand hypothetical, some kind of thought experiment. But it wasn't. It was her life. She waited for the fretfulness, but instead, her palms began to tingle.

"Why the doctor, though?" Esme asked, her face thoughtful. "What does he have to do with this?"

"And how would anyone even know he was going to be there?" Daniel asked. "Cecily had barely been home for twelve hours."

"Well," Oliver said, as if he were being perfectly reasonable but also bracing for dissent, "it seems to me the only way to know for sure is to get them to come out of the shadows so we can ask."

Everyone's eyes turned to Cecily, and she took a step back, stifling the urge to flee.

Daniel's expression grew thunderous. "We're not using her as bait," he snapped, and Cecily was both taken aback and gratified by this quick leap to her defense.

"Not bait," Oliver said quickly. "More like… incentive."

"Oliver," Esme said, "you're being mercenary."

"Esme," he replied, mirroring her tone, "you're being naïve. She's a valuable asset. Besides, she stands to benefit more from finding the actual killer than any of us!"

"She's not an asset," Daniel said, his voice rising. "She's a person."

"She wouldn't be in any real danger!" Oliver said. "If this person… these people… whatever are enemies of the RPC, we likely have at least some common goals and interests. They could be potential allies."

Daniel raised his eyebrows. "Allies we would expose to clear Cecily's name?"

"I don't know!" Oliver said, throwing up his hands. "We could at least put out feelers! Quietly spread the word that she's still in the city. See what turns up. And if someone wants proof, say a small demonstration of her power …" He trailed off, leaving it to everyone else to figure out how beneficial such a scenario could be, and it was that, the casual assumption that everyone would be on board with this plan, that sent Cecily over the edge.

"I don't want this!" she exploded, planting her hands on the table. "I've never wanted it! You keep talking about it like it's something useful, but I've spent my entire life just trying to find some semblance of control so I don't have to be afraid of it all the time. And even that hasn't been enough! I'm not a crusader for justice or whatever it is all of you are trying to be here. I just want to figure out who did this so I can go home and forget this ever happened!"

Then her hands were alive with electricity. The writhing threads arced over and around her fingers, blackening the table where she gripped it, and a stray spark leapt onto the stack of papers nearby, setting them alight. Oliver grabbed a nearby trash can and scooped the papers into it, poking at them with his cane until the fire was out.

The silence in the room was very loud. Heat rushed into Cecily's face as she snatched her hands back, cradling them to her chest. The burst of fury had subsided, but an overwhelming tiredness and a heavy sense of shame had taken its place. She took a step back.

"Please—" Her voice came out strangled and tight. She swallowed and tried again. "Please excuse me."

Then she turned and fled the room.

CHAPTER 9

DANIEL

"Well, that could have gone better," Oliver said.

Daniel gaped at him. "Yes, I imagine it could have if you hadn't essentially poked her with a sharp stick until she exploded!"

"I'll say this," Esme said, her gaze on the door Cecily had just exited. "Her parents are right about one thing. As it stands, she is dangerous. That much power with no training…" She shook her head. "Something needs to be done immediately."

Oliver's shoulders slumped, his expression contrite. "Daniel's right. This is on me. I'll go talk to her, apologize."

Daniel would have found that gratifying under any other circumstances, but not now. "No," he said firmly. "I'll go. She's more likely to listen to me." Probably. Possibly. Sighing, he ran a hand over his face and moved toward the door.

He checked Esme's dressing room first, then went up to the Lounge, since those were the two places he knew Cecily had been before, but there was no sign of her. As he was heading down to the main dining room, he noticed that the stage door was ajar. That wasn't terribly unusual—people were constantly going in and out during the day—but he slowed his steps anyway and caught a glimpse of a narrow back and dark hair. After a pause, he made his way through the wings and onto the stage itself. Cecily was perched on the edge with her feet dangling into the orchestra pit, back straight but head bowed. She didn't move as Daniel sat down beside her.

"I'm sorry," she said, eyes on the hands that were twisted together in her lap.

"It's all right," Daniel replied. "None of us really liked that table anyway."

The corner of her mouth ticked up, seemingly against her will. After a moment, her frown settled back into place. "I just..." She dropped her hands to her sides, flexing them against the wood of the stage. "I don't usually lose my temper like that. I don't know how to keep it under control."

"I know," Daniel said.

It felt achingly familiar, sitting with her like this, soothing a hurt that someone else had inflicted. If he closed his eyes, he could almost imagine they were back in Dearborn House, hiding in the library. But he didn't close his eyes. Instead, he glanced down to where their hands rested next to each other on the wooden boards, little fingers almost touching. Instinctively, he shifted his hand away.

In his peripheral vision, he saw her head turn toward him, attention drawn by the movement. From the moment she'd opened her door at the boarding house, he'd been aware that her defenses were up, but now all her fortifications seemed to give way at once.

"What happened to you, Daniel?" she said, and there was hurt in her tone, mixed in with the confusion. "It's always nagged at me. One day, you were just... gone. And I never found out why."

Daniel had turned to her, his own pain warring with surprise. "You mean you didn't know?"

Cecily shook her head, wide-eyed. "Didn't know what?"

Daniel sighed and dropped his gaze to his hands, rubbing them together. "Your mother saw us together," he said quietly. "Out in the garden."

The two of them had spent so much time out there over the years. The fact that it had taken Mrs. Dearborn so long to notice only highlighted how little attention she had paid to her daughter back then.

"She began snooping around and figured out that we were close. So she fired my father. Said having me around was a bad influence on you."

Cecily's mouth fell open in shock. After a moment, she put forth a visible effort to collect herself. "I am so, so sorry," she said. "I had no idea."

"It's all right," Daniel muttered, which was a bald-faced lie. It was not all right. It had never been all right. But it wasn't Cecily's fault. In fact, to his surprise, he could feel a small part of him—one that he hadn't even realized was still broken—knitting back together in the wake of her reaction. He'd known she wasn't responsible for what happened, but on some level, he'd believed that when she'd found out, she hadn't cared. If she had she would have done something, at least tried to find him. Her silence had been the biggest blow of all. And now he knew she hadn't known after all. She hadn't willingly let him go.

"What did the two of you do?" she asked. "Afterward."

"Pop tried to find work in the city," Daniel said, "but palatial mansions with formal gardens are pretty thin on the ground, and the few options he had were already fully staffed. He even checked into some houses up toward the strait, but it was hard to get an in without any existing contacts and no letter of reference." He felt her tense then, at the insult of dismissal doubled by the denial of a recommendation for further employment. He was surprised that she would even recognize it; most of her set wouldn't. But that was what had always drawn him to her, wasn't it? "Eventually, he started working down at the docks. The pay was abysmal, but then he had a stroke of luck and found something making decent money." He paused, the old hurt resurfacing. "What he didn't tell me was that the pay was good because the working conditions were so bad. They made him sick, and then he couldn't work at all, which meant we didn't have any money for a doctor. And then…"

Tentatively, Cecily reached out and touched his hand. "I really am so sorry, Daniel."

He nodded, shrugging one shoulder. "Yeah, well, it's not like we were special. These things happen all the time."

Cecily withdrew her hand, but he could still feel her eyes on him.

"What about your brother?" she asked. "Couldn't you have gone to him for help?"

"Patrick was in the merchant marine by then. He sent us what he could while Pop was sick, but afterwards…" Daniel shrugged. "Even if I'd wanted to reach him, I didn't know that I could—it was tricky catching him in port. Plus, what was he going to do with a kid brother in tow? I didn't want to burden him with it. I decided to just handle things myself."

"By what, living on the street?" For the first time, her voice held a hint of, what… disapproval? Judgment?

"For a while," he said, and he hated the note of defensiveness that even he could hear. "I'd get a bed for the night, doing odd jobs here and there, and I found some forgotten corners that were almost safe if I was desperate. I spent a lot of time at the library." He thought back to those long days, sitting at a wooden table and looking at art books filled with gorgeous color plates, the kind librarian pretending not to notice. "I got by."

"How did you end up here?"

"I tried to pick Oliver's pocket."

That elicited a startled laugh from her. "Really?"

"Really," Daniel affirmed. "In my defense, he seemed like an ideal mark. That pristine suit and pomaded hair, the carnation in his buttonhole. Easy money.

"But as soon as I dipped my fingers for his wallet, he grabbed my wrist and shoved me up against the building we were passing. So, there I was, face pressed into the bricks, cussing a blue streak and swearing up and down I hadn't done anything wrong." He shook his head at the memory. "He had me dead to rights with my hand in his pocket, and I flat out would not admit what I was doing. It tickled him. He told me later that he admired my commitment.

"He's only three years older than me, but that was a much bigger deal when we were thirteen and sixteen than it is now. He decided to take me under his wing. Thought it would be a lark. So he brought me here to meet Esme. It was different then. Esme had been telling fortunes for a while at that point, had built up a solid client list, but the club was just starting out, and money was tight. It didn't matter. She welcomed me like I was her own, fed me the first hot meal I'd had in days, and gave me a safe, warm place to sleep. I've been here ever since."

"And you work for them?"

"I suppose you could say that," he said. "Although Esme insists it's 'with' rather than 'for'. She has the last word, but she likes to hear from all of us when she's making plans, whether it's for the club or circumventing the Embargo."

"She trusts you," Cecily observed.

He nodded. "It's a compliment I don't take lightly."

"And Oliver? Does he still see himself as your… mentor? Protector?"

Daniel smirked. "He would claim something more like 'guru' or 'overlord,' because he's insufferable. But I watch his back as much as he watches mine these days, however much he hates to admit it."

"He seems a bit… mercurial," she said, smoothing her hands over her skirt.

Daniel shook his head. "I'm sorry about what happened in there. He gets carried away sometimes."

"But didn't you say he could sense how people are feeling?" she said. "Couldn't he tell that I was getting upset? It seemed like you could, and you don't have any powers."

"He was excited about his theory," Daniel said, neatly sidestepping the incisiveness of her observation for the time being. "Sometimes, when his own emotions get keyed up that way, it messes with his perception."

"That seems inconvenient," Cecily said, then her voice shifted, taking on a note of disdain. "Or I guess it could be just the opposite. It would be handy to have something like that in your back pocket to excuse any bad behavior."

Daniel chuckled. "Tell me about it. Although, sometimes, it's not a matter of making excuses—he just doesn't care." He sobered a bit. "I asked Esme about it once when I was mad at him, how he could get especially vicious in an argument, determined to get the last word. She told me it was a survival tactic. He can never turn his power off, so he had to figure out how to turn off his concern about how other people feel sometimes. It's what keeps him sane. And as the people he feels safest with, who he knows will forgive him, we get the brunt of it."

Cecily stared at him. A variety of emotions swept over her face in rapid succession, so quickly he couldn't identify them and suspected she couldn't either, really. Then she started to laugh. It wasn't a frantic, hysterical laugh, for which he was grateful, but there was a touch of bitterness in it—as if she had resigned herself to the absurdity of her fate because she knew she had no choice. The cynicism of that made his heart ache.

"All of this hardship, all this trouble," Cecily said finally, catching her breath. "And Esme says it's because of rocks from outer space."

Daniel shifted awkwardly. It did sound far-fetched when she put it like that.

"Do you believe it?" she asked, turning her full attention to him. "What she says about this cosmic struggle between good and evil?"

Daniel sighed. "I don't know. I've seen a lot of strange things over the last few years, things that have made it all seem possible, if just for a moment. Then we settle back into our normal routine, and there's errands to run and bills to pay, and it begins to seem outlandish again." He shook his head. "The thing is… I don't care if it's true."

Cecily raised her eyebrows. "You don't?"

"No," Daniel said. "Maybe the truth is out there with great god-like beings that are connected to the magic in our world, and maybe it isn't. If those beings showed up here tomorrow in their spacecraft or whatever, I suppose it would make a difference, but for now, they don't affect my day-to-day life. You know who does?" He met her eyes. "Esme. She is kind, and she is brave, and she always tries to do what is right. She saved my life all those years ago, and she's saved so many other people since then." He paused, letting his gaze drift back out to the empty tables. "That's why I stay here. Not for any grand crusade or crazy war in outer space. For her. And Oliver and all the others. They're what I believe in."

He realized then that he'd never quite put his feelings into words like that, even to himself, but all of it was true. Maybe he would have felt that way about anyone who'd gotten him off the streets, but he doubted it. Esme had given him a purpose as well as a home. Together, the makeshift family she'd created had gotten him through the grief of losing his father, his home, and his best friend.

And now, somehow, one of those things had returned.

The revelation that Cecily hadn't known about her mother's actions had changed so much. Now he could admit, even if only to himself, that he had been hoping desperately to have her in his life again. That he'd wanted it from the moment he agreed to go back to that miserable house that had taken so much from him. With the air cleared between them, maybe, just maybe, they could begin again.

Cecily sat quietly for a moment, digesting his words, then she sighed and ran a hand over her face. "Ugh, I suppose I need to go apologize for my outburst. I'm so embarrassed that everybody saw that."

Daniel had to smile. "They sent *me* to apologize to *you*."

"Really?" After a beat, she smiled too. Daniel got to his feet and held out a hand to her.

"Come on," he said, helping her to her feet. "Let's go get this sorted out. We have your name to clear."

CHAPTER 10

CECILY

As they approached the door to Esme's office, Cecily braced herself, preparing for what she anticipated would be a painfully awkward confrontation. But as it turned out, she needn't have bothered. The room was empty.

"I must have been gone longer than I realized," Daniel murmured. "I guess they decided to go do something productive instead of just waiting." He turned to Cecily. "Will you be all right in here while I go find Esme?"

Cecily rolled her eyes, but she couldn't fight back a fond smile. "Yes, Daniel. I think I can manage sitting here in an empty room on my own." She deposited herself on the edge of a chaise lounge upholstered in sapphire silk, crossing her legs at the ankle. "I suppose a herd of stampeding wildebeests or some similar threat might descend while you're gone, but I will do my best."

Daniel stared at her for a moment, seemingly at a loss for words, then shook his head and turned toward the door. But she thought she glimpsed a smile on his face as he went.

Once he was gone, she let her gaze drift around the office, taking in what she had been too preoccupied to notice when they'd first arrived. The space was more formal than Esme's dressing room, with fewer personal touches, but Cecily could see the same hand in the decor. The room was warm and inviting, boasting tall bookshelves and framed prints of flowers and birds. The wallpaper was patterned with green-and-gold arches that complemented similar colors in the large Persian carpet. Besides the chaise lounge, there were some russet leather club chairs and a desk with smaller wooden armchairs. And, of course, the table she'd nearly destroyed.

She gave the table a sidelong look, feeling a bit of the familiar shame and embarrassment, but not as much as she likely would have before speaking to Daniel. A few newspapers were still scattered over its surface, and part of her was tempted to go over and read them, to find out exactly what they were saying about her. But she knew it was likely just variations of the story Daniel had read to them, and she didn't have the energy for that. Her plate was overfull as it was.

Just then, the door flew open, and Cecily jumped to her feet, spinning toward the sound. When she turned, though, it was not Daniel or Esme she saw. It was Oliver.

"Oh," he said, stopping short, his face reflecting her own surprise. "I didn't know you were in here."

"Well," she said, somewhat feebly, "I am."

"Yes, I can see that now," Oliver said.

There was a beat of silence during which Cecily could practically see him reassuming his mask, the one he'd worn the previous night. She understood now that his demeanor earlier, which had seemed so different from their first meeting, meant that he had accepted her as someone he could be himself with, who he didn't have to con. Now, she was seeing his public face again. The one he showed to those he wasn't sure he could trust. And well, that was fair enough, she supposed.

"Please excuse my lack of hospitality," he said, his voice smooth now, meant to charm. "Seems a bit early for a drink, but maybe you'd like something from the kitchen? Perhaps some fresh coffee?"

"No, thank you," Cecily said. "I'm fine."

"Are you sure? Alphonse just arrived, and he is a virtuoso with pastries. Belleterre-trained and everything—you should feel right at home."

"Truly, it's not necessary."

"I insist," he said. He crossed to the wall and pressed a button near the light switch twice—a buzzer to the kitchen, she realized. Then he propped himself against the edge of the desk, hands stacked atop his cane.

"It will be here shortly," he said, shifting his weight to rest more comfortably. "How has it been for you, coming home? I imagine it's quite the transition, even without the brutal murder thrown in?"

Cecily couldn't help but huff out a short laugh. "It has been quite the culture shock." She gave him an assessing look. "Have you ever visited Belleterre?"

He shook his head. "Sadly, no. I've never strayed past New Avalonian shores, more's the pity."

"I just wondered. Since you were speaking Belleterran last night."

Oliver grinned. "Ah, that. Daniel has accused me of only knowing the romantic bits, which is, if I'm being honest, not far off the mark. An occupational hazard, I suspect—picking the low-hanging fruit that will come in the handiest rather than pursuing the language in earnest."

Cecily cocked her head. "And what precisely is your occupation?"

He waggled his head back and forth, as if searching for just the right term. "I guess you could call me a master of ceremonies. The club's major domo and all-around head *bon vivant*." He emphasized pronunciation of the last term to almost comic effect, then leaned toward Cecily with a conspiratorial air. "Do you see what I did there? With the Belleterran?"

Cecily couldn't help but smile. She was keenly aware of the fact that this was a performance, intended to put her at ease so she was more malleable, but it was still working. He was *good*. "Yes, I saw."

He straightened, looking pleased.

"How did all of this"—she gestured at the building around them—"get started anyway?"

Oliver shrugged. "When the Embargo passed, Esme decided we

had to do something. As you're probably aware, there was plenty of anti-magic sentiment out there before that, but the new laws took everything to a whole other level. For our own sakes and for others', we couldn't just sit back and do nothing. So she and some like-minded adepts set up a loose network to help practitioners who ran into trouble, and there were some successes here and there. But to make any serious progress, we needed money. That's when Esme opened this place and started telling fortunes. It was slow, hard work, but over time, we built it to what it is now."

He stood a little straighter. "Using magic to protect magic feels especially mutinous. It's extremely satisfying."

"Why a nightclub, though?" Cecily asked. In much of the world, and even in New Avalon before the Embargo, practitioners ran many different businesses that made use of their abilities, from bakeries to greenhouses to ferries. Perhaps the most lucrative were clinics—or "spas", as they were often called—where clients could receive treatments for their physical and mental well-being. Based on what Daniel had told her, the crew Esme had assembled seemed suited to that kind of work.

"Well, for one thing, a nightclub is just more fun." Oliver flashed that grin again. "But there is a strategic aspect to it as well."

"How so?"

"The Embargo is very clear about the use of magic being forbidden, for the good and safety of all." His lip curled in distaste at the trite platitude. "But that's not how it goes in reality. Taboos are, by their very nature, tantalizing; people are drawn to the mystery and sense of danger. Specifically, people with money to spare and too much time on their hands. The authorities understand that there's a demand for what we provide and will continue to be, for as long as magic is outlawed. The way they see it, as long as charm schools keep the rich patrons happy—and keep coppers on the payroll—it's only a bit of harmless mischief. The customers indulge, then go back to their everyday, respectable lives where magic has no place." His face darkened. "Where adepts are circus acts and not neighbors."

"If you're simply an amusement, you can't be a threat," Cecily said.

Oliver nodded. "It's not exactly hiding in plain sight, but it is sleight of hand. If the authorities think Esme is just an entertainer, they're less likely to do any real digging and find out what's happening under the surface."

"Which is the systematic defiance of the Embargo," Cecily said, all the pieces clicking into place.

"Precisely," Oliver said smugly.

Cecily considered him. He was dressed more casually than he had been the night before, in a vest and shirtsleeves rather than a suit. In fact, the general style was similar to Daniel's, but there were subtle, telling differences. The fabrics were finer, the tailoring was more polished, and the carnation and watch chain were present and accounted for. Cecily had known from the moment she'd met him that he was a man who put a lot of stock in his appearance, and she hadn't faulted him for it; she knew what it was like to trade in that currency. But she could also see now that everything he put on was camouflage, his own particular brand of misdirection. If he was the one in charge of determining how others saw him, he'd have the upper hand in any situation.

She'd always thought herself accomplished at adapting to her environment, making snap judgments about people's expectations of her and charting her course accordingly, but he put her in the shade. On some level, she'd always envied adepts like Oliver, whose powers were invisible. They were indistinguishable from non-practitioners in a crowd. *Normal*, or close enough to it. But she hadn't thought about what it would be like to have a power that was on all the time. To have to be on her guard every minute. She lived in fear of her outbursts, but they were relatively rare and never lasted long. What if that weren't the case? If every touch had the potential to hurt or destroy?

Her own strategy for dealing with her power had been to try pushing it down and subduing it. It had, in the long run, not been particularly effective. Oliver, meanwhile, had figured out a way to endure. And if he was a handful, if he was temperamental and unpredictable and cunning, he was also compassionate. Like Esme and Daniel, he had devoted himself to kindness and protecting people with nowhere else to go. There was nobility in that, which was more than she could say for herself.

"I'm glad Daniel found you," she said.

Oliver's face sobered, a bit of the mask slipping away. "So am I. He's very important to the work we do. He's also the closest thing I've ever had to a brother."

The vulnerability of that answer surprised her. She felt herself warming to him even more and wondered if the feeling was mutual, if she had unknowingly passed some kind of test. She decided to experiment, to see how far he'd let her go. "Can I ask you a personal question?"

Oliver smirked, some of his swagger returning. "Sure, as long as you buy me dinner first."

Cecily rolled her eyes but pressed on. "Why do you call your mother by her first name?"

Oliver leaned toward her, as if he was imparting a secret. "Let me tell you something about Esme—the woman is irredeemably vain. Once I hit puberty, she didn't want anyone to know she was old enough to have a son my age, so she initiated evasive maneuvers."

Cecily raised an eyebrow, dubious of his answer and a little sad. He must have picked up on her disappointment, because his face softened a bit.

"Seriously, though," he said, and there was a note of earnestness in his voice that Cecily hadn't heard before, "when I was thirteen, she sat me down and told me we weren't going to stand on the ceremony of hierarchy anymore. That since she took care of me and I took care of her, we were basically the same, so I should call her Esme instead of Mom."

"That's a lot of responsibility to place on you," Cecily said. "You were just a child."

Oliver shook his head. "It wasn't like that. It wasn't a burden. It was more like... I had earned the right to be considered her equal."

Cecily pondered that. She tried to picture her parents doing anything remotely similar for her and found she couldn't. The entire notion was laughable. To be treated with such care and respect by a parent. To be valued as a person and not a pawn.

"That's hers, you know," Oliver said, pulling Cecily out of her thoughts.

She had been so deep in her own head, she'd lost track of the conversation. "I'm sorry?"

"The necklace," he said, nodding toward her throat.

"What? This?" She reached up to touch the locket Daniel had given her.

Oliver nodded. "When Ebony said she needed something to infuse with that charm, Esme went and got it from her jewelry box." He smiled. "She said she thought it might suit you better than some of her more ostentatious pieces."

Cecily rolled the pendant between her fingers. She was nobody to Esme. Well, perhaps not nobody—she was connected to Daniel, and Esme had admitted to having a professional interest in her. But still, she was a stranger, and Esme had been nothing but generous to her. She'd given Cecily shelter, protection, something like friendship. And now, a piece of her past. A piece of herself. Nobody except for Daniel had done anything close to as much for her before. And in that moment, she decided. She chose to take a stand.

"I'll do it," she said. "I'll help you."

Oliver's eyebrows shot up. "Really?"

Cecily nodded. "Really. And not just to clear my name. If I can do something to undermine the Embargo and the people who benefit from it..." She took a deep breath. "I want in."

Oliver smiled at her—a genuine smile that reached his eyes—and she could see how many a heart would melt in the face of such a thing. If he was ever willing to let someone see so much of him. "Esme will be happy to hear it."

"Happy to hear what?" Esme asked as she came through the door, Leo and Daniel just behind her.

When Daniel saw that Cecily was there with Oliver, he shot her an alarmed, questioning look. But she gave a brief nod and held a reassuring hand up where only he could see it, and he relaxed.

"Cecily has decided to help us take down those sniveling RPC bastards," Oliver said, a note of pride in his voice.

Esme's eyes widened, and she turned to Cecily. "You have?"

"Well, I wouldn't have put it quite that way. But yes." She paused. "I want to help."

"Are you sure?" Esme asked, and Cecily knew it was a genuine question. She could say no, and this woman, these people, would still help her, no questions asked. But she didn't want to.

"I am."

"Well then," Esme said with a smile, "let's get to work."

CHAPTER 11

DANIEL

Claudia showed up with coffee and pastries just as everyone was settling back in to talk. Daniel brought Cecily a cup and saucer, then joined Cecily on the edge of the chaise. One by one, the others took the club chairs—an unspoken agreement to steer clear of the scorched table.

While Esme fussed at Oliver to stop being so fiddly with his coffee so they could get started, Cecily held up a palmier, examining it before she took a tentative bite. Daniel tried very hard not to notice how her eyes drifted shut in pleasure as she chewed.

"Oliver was right," she murmured. "These are amazing."

Daniel nodded. "Alphonse is a genuine artist." It was true, and they all revered him for it.

"So," Esme's bright voice cut in, bringing the session to order, "where were we?"

"Oliver was explaining how this might not be about Cecily at all, except it also is kind of about her," Daniel said.

Oliver shot him a scathing look, which Daniel ignored.

"Right," Esme said. "Oliver, remind us how that is."

Oliver sighed. "I really think that this is about going after AG and the RPC in general, and Cecily is just a convenient scapegoat. But because she's involved now, we may be able to draw the killer out with the prospect of getting their hands on her so they have more control of the situation."

Esme mulled that over, fingers drumming on the arm of her chair. "I don't know. Even if you're right, I still don't think the doctor was chosen at random. There's something else at play there."

"There's a reason Dearborn hired him," Leo said. "If he's in tight with the RPC, it could have put a target on his back for reasons that are unrelated to this larger scheme you're proposing."

Oliver snorted. "You mean aside from being a despicable crackpot?"

"All harmonic therapists are despicable crackpots," Esme said. "What made this one special enough that he ended up dead?"

"Has he been attached to any of the adepts we've worked with lately?" Daniel said.

"I don't think so," Oliver replied. "He wasn't one of the flashy types who advertises in the papers and riles up crowds at political rallies. I might have come across his name once or twice, but nothing about him stands out."

"Some of the less sensational articles went into his history and qualifications," Leo said. "He seemed to have a bit more credibility than a lot of these guys. Studied neurophysiology in med school. Did some work on brain injuries before he went into private practice."

"How does someone like that end up in the harmonic therapy racket?" Daniel said.

"Think about who hires harmonic therapists," Oliver said, holding up his pinched fingers and rubbing them together. "Always follow the money."

"Maybe his expertise was why the RPC was interested in him," Esme said. "To lend a veneer of legitimacy to their anti-magic efforts. Teasley's been as intractable as ever, but it seems like other voices are trying to make their message a little more palatable. Like that new program Vandermark proposed. What's it called?"

"Partners in Progress," Leo said.

Esme snapped her fingers. "That's the one. With the 'successful' harmonic therapy patients mentoring the new ones through the transition. Putting a kinder, more nurturing face on their bigotry."

"Oh, yeah," Oliver said. "Teasley must have had to hold his nose to take that medicine. But he did get to appoint that other RPC hardliner to 'help' oversee it and keep Vandermark from getting too far into the weeds—Eleanor Bradshaw." He snorted. "Claims her son died because of magic when it was probably overindulging in gin and going for a joyride."

"Oliver," Esme said in a quelling tone.

"What?" Oliver said. "I mean, it's sad that he died, but there's no reason to pin it on us because she doesn't want to face the fact that her son was an idiot."

Daniel had encountered Matthew Bradshaw from a distance once or twice as a kid because he had been one of Herbert's friends. He had always struck Daniel as a reckless, self-involved sort of guy intent on pursuing his own enjoyment. Nobody was one hundred percent sure what had happened on the night he died. There had been rumors he'd frequented charm schools, even taken up with a female adept he'd met in one, but Daniel agreed that it was far more likely that he had just drunk himself stupid and gotten behind the wheel of an auto, convinced he was invincible.

His mother, who had always been a politically temperate woman, was consumed by grief upon his death. Adamant her son had been a victim of some sort of adept conspiracy, she had become a passionate supporter of the RPC. That fervor had recently led to her being elected to the National Congress as one of only a handful of women serving in the governing body. She had quickly become a thorn in the side of all practitioners.

"In any case," Esme said, drawing the conversation back around to the problem at hand, "if Fairchild really was involved with RPC efforts at that level, it could have attracted the wrong kind of attention."

"We need more information," Leo said. "If we're lucky, the authorities may not have searched his offices yet. I'd say it's worth a look."

"I'll go." Daniel looked at Oliver. "You in?"

Oliver nodded. "I'm game after second dinner service tonight."

"Excellent," Esme said. "Hopefully, that will give us more to go on."

"There is one other thing," Leo said. "Shining Light released a statement this morning."

Everyone in the room groaned.

"Hells, what are they up to now?" Oliver asked.

Leo shrugged. "The usual. They didn't come right out and claim they were responsible for Fairchild's death, but they didn't confirm that they weren't either. Just the same old 'Ignorance will be punished —magic will rise!' nonsense."

"Do you think there's anything to it?" Daniel asked.

"No," Leo said. "But it might make law enforcement jumpy, so it's something to keep in mind."

"All right." Esme turned her gaze to Cecily. "Now it's time to see about you."

Cecily stiffened next to Daniel. "How so?"

"You need some training," Esme said, her voice kind but firm. "Otherwise, there may be more incidents like the one this morning, and we may not be so lucky in terms of containing the damage."

Daniel knew Cecily must have been nervous about the prospect, but she didn't argue, just took a shaky breath and nodded.

"Ideally, we'd pair you up with someone whose power resembles your own," Esme continued. "But we don't have any energy users on hand right now, so I think our best bet would be Paloma."

Oliver let out a supremely unhelpful cough. Daniel sighed as Esme looked over at him, lifting a brow.

"Do you have an objection, Oliver?"

To most onlookers, Oliver would have appeared unruffled, but Daniel could see the battle waging inside him. There were now two outcomes to this situation—tell Esme what Paloma had said about Cecily the night before, condemning her to the special agony of Esme's disappointment and censure, or say nothing and allow Esme to move on with this plan. Paloma wasn't going to like either of them.

In the end, Oliver must have decided that discretion was the better part of valor, because he just said carelessly, "Not at all."

Esme looked dubious, but after a moment, she turned her focus back to Cecily. "Also, with all the attention right now, it might be better for you to stay here rather than going back and forth to the boarding house. We don't really have any existing accommodations on-site, but I think we can manage—"

"She can have my bed," Daniel cut in, then felt his face heat when all eyes turned to him and he realized how that sounded out loud. "I mean, it's comfortable enough and mostly private. I don't mind."

Cecily's brow furrowed. "But then where will you sleep?"

Daniel shrugged. "I'll grab some blankets and make up a pallet somewhere. I don't need much."

But Esme shook her head. "I need you sharp, Daniel. I don't want you making sloppy mistakes because you haven't had enough rest. Why don't you stay at the boarding house, instead? There's less chance of attracting notice if it's you going back and forth."

Daniel wanted to object but found that he had no effective counterargument, only a bone-deep resistance to the idea of leaving Cecily there without him. First and foremost, he knew that admitting this would do absolutely nothing to sway Esme, but he was also reluctant to give voice to it in Cecily's presence. The admission felt too raw and overpowering for the fragile structure of their rekindled friendship.

Esme's eyes softened in understanding. "She'll be safe here with us. You know she will."

And he did, so he nodded, not letting himself meet Cecily's eye.

There was a knock at the door, and a frazzled man with a pencil mustache poked his head inside.

"Leo," he said, "there's someone here who says he came to talk about a place in the orchestra?"

Leo pulled out his pocket watch and checked the time, cursing under his breath as he tucked it away again. "I didn't realize it had gotten so late. Do you want me to tell him to wait?"

"No," Esme said. "I think we're done here for the time being."

Leo nodded and walked out the door, closing it behind him with a soft click.

Oliver stood and stretched. "And I should probably go check on the guest list for tonight."

"That's fine." Esme got to her feet and turned to Daniel. "In the meantime, you two can go back to the boarding house to pick up Cecily's things."

Daniel and Cecily exchanged a look.

"What things?" he asked.

Esme frowned. "You know," she said, gesturing toward Cecily. "Her... Wait. That's what you were wearing yesterday."

Cecily looked down at herself. "Yes?"

Esme rounded on Daniel. "You didn't get any other clothes for her?!"

Oliver did a less-than-exemplary job of smothering a laugh as he made his way to the door, and Daniel glared at him before turning back to Esme.

"We were in a bit of a hurry. I didn't exactly have time to stop and pack her steamer trunk."

"But you didn't think to find her something later?"

"Well, you didn't either!"

"I was busy working with Ebony on the protection charm, and contacting Doris about the boarding house, and oh, yes, running the club!" she shot back. "Plus, I did give you a coat. That didn't spark any inspiration?"

Daniel started to argue, but in hindsight, it did seem an obvious lapse. From the corner of his eye, he could see Cecily trying hard not to look amused, and his face burned. He pressed his lips back together and met Esme's gaze. She seemed to recognize his lack of a retort as the best she was going to get in terms of acknowledgment and had the decency not to look too smug about it. Unlike her son, Esme knew it was bad form to gloat.

"Okay," she said benevolently. "I'm sure we have some things around here that will do. Right now, take Cecily upstairs and get her settled. I'll go see about Paloma. This is about the time she usually practices, since she has the stage to herself."

"Yes, ma'am," he said, pride still stinging.

Esme gave them a smile and left.

After a beat, Cecily clapped her hands once. "So," she said cheerfully. "Let's go see my new digs."

CHAPTER 12

CECILY

Cecily followed Daniel up the stairs to the large space she had glimpsed the night before. When they reached the door, he led her to a corner that was sectioned off by screens. A curtain hung over the gap between them, creating a sort of improvised door. This was Daniel's "room," she realized with a jolt.

"Well," he said, sweeping the curtain aside, "here it is." He paused. "I guess I'll just..." And he popped through the improvised doorway to grab a few items of clothing from the rod in the corner.

Watching him, Cecily had a sudden pang of conscience. "Daniel, you don't have to—"

He cut her off with a shake of his head. "Make yourself at home," he went on, coming back into the larger space of the Lounge. "The bathroom is down the stairs and to the left, in the dressing rooms backstage. The hot water can be temperamental—you have to turn the tap as far as it will go, then ease it back so you don't burn yourself. Like Esme said, someone should bring you some clothes soon." Then there was really nothing else to say. He took a few steps toward the stairs but seemed reluctant to go.

"Thank you, Daniel," Cecily said, hoping he could hear the sincerity in her voice.

His cheeks colored a bit, but he only said, "See you tomorrow." Then he was gone.

Slowly, Cecily made her way into his makeshift home. She hung her borrowed coat on the rod, then sat gingerly on the bed. In an instant, she was acutely aware that this was where Daniel slept; being there without him almost seemed like a violation. And it wasn't just the bed. Being here among all of his things felt keenly intimate.

Her gaze drifted over the posters and clippings pinned to the walls, Daniel's remaining clothes, his dishes, and his books. She noticed that several of those, while they were different sizes, had almost identical bindings—dark blue with subtle embossed flourishes on the covers. Curious, she picked one up and, upon flipping through it, realized it was a sketchbook. Immediately, she snapped it shut and replaced it on the shelf. She remembered Daniel's sketchbooks, of course; he'd always had one with him, when she'd known him before. But they'd been cheap things bound in thin gray paperboard, not elegant objects like these. After a moment, she began to feel a little silly. After all, he hadn't told her she *shouldn't* look at them. Even so, she couldn't bring herself to pick the book back up. She found that she wanted to be invited. That she wanted him to make the choice to share them with her.

At the thought, her own cheeks warmed, and she got to her feet, suddenly eager to be out of his space. Smoothing her hands down her skirt, she decided this was as good a time as any to find Paloma and went down the back stairs to investigate.

As Cecily reached the ground floor, she could hear strains of music in the air. She passed the dressing rooms and made her way through the darkness of the wings until she was standing just outside the reach of the spotlights someone had turned on. The music was coming from a phonograph on a cart that had been wheeled to the back of the stage. The tune was a modern one, syncopated and a little bit naughty, with lots of horns and a sly piano. And in the center of the spotlight, Paloma worked wonders.

She wasn't wearing a fancy costume now—only a plain black gym suit that left her limbs bare—but her movements were still mesmerizing. Her body exhibited a grace that rivaled that of the prima ballerinas in Ville du Soleil as she leaped and spun, but the real triumph was the water. Two tubs had been placed on opposite ends of the stage, and with undulating motions of her hands, Paloma summoned the liquid from them, sculpting it into fantastical shapes and patterns that swirled and jumped as she danced but never touched her. It looked like something from a fairy tale or a dream, and Cecily watched with equal parts awe and longing. She couldn't imagine what it would be like to not only have that degree of control over what she could do, but also be able to create something so beautiful with it.

The tempo of the music slowed, winding down to its conclusion. Accordingly, Paloma's movements became looser, more relaxed, and the water retreated into the tubs, not a drop left on the wood of the stage. Eventually, she came to rest in a pose that left her bowed at the waist, arms swept out in the imaginary audience's direction, and a beat later, the song came to an end. There was a moment of perfect stillness, then quiet static hummed from the phonograph as the record continued turning around and around, the needle stuck in its final groove. For a moment, Paloma didn't budge, but then, responding to some sign or impulse that Cecily couldn't identify, she straightened, then walked to the phonograph, lifted the needle arm, and settled it back into its cradle.

"You don't have to hide in the shadows back there like a creep," she called out.

Cecily swallowed. She took a few steps forward until she was in the circle of the stage lights, clasping her hands in front of her to hide her nervousness. "You're very talented."

Paloma turned to face her, crossing her arms over her chest and looking Cecily up and down. "So, apparently. Esme wants me to train you."

So much for niceties. "That is my understanding, yes."

"Well…" Paloma tilted her head expectantly. "Let's see what you've got."

Cecily's stomach sank. "What, right now?"

Paloma lifted her chin, eyes serious and dark. "Right now."

Cecily nodded, taking a step forward. This was obviously a challenge, and she couldn't afford to flub it. She lifted her hands, holding them in front of her at roughly chest level, picturing flickers of electricity wreathing them and willing her power to appear.

Nothing happened.

She took a deep breath and tried again. She had spent most of the night replaying the vision Esme had shown her over and over again, and she tried to summon that sense of elation, the feeling of not only being in command of her power but delighting in it. Of turning it to her chosen purpose. Her brow was creased with effort, and a drop of sweat slid down her back, but she thought she felt a small flash of power in her hands. She latched on to it, and with one last push of effort, a spark flared to life between her palms.

It fizzled out immediately.

She stared at the empty space where the spark had been, crestfallen. Then she heard Paloma make a noise, very softly. Something between a laugh and a scoff. A sound of judgment and dismissal that stirred the banked embers of Cecily's anger.

Well, it was anger that usually set her off, wasn't it? She could work with that.

Focusing on her hands again, she drew on all the stress, helplessness, and general wrongness of the last few days. She remembered how she had dreaded the reunion with her parents. How she'd lain awake in the darkness, petrified of what Dr. Fairchild had in store for her. How she'd sat next to his mangled body, knowing someone had done this because of her, *to* her, just because of who she was and what she could do. One life snuffed out and another ruined, and it was all so cruel and *unnecessary*—

Without warning, bolts of lightning shot out of her hands, arcing forward toward the stage. Paloma shrieked and jumped back just in time for the electricity to miss her feet. Instead, it scorched the smooth boards where she'd been standing, leaving a mark that smoked slightly in the quiet room.

Cecily's hands flew to her mouth as she stared, horrified, at the black spot before her. Paloma, likewise, peered at it with wide eyes before shifting her gaze up to Cecily's face. They stood there like that for a long, silent moment, Cecily's stomach roiling with self-recrimination. She scrambled for something to say, anything that would make it feel like less of an appalling disgrace of a failure.

Then Paloma burst out laughing.

Cecily's anger surged back to the surface, but after a moment, she realized Paloma's laughter wasn't bitter or mocking. Rather, it was surprised and a little self-deprecating, the laugh of someone faced with a truly wild and unexpected turn of events. As Cecily watched, she stepped forward and leaned down, examining the mark, a look of concentration on her face.

Eventually, she glanced up at Cecily. "Not bad."

Cecily flushed with... Oh, she couldn't even tell anymore. "Thank you?"

Paloma straightened and gave her a wry smile. "If we're going to do this, we could probably do with a change of venue. Go get your coat and meet me at the stairs in five minutes."

With that, she vanished into the wings, leaving Cecily to stare after her in astonishment.

After a moment, Cecily managed to collect herself and reclaim her coat. And sure enough, five minutes later, Paloma joined her, her practice outfit replaced by warmer clothes topped with a coat and scarf.

"All right," she said, climbing the first steps. "Up we go!"

"Up to where?" Cecily asked, placing her hand on the banister and following. As far as she knew, the Hierophant only had the two stories, and she had seen nothing on the second floor the night before that looked conducive to practicing with her powers.

Paloma sighed impatiently. "Just come on." And she rounded the first landing and disappeared.

They passed the second floor without slowing, and when they reached the last of the stairs, Paloma pushed open a metal door, letting a gust of cold air into the stairwell. Then the two of them stepped out onto the roof.

The building may have only had the two floors, but the ceilings were high, so the roof gave Cecily a more elevated vantage than its neighbors. The little shed-like structure they'd just come out of sat on one of the back corners. Farther down was a trellis covered in desiccated climbing branches that Cecily suspected would be alive with roses in the summer. Along the front side were the billboard and water tank she remembered seeing from the street. Strings of lights and a series of ropes had been rigged up between these structures with tarps draped over the latter to create a sort of makeshift pavilion that provided shade and some protection from the wind. Some smaller pieces of stage scenery and props had been dragged up here—a dressmaker's dummy, a lamppost, some kind of giant mushroom - the choices likely dictated by what would fit up the stairs. Some battered metal furniture and rather forlorn cushions patched together from scraps of canvas took up much of the rest of the space.

Cecily was enchanted. It felt like something from a storybook, one of the adventure novels that Herbert had passed off to her once he'd gotten bored of them, which rarely took very long. It was a tinker's workshop, a pirate cave, a house in the trees built by castaways on a deserted island. She and Daniel had spent hours lost together in those places, once upon a time.

"Okay," Paloma said. "The weather is being fairly cooperative today, so that's good."

The air did feel a bit warmer than it had since Cecily had come home. It was definitely still cold, especially when the wind came off the harbor, but it was a few degrees above freezing, which was apparently suitable for what Paloma had in mind.

"Now. Watch." Paloma held her hands out in front of her, and a small sphere of water coalesced in the cradle formed by her palms, ripples swirling over the surface. It was so simple compared to what she had done onstage, but it was still wonderful—a tiny, perfect miracle.

"How are you doing that?" Cecily asked.

"I'm collecting moisture from the air," Paloma said. "It's harder than working with water that's already liquid, and I don't have as much control, but it gets the job done." The corner of her mouth quirked up. "Claudia gets so mad when I do it like this at home. She says it dries out her skin." Her eyes flicked to Cecily, and she pulled her hands apart with a flourish, dispersing the sphere in a flash of mist. "Okay, your turn."

Cecily took a step back. "I'm not... Are you sure?"

"You say you want to learn control," Paloma said. "And the only way to do that is to practice." She grabbed Cecily's wrists, pulling her hands forward. "Come on. No time like the present. And if you set something on fire, it will be much easier to put out up here."

Cecily's eyes went wide with horror.

"I'm kidding!" Paloma said, voice bright and, evidently, meant to be encouraging. "But seriously, let's move away from the tarps a little."

Cecily swallowed. Deeply ingrained feelings of inadequacy—and yes, all right, fear—swirled inside her, especially given her display downstairs. But Paloma was right. If she had any hope of controlling her powers—and her life—she had to see this through.

"Okay. What do I do?"

"I'm no expert on electricity," Paloma admitted as she spread Cecily's arms wide. "But I imagine the basics are the same as water. First, take a deep breath." She demonstrated by closing her eyes and pulling air in through her nose, then letting it out slowly through her mouth.

With some surprise, Cecily recognized the process from the calming exercises her doctor had taught her years before. She followed Paloma's example.

"Now," Paloma said, "imagine the ambient energy surrounding you like a cloud. It likes you. It's your friend."

Cecily couldn't suppress a smile at the enthusiasm in her voice. She felt Paloma bring her hands back in front of her, sides pressed together at waist level.

"Now open your eyes," Paloma said. "And concentrate on pulling the energy from that cloud toward you. Ask it to gather in your hands, the way I did with the water."

Cecily took another breath and stared at her palms, trying to summon the crackling light that often sprang from them whether she liked it or not, but willing it to be stable. Calm.

Nothing happened. Cecily's brow furrowed in frustration, and Paloma reached out, using her hands to support Cecily's forearms.

"Don't force it," she said, her voice as gentle and soothing as her touch. "Invite it. Let it connect with the energy inside you. The stuff that makes your brain think and your heart beat."

Cecily focused on making herself relax, releasing the tension in her shoulders and her jaw. Then she tried again, reaching out to the air around her, picturing her body as a circuit and letting the energy flow through it.

In her hands, a flicker of blue sprang to life. Instead of instantly winking out like before, it held steady. She gasped, and Paloma's grip on her arms tightened ever so slightly with excitement.

"There it is!" Paloma said, clearly fighting to keep her voice quiet so as not to disturb Cecily's concentration. "You did it! Now keep going!"

Cecily took a shaky breath and held it, willing the flicker to remain. It felt different than what she was used to. Almost… friendly, just like Paloma had said. She tried to feed her good will to the flicker, like a handshake or a kiss on the cheek. Slowly, the flicker grew, shifting and expanding until Cecily had a delicate globe of light cupped in her hands. Paloma withdrew her hands, but the globe remained, glimmering softly.

"Okay," Paloma said, barely a whisper. "Now let it go."

Cecily began to pull back her intention, but not the warmth that had settled in her chest. As she watched, the ball began to dwindle and fade, then it disappeared. Peacefully, like something falling asleep.

Cecily dropped her hands, air escaping from her lungs in a rush.

"See?" Paloma said, beaming. "You can do it."

As Cecily fought to catch her breath, tears sprang to her eyes. She could do it. She could *do* it. Whether she could do it consistently remained to be seen, but now she knew, really knew, down in her bones, that she could work with her power. She didn't have to fight it anymore. She didn't have to be afraid.

She turned toward the back of the roof as the tears fell, embarrassed, but Paloma was too quick for her.

"Hey," Paloma said, real concern in her voice now. "Are you okay?" She stepped forward and rested a hand on Cecily's elbow.

"Yes," Cecily said weakly, wiping at her cheeks. "I am. It's just..." She couldn't find the words to finish the sentence, so she resorted to waving nonsensically.

Paloma's face softened, and she squeezed Cecily's arm. "Yeah. It is."

She pulled a handkerchief out of her coat pocket and handed it to Cecily. The two of them were quiet for a moment as Cecily collected herself.

"Thank you." She carefully folded the hanky into a neat square. "I think that might be enough practice for one day." She was expecting Paloma to make some breezy remark of agreement, but no remark was forthcoming.

Cecily lifted her head to find Paloma gazing at her, assessing her.

"What?" Cecily asked.

"You know," Paloma said, "I was really prepared not to like you."

Cecily twisted the hanky in her fingers. "Well, it's very... forthright of you to share that."

"But you're not what I expected," Paloma continued. "In another situation, we might even have been friends."

Cecily raised her eyebrows. "Only in another situation?"

For a moment, Paloma just looked at her. Then she smiled. "Okay. Maybe in this one, too."

CHAPTER 13

DANIEL

Several hours later, Daniel pulled his auto, headlights off, into the mouth of an alley a few neighborhoods over from the Hierophant, then backed into the shadows provided by a stand of trees and killed the engine. Across the street stood the office of the late Dr. Ernest Fairchild. Daniel considered the building, head tilted to the side in thought. It was elegant but understated, in a neighborhood that was posh, but not too posh. Detached, rather than a row house. Respectable, discreet. Orchestrated to attract a very specific type of clientele.

Ad Astra Law Enforcement should have been there already, but then again, they thought they'd already identified their perpetrator, so Daniel was ninety-nine percent sure they hadn't bothered. He'd never thought much of the city's authorities, but in this case, their ineptitude worked in his favor, so he wasn't going to complain.

"What do we think?" Oliver asked from the passenger seat. "Any heightened security?"

Daniel shook his head. "No. He was the type who couldn't even fathom the idea of someone trespassing in his domain. The sense of entitlement was stifling."

"So, a standard B and E?"

"Sounds about right."

"Is this what y'all normally do?" Aaron asked, leaning up from the back seat to poke his head between them. "Casing the joint? Am I saying that right?"

Daniel looked at him then shifted his gaze to Oliver. "You had to bring him?"

Oliver threw his hands up. "I told you—he latched on to me as I was headed out the door, and I don't know if you've noticed, but he's very persistent. I could have stood there arguing with him, but it was much quicker to just agree that he could come along."

Daniel swung his attention back to Aaron. "And why did this seem like a good idea to you?"

"It's not fair that we all have to stay behind at the club while you two get to go out and do all the cloak-and-dagger stuff," Aaron said. "I just wanted to see what it was like."

"It's not a wireless serial, Aaron," Daniel said. "This is a real job. It takes skill, finesse."

"I'm brimming with finesse!" Aaron protested. "Come on, just give me a chance."

Daniel and Oliver exchanged a look. Oliver lifted his eyebrows in a "How bad could it be?" sort of way, and Daniel sighed.

"Fine," he said.

Aaron beamed. "All right, what do I get to do?"

Daniel reached into his pocket and pulled out something that looked vaguely like a wooden kazoo. Reaching into the back seat, he slapped it into Aaron's palm.

Aaron stared at it. "What is this?"

"Bird call," Daniel said. "Sounds like a barrier owl. Your job is to sit in the car and keep an eye on the street. See something suspicious, that's one hoot; if someone approaches the building, hoot twice."

The barrier owl, which was native to the area around Ad Astra, was notoriously loud and considered an insufferable but unavoidable pest in the city. Daniel and Oliver had discovered that its call was the only sound they could use as a signal that would carry enough to be heard without arousing suspicion.

118

Aaron did not look impressed. "Are you serious? I'm just going to sit in the car? Why can't I do something to actually help?"

"You *will* be helping," Oliver said. "Because if you're sitting in the car, that frees both of us up to go into the office, which means we'll be in and out more quickly."

Aaron's face screwed up in distaste, and Oliver sighed, clearly losing patience. "Look, you wanted to come. It's not like we twisted your arm."

"Okay," Aaron grumbled, then pointed at the back of Oliver's head. "But I am sending you some *vicious* emotional energy."

"I'm aware," Oliver said blithely.

That settled, Daniel and Oliver slipped out of the car and crossed the street to Dr. Fairchild's office. They climbed the stairs onto the low porch, and Daniel dropped into a crouch in front of the door, sliding his lock picks from his pocket and getting to work.

Next to him, Oliver slouched languidly against the wall, hands stacked atop his cane. He looked entirely casual, as if he stood outside office buildings in the middle of the night as a matter of course, but Daniel knew he was watching the street with an eagle eye.

"You seem to be taking your time with that," Oliver said. "One might think you had all night to do it."

"Nobody asked you," Daniel grumbled.

This sniping wasn't exactly new to them. The truth was that Oliver was the more skilled of the two at locks, by far, but his leg made it difficult for him to stay hunched down at the doorknob's level for long. His impatience at having to wait on someone less capable to get the work done made him testy. Daniel knew better than to take the bait, but the awareness that Oliver was standing there judging him made his own fuse short. Times like this emphasized to Daniel that Oliver really was a brother to him, because only his actual brother had ever needled him quite so successfully.

Eventually, the lock's tumblers obeyed his picks. In a matter of seconds, Daniel was on his feet and inside the building with Oliver close on his heels, pulling the door shut behind them. In the office's thick darkness, Daniel reached into his pocket and pulled out an elec-

119

tric torch—one of the very latest designs on the market and quite expensive, which Esme never let him forget. He flipped the switch on the torch's handle and swept the resulting beam of light over a modest but comfortable waiting area and a staircase leading to the second floor. Daniel jerked his head toward the stairs, and Oliver nodded.

They made their way up the stairs and down a short hallway to a door where Dr. Fairchild's name had been painted in gold, though in a far less ostentatious fashion than Esme's. This door was unlocked, a surprisingly basic oversight. Still, as Daniel had said in the auto, the doctor had seemed the type to expect his life, professional or otherwise, to move along smoothly, undisrupted by something as uncouth as burglary. Though when he'd last left the place, he also hadn't known he wouldn't be coming back…

Daniel's mood sobered a bit as they entered the office, and after checking the window in the torch's light to make sure the curtains were drawn, he turned on a lamp to get the lay of the land.

The furnishings in this room were of noticeably higher quality than those downstairs, all mahogany and leather. After a moment, Oliver moved to a row of metal file cabinets against one wall. He dragged over a tufted ottoman from the conversation area in front of the fireplace and sat down to comb through one of the lower drawers. Daniel, meanwhile, rounded the massive desk and began examining its contents.

An elegantly tooled green leather pad with a coordinating marble clock, pen holder, and letter opener covered most of the desktop. There was also a neat stack of papers and another of medical journals. The topmost journal, *The Selective Heredity Review*, featured an article by Dr. Fairchild himself entitled "Adept at What Cost?: A Theory of Human Pedigrees Liberated from the Strictures of Magic."

Daniel scowled, but dutifully flipped through both stacks looking for anything useful. When that search was fruitless, moved on to the desk's drawers. The center drawer yielded only pencils, paper clips, and other supplies, while the larger drawer to the left contained stationery, a large silver flask, and a blank racing form. The drawer to the right held several hanging files, presumably more pressing or recent than those in the cabinets Oliver was checking. Daniel inspected these as well and found nothing interesting. But just as he was about to move on, he spotted a flat metal box wedged into the back of the drawer, partially concealed by the file folders. Carefully, Daniel extricated the box and sat it on top of the desk.

Unlike the office door, the box was locked, but Daniel made quick work of it and lifted the lid eagerly. Inside, he found a small ledger book and a stack of invoices, all labeled with the name Center for a Flourishing Humanity. Daniel skimmed the book and the documents, but aside from the weirdly utopian name, nothing leaped out at him as incriminating or suspicious. He was beginning to despair when he took one last look inside the box and found a plain white envelope nestled in the bottom.

He lifted the envelope out of the box and looked it over. It lacked an address or any other distinguishing marks. As he opened it, though, he noticed that the paper was creamy and thick, clearly expensive. The slip of paper he withdrew was similarly impressive, trimmed in a tasteful gold border, though it bore no identifying letterhead. Someone had written on it in deep-blue ink, presumably with the same sort of fountain pen as the one on the desk.

Fairchild—

As we discussed, I contacted T. to bring him up to speed on the project. He was delighted to hear of your progress and would like to arrange a face-to-face meeting with you soon to discuss further steps. You know I have always believed that your efforts represent a turning point in our nation's—nay, our very world's—future. I think others may finally recognize the significance as well.

Stay the course, my friend. The reward will be great.

Yours,

A. Sutterfield

"Well, isn't that interesting," Daniel murmured, leaning back in the desk chair.

"What?" Oliver asked, standing and moving to the desk.

Daniel held out the letter. Oliver read it silently, then let out a low whistle. "Who do we think this 'T' is? Teasley?"

"I'd say the odds are good," Daniel said. "I guess it could also by Turner-Hoff, but that leads us to basically the same place."

"What do you make of 'further steps'-"

Oliver cut off abruptly as Daniel held up his hand. Outside, they heard a single hoot of a barrier owl. They waited a moment to see if another would follow, but all was quiet. Even so, they knew their time was up.

"Let's go." Daniel stuffed the box inside his jacket and zipped it up.

The two of them made one final inspection of the room to ensure everything else was just as they'd found it. Then Daniel turned off the lights, and they slipped out the office door. On the ground floor, they approached the windows with care and peered cautiously through the lace curtains, checking for whatever threat Aaron had spotted.

"Should we wait a bit?" Oliver muttered.

"No," Daniel said after a moment. "Aaron would have signaled again if it wasn't safe. Let's make this quick."

For once, Oliver didn't argue. Instead, he nodded, and the two of them moved swiftly to the front door. Seconds later, they were across the street and settling back into the car.

"What did you see?" Daniel said. "Did anybody try to get into the office?"

"No," Aaron said. He was more serious now, presumably, because he'd realized that they actually had given him a legitimate job rather than just leaving him behind for kicks. "There was a car coming down the street—black, no plates. It slowed down in front of the building, and I thought I saw someone in the passenger seat looking up at the second floor, but then they kept driving."

"Do you think they saw us?"

Aaron shook his head. "The curtains hid most of the office, but a little light seeped out around the edges. That's probably why they kept driving." He swallowed. "I think there was someone in the back seat with a rifle."

Daniel bit his lip, considering. "Doesn't sound like coppers."

"Nope," Oliver said. "RPC?"

"Maybe," Daniel said. "Or Shining Light coming to see if there was anything they could use to stir up trouble. Either way, we don't want to be here if they come back." He started the engine and glanced at Aaron in the rearview mirror. "This cloak-and-dagger enough for you?"

Aaron was quiet as Daniel took them back to the Hierophant.

CHAPTER 14

CECILY

"That's it," Paloma murmured, lowering her hands slowly. "Hold it steady."

She had been spotting Cecily, which was more a thoughtful gesture than a real precaution, since it was unclear what precisely she would do if Cecily's magic went haywire. But now, she took a step away, ceding the floor entirely to Cecily.

Cecily barely noticed. Her attention was on the sphere of energy cradled in her hands, an orb of crackling blue and white. With Paloma's help, she had gotten to the point where she could call the energy with relative ease. It was maintaining control that was difficult. Now, Cecily poured her intention into the sphere. As they both watched, it began to move, turning erratically, juddering in Cecily's hold. Distantly, Cecily heard Paloma make a soft sound of triumph. It wasn't much, but it was more than she'd been able to muster thus far that day.

Cecily pushed the distraction away and narrowed her focus, trying to smooth the sphere's motion and settle the snapping tendrils of electricity that covered its surface. For a moment, she thought she had it. Then something inside her went tight, and the tendrils all seemed to leap outward at once. Cecily dropped her hands and jumped back as the sphere flared, turning inside out. A moment later, it fell back in on itself to wink out of existence, leaving behind a scorched scent of ozone.

Paloma peeked out from underneath her arm, which she had instinctively thrown up to protect herself. "You're trying too hard."

"I don't see how there is any 'too hard' in this situation. It's sort of important that I get a handle on this."

Paloma gave her a sympathetic look. "I know. But magic isn't a misbehaving child. You can't *force* it to do something."

Cecily sighed. "I suppose that's just as well. I've never been especially good with children."

They were on the roof again, having spent a good chunk of the afternoon practicing. Cecily rubbed the back of her hand across her forehead, warm despite the chill in the air. She largely had her clothing to thank for that. Esme had made good on her promise, and she'd returned to Daniel's nook after her first visit to the roof to find a collection of dresses, shoes, and other assorted odds and ends laid out on and under the bed. They had all more or less fit, and something about the haphazard nature of them made her look rather avant-garde. Like an artist. She found that she quite liked it.

Paloma, however, had taken one look and declared everything unsuitable for practice. She had then somehow procured trousers and boots for the pair of them to wear during their extended periods in the elements, and they both had them on now underneath their coats. Cecily had long ago abandoned her scarf to one of the metal chairs, and neither of them wore gloves, as they needed their hands free to work.

"Remember," Paloma was saying, voice patient, "a failed attempt is just—"

"A new hypothesis," Cecily finished. "I know."

During breaks in Cecily's training, the two of them had discovered a shared love of science. Cecily had always focused on physics, since that was relevant to her powers, while Paloma was more interested in biology and the human body, but their interests gave them a common frame of reference, a common language, to draw on as they worked.

Cecily had rarely had someone to share her passion with, and she found she enjoyed their conversations very much. But then she'd brought up university.

"Why aren't you in med school?" she'd asked. "You'd make a fantastic doctor."

Paloma had just laughed. "I would love to go to med school. But most of the ones in New Avalon still don't admit women. And even if they did, they might not be open to an immigrant woman with no money." Her tone was rueful, but seeing the look on Cecily's face, she'd softened. "I'm making enough money from the club that I can put some away in savings. Maybe I'll get to go one day. I'm good for now. Come on, let's get back to work."

Cecily had followed Paloma's lead, but her cheeks were burning, in no small part because Paloma had felt compelled to comfort *her*, when she was the one who had misstepped. She'd never had to worry about anything like that. Talking her parents into letting her go to Belleterre had been the hard part; actually getting into university had been easy. Cecily had always known that she had advantages that others did not, but facing it so directly left her feeling flustered and embarrassed. She did her best to shake it off and focus on the work.

Now, she watched as Paloma stretched and looked up toward the sky.

"Ugh," Paloma said. "I wish it would either snow already or clear up so we can have some sun again. I hate this lingering gray overcast business."

"I like it," Cecily said. "I think it's kind of… mysterious. Romantic."

"You would," Paloma said with a sigh, but her words were good natured.

Cecily smiled. "Shall we go again?" she asked. A part of her longed to head inside to rest and get warm, but as she's just said to Paloma, she felt a driving sense of urgency to do as much as she could as quickly as she could to make herself of use.

Paloma pulled a watch out of her coat pocket and checked the time. "No," she said, and Cecily felt a mixture of regret and relief. "I think that's enough for now. I have a wardrobe issue I need to address with Charmaine, and it's almost time for me to meet with her. Besides"—she cast a knowing look at Cecily—"you seem like you could do with a breather."

Cecily's face burned at the realization that she hadn't been projecting as much dogged stoicism as she'd thought, but she accepted the reprieve for what it was, and as she followed Paloma inside and down the stairs, she realized she was starving. When she reached the ground floor, she turned her steps toward the kitchen.

Preparations were already underway for the first dinner service, but among the hustle and bustle, she managed to catch the eye of Bao, one of the junior chefs who had been friendly to her.

"Anything I can get for you, Miss Dearborn?"

"Bao, we've been over this. Please call me Cecily. And I'd like a cup of tea, if it's not too much trouble."

"Coming right up." He grinned, turning toward the shining appliances just as a deep voice called out, "Ah, *ma chérie, tu es arrivée!*"

When Cecily had finally gotten around to meeting the famous Alphonse, they had hit it off right away. After she'd explained that she had just returned from Belleterre, he had grasped her hands and waxed poetic about the wonders of his beautiful homeland, delighted to find someone who knew it well enough to share in his appreciation, and in his own language, no less. Now, the stout, dark-haired man, whose impeccably curled mustache was quivering with excitement, hurried toward her. He took both of her hands in his and kissed her expansively on each cheek.

"*J'ai quelque chose à vous montrer que seule une femme comme vous pourrait pleinement apprécier,*" he said, leading her over to the pastry station.

Atop the marble counter sat a tower of delicate, beautiful macarons in alternating layers of ivory and pink. Cecily sighed in pleasure. The patisserie near her flat in Ville du Soleil had made the most divine macarons. They had been one of her favorite indulgences while she'd lived there, and while she'd had much bigger issues on her mind as she had hastily prepared for her return, a tiny part of her had still despaired at finding anything comparable when she returned to Ad Astra.

Now, she gazed on Alphonse's wonderful confections with a kind of rapture. *"Ils sont merveilleux, mon ami. Vous vous êtes surpassé."*

Beaming, Alphonse retrieved a delicate saucer and transferred six macarons to it—three pink, three ivory—before holding it out to Cecily. She put up a token protest, but he refused to take no for an answer, so finally, she conceded.

"Merci," she said, accepting the saucer. *"Tu es un prince parmi les hommes."*

Alphonse gave her a slight bow, then turned toward the oven, where some sort of timer was shrilling. A moment later, Bao appeared with Cecily's tea, and she took everything to the small dining room attached to the kitchen where the staff often took their meals.

Settling into one of the chairs at the table, she took a sip of tea and examined the macarons. After a moment of consideration, she selected an ivory one. As she took a bite, the light, crisp meringue of the outer shells shattered against her tongue, giving way to the rich, almost smoky sweetness of the vanilla buttercream inside. Cecily gave a quiet moan that would have been embarrassing if anyone had been there to hear it.

Truly, Alphonse had a gift.

She took a second bite, followed by another sip of tea. It could have been her imagination, but it seemed between the warm drink and the sugar, she was already beginning to feel restored. She had just popped the last of the macaron into her mouth when she caught a flash of movement through the open door, only realizing after the fact that it was Daniel rushing past. He must have had a similar delayed moment of awareness, because after a moment, he backtracked, pausing in the doorway to look at her.

"Hi," she said and lifted her teacup for another sip.

"Hi, yourself." He came into the room, hands in his pockets. "Wasn't expecting to find you down here. What are you up to?"

"Just having a little pick-me-up. Paloma and I were out training."

"Oh? How's that going?"

"All right, I guess." She shrugged, wishing she had something more encouraging to tell him. "How about you? What are you busy with today?"

"I've been with Esme and Oliver, going over what we found at Dr. Fairchild's office last night."

"Oh," Cecily said, suddenly more alert. "Anything helpful?"

"Maybe," Daniel said. "It's hard to tell anything for sure, but Esme reached out to one of our contacts to see if he can help us make sense of it. I'll be meeting with him later tonight."

"You mean there wasn't anything conveniently labeled 'Incriminating Evidence'?" she asked

Daniel shook his head. "Sadly, no. They're going to make us work a little harder for it than that."

Cecily nodded in commiseration and picked up another macaron.

"What are those anyway?" he asked as he pulled out one of the other chairs and sat down.

"Macarons. Vanilla and"—she picked up a pink one and passed it under her nose, inhaling—"raspberry, I think. I had them all the time in Belleterre, and these are excellent."

Daniel huffed a laugh. "Fancy. I guess you can take the girl out of society, but you can't take society out of the girl." His tone was matter-of-fact, with no hint of malice or bitterness, but it still hit Cecily like a blow. It took her a moment to sort through the feelings his words conjured up, but the main one felt something like… betrayal? It had felt as if they were bridging some of the distance between them, but now it seemed they were back to square one.

"What's that supposed to mean?" she asked, her voice sharp with emotion.

Daniel looked up, surprised by her reaction. "Well, you've always liked fine things. And people have liked giving them to you. I mean, Alphonse has never made these for any of us."

"And that's my fault?"

"No," Daniel said, looking increasingly out of his depth. "Obviously not. I just meant that you seem to manifest a little of the luxury you were born to wherever you go. Even when it seems like you're at rock bottom. It's kind of impressive."

"What should I be doing? Wallowing in a hovel? Wailing and gnashing my teeth?"

"No, but—"

"I like good food," Cecily said. "I like good art. I like wearing nice clothes. What's wrong with those things?"

"Nothing," Daniel said, getting exasperated. "But are they worth everything that comes with them?"

"Like what?"

"The greed. The arrogance. The graft. I don't know why I'm having to explain this to you—you've seen that ugliness your whole life."

"I have. But I'm still not sure how Alphonse making me a snack comes into play."

Daniel blew out a frustrated breath, throwing up his hands. "Because that's not how things work here! We've all had to fight tooth and nail to get where we are. Nobody gave us anything."

"And where is it that you are?" Cecily asked. "A cloister where you've retired to seek spiritual enlightenment? A hermitage out in the woods where you reject worldly concerns? Because to me it looks an awful lot like an illicit nightclub that caters to the very people you're complaining about."

"Esme explained that to you. It's a means to an end."

"Oh, really? So Oliver suffers through wearing custom tailored suits for the cause, is that it? It's penance for Esme to decorate her office with teak and silk?"

Daniel glowered at her, but beyond his frustration, he seemed perplexed. And despite her own indignation, she understood. They'd never fought, before. Now, though, it seemed they were both prone to lashing out at even inadvertent slights. Where once they'd been quick to forgive, now they were wary. And while she suspected they both wanted to break the impasse, neither was willing to make the first overture.

"Are you seriously trying to say that Oliver and Esme are like your parents and their friends?" Daniel asked.

Cecily scoffed. "Not even a little. Like you said, they worked hard for what they have. I'm just pointing out that things aren't as black and white as you are making them out to be."

Daniel sat back in his chair. "What about me, then?"

Cecily's brow furrowed. "What about you?"

"I don't have any antiques or elegant clothes. I'm the same old Ogygian street rat I've always been, just like all the others crowded into tenements and barely scraping by in this city. Nothing about that has changed."

Cecily felt a stab of tenderness then, seeing what so much struggle and loss had done to the sweet boy she'd known all those years ago. But she wouldn't let his flawed assertions go unanswered, either.

"If that's true," she said, voice even, "why aren't you still using the flimsy sketchbooks from when we were kids instead of those beautiful blue ones with the nice, thick paper?"

If the look on his face was any indication, it was Daniel's turn to feel betrayed. For a moment, he just sat there, stunned and slack-jawed. But then his mouth snapped shut, eyes blazing.

"Let me get this straight—*you're* accusing *me* of extravagance?!"

"I'm not accusing you of anything. I'm just making an observation."

"You don't know what you're talking about," he said, voice edging close to a growl. "I don't even have a proper room of my own. I'm essentially homeless."

"That," Cecily said, "is nonsense. This is obviously your home, and based on what Oliver and Paloma have told me, the only reason you still live upstairs is because you choose to."

Daniel scowled.

"You know," she said, voice softer now, "it's okay to want something for yourself."

"Yeah?" Daniel said. "And what is it that you want?"

Cecily blinked, somewhat taken aback. For so long, her answer would have been control of her powers. With that, she'd thought she could live a normal life—one without the fear and shame that had been her constant companions since she was twelve. But now that that control was finally within her grasp, she had no idea what was going to come next. Even if they managed to figure out who had killed Dr. Fairchild, what would her life look like afterward? She'd never be entirely free of this murder, at least not in the court of public opinion. People would always wonder and whisper, no matter how much evidence she produced. And she had started building connections here that she didn't want to just abandon once she was cleared. Those things didn't lend themselves to any kind of "normal" that she was used to.

"I don't know," she said. "Everything is different now."

Something about that candor seemed to mollify him, and his shoulders relaxed a bit. "If you could pick something new—anything you want, no restrictions—what would it be? There's aviation, moun-taineering, spelunking…"

Cecily raised an eyebrow. "Spelunking?"

"It's kind of the opposite of mountaineering—you know, exploring caves, looking at stalactites and stalagmites."

"I know what it is," she said. "I'm just wondering why you thought it would be something I'd enjoy."

"It was just an example!"

"Not a particularly good example."

"Seriously, though," he said. "What would you choose?"

Cecily paused, thinking hard, and a plan began to take shape. "I think I'd live on a train."

Daniel stared. "You'd what?"

"Live on a train. You know, one car could be my living room, one could be my bedroom, et cetera. I could travel around and always be seeing new sights and meeting new people. I'd get to know the whole country."

"Wouldn't that be lonely?" he asked. "Riding the rails all by yourself?"

Cecily considered that for a moment. "I'd invite the friends I made to come along, so we could have adventures together."

"There's still big stretches of nothing out there," Daniel said, eyeing the plate between them. "No place to get luscious desserts."

"I could hire Alphonse. He'd travel with us. I'd give him two cars—one for a kitchen and one for himself."

"Sounds like a sweet arrangement," Daniel conceded.

"It would be." A feeling of wistfulness settled over her. She met Daniel's eyes. "I would be free."

Her words hung in the air between them for a moment.

Daniel looked at her as if she were something rare and mysterious, not someone he'd known for years. Then he looked away. "What would happen when you ran out of track, after you'd been all over the country? Would you just start over?"

"Maybe," Cecily said. "But eventually, I'd like to settle down. Perhaps find a small city in the mountains or on the coast of Calafia with a university. I could buy a little house and rent out my train to other wanderers while I studied and taught and became a world-renowned physicist. And I'd have a cat." She nodded once for emphasis. "Maybe a calico. I'd name her Anomaly."

Daniel blinked at her. Then he shook his head. "You are a woman of singular vision, Cecily Dearborn."

Hearing the fondness in his voice, she smiled. "I try." She pushed the plate in his direction. "Macaron?"

CHAPTER 15

DANIEL

That night, Daniel drove down toward the harbor and parked his auto in the shadow of an abandoned warehouse. Turning his collar up against the cold, he walked a few blocks down the ramshackle street to an all-night diner with a red neon sign proclaiming "COFFEE—BURGERS—PIE." It was the last that had made him choose this particular establishment rather than any of the similar joints in the neighborhood. The place may not have been a lavish Belleterran patisserie, but it had the best coconut cream in the city, and soon he was ensconced in a booth with a slice and a cup of far less impressive coffee to wait.

He took his time eating, watching any new customers carefully as they hurried in from the cold, but none of them spared him a glance. By the time he'd finished his pie, all was still quiet in the diner, so he called for the check. He was a little annoyed, if he was honest. He'd been hoping for more of a distraction.

As the waitress rang him up, Daniel stared at the reflection of the counter in the plate-glass window, turning his conversation with Cecily over in his head for the umpteenth time. Maybe he'd been naïve to assume they would fall back into their old camaraderie once they'd started opening up to each other again, but their conversation that afternoon had still felt wrong. They'd never argued as children. And of course this one had been about money. Of course it had. Because that was the elephant in the room, wasn't it? It always had been.

The closest they'd ever come to having a real fight was on one memorable occasion when he'd been almost sick with jealousy because Cecily attending the opening of the new Ad Astra Museum of Art. He'd been ashamed of his envy and tried to hide it, but that hadn't gone especially well. He'd been short with Cecily, temperamental, and she'd just looked at him with wide wounded eyes. She'd known why. How could she not, when she knew him so well?

The day after the opening, she had grabbed his hand and led him to the old maple tree behind Dearborn house. The two of them had lain in the grass, heads together as they stared up at the spring sunshine filtering through the leaves, and she had described every painting she'd seen in exacting detail, giving him as much of the experience as she could. Years later, he had finally gotten to attend the museum on his own. That was after he had come to live with Esme and Oliver, when he had locked his bond with Cecily away into a secret part of himself that he could ignore as he went about his day-to-day life, but even so, on that visit, none of the paintings had lived up to the visions he'd constructed in his mind based on her whispers.

It seemed this would always be their path. When it was just the two of them left to their own devices, it was so easy to forget the difference in their circumstances. They would choose each other, again and again. But nobody else seemed willing to let them ignore those divisions, and growing up had only made the situation more fraught.

Finally, the waitress brought Daniel's change, and, leaving a generous tip, he got up and walked out the door. The wind hit him like a physical thing, and he paused, wishing he'd remembered to wear a scarf. His eyes scanned the street, and still, he didn't see anyone who looked like a contact. This was getting ridiculous. These covert rendezvous were, by design, unpredictable and difficult to gauge, but it was cold as hells, and he was going to attract attention if he lingered much longer.

Playing for a bit more time, Daniel strolled to the corner and lit a cigarette. He didn't especially care for smoking, but it gave him something to do with hands and made him less conspicuous than he would have been just standing there twiddling his thumbs. The diner was on a slight rise, and before him, the streets sloped down toward the water. As he exhaled, he gazed over the harbor, taking in the lights of the docks and the handful of boats that were out on such a cold night.

One craft in particular caught his attention. It was farther out than the other boats, though still within the curve of the barrier islands that separated the city from the ocean proper, and it sat on the water like a precious bauble on a length of velvet, a single green light at its bow. In the low light of the moon, he could make out something if its shape—sleek and low slung, probably a yacht. Cecily's people. Not her actual family, of course; Mrs. Dearborn would never be so gauche as to take the boat out with everything going on. But her circle. The ones he hated so deeply but couldn't seem to shake. Even here among the warehouses and run-down offices, in what they would inevitably call the "rough" part of town, he wasn't free of them.

Pushing away those thoughts, Daniel took another drag. He was debating whether it was time to just declare the whole night a bust when a big man with a bushy mustache and a bowler hat strolled up the sidewalk in front of the diner, blowing on his hands to warm them.

"Hey, friend," he said, patting his pockets as he approached Daniel. "Could you spare a light?"

Daniel nodded and put his own cigarette between his lips to light the one the man withdrew from the depths of his voluminous coat. For a moment, the two of them stood there wordlessly, the crackle of tobacco and paper mingling with the far-off sounds of the harbor.

The man blew a series of smoke rings that hovered for a moment before they were carried off by the wind. As they disappeared, he murmured quietly, so only Daniel could hear, "Count twenty and follow." Then, more loudly, he said, "Much obliged, pal. Have a good night." And without so much as glancing in Daniel's direction, he strode away.

Daniel took a final puff, dropped his cigarette to the sidewalk, and crushed it with the toe of his boot, all while counting in his head. When he reached twenty, he ambled off in the same direction the man had gone. He tucked his hands into his pockets as he went, keeping his pace casual and his gaze straight ahead, but he was nevertheless on high alert for any sign that he was being watched or followed. This lasted for five or six blocks until he caught sight of a scrap of cloth snagged on the fence post at the mouth of an alley. When he reached the fence, he snatched the cloth off the post without breaking stride and turned into the shadowy recess of the alley. In the low light, he saw the man in the bowler hat standing next to a big new auto. As Daniel approached, the man nodded and opened the rear passenger door, gesturing for Daniel to get in. Daniel did, and the door swung shut behind him.

There was another man in the back seat of the car. He was smaller than the man in the bowler, lanky and thin with a mop of thick dark hair and spectacles that reflected the alley's meager light. He wore a heavy coat and fingerless gloves that were discernible primarily because of the way they obscured the pale-golden skin of his hands. His foot tapped absently on the floorboard, as it often did in these meetings. Ignotus had a hard time sitting still.

Ignotus wasn't his real name, of course. Daniel had no idea what it was, which was the whole point. It was safer that way. Whatever he went by, this man was one of the most wanted conjurors in New Avalon. His knowledge of magic and those who practiced it on the continent was virtually encyclopedic. If anyone had insight into Dr. Fairchild's dealings and how the RPC might have been involved, it would be him. That was why Daniel was willing to put up with his trying demeanor. The first time they had met, he had introduced himself by saying, "Ignotus is fine for our purposes. It means 'not known.'" He'd chuckled a self-satisfied chuckle and said, "A little joke there, you see. Because it's not really my name," as if Daniel were wholly incapable of figuring this out on his own. That had more or less set the tone for their entire relationship.

"Daniel," Ignotus said now by way of greeting, and Daniel sighed. Everyone called him Daniel—it actually *was* his name, after all—and yet, whenever Ignotus said it in his plummy Avalonian accent, it felt like he was an old-timey schoolmaster and Daniel was his misbehaving pupil. It was maddening.

The man in the bowler slid in behind the wheel, pulling the passenger door shut with a bang. He turned slightly to speak over his shoulder.

"Do you need anything else right now, sir?"

"No, thank you, Douglas," Ignotus said. "Just keep us moving."

The man nodded and started the car. Ignotus, meanwhile, reached into his pocket and withdrew something that gleamed in the darkness. As Daniel watched, he placed a coin on the back of the front seat, then knocked a tuning fork against his thigh, filling the car with its gentle ring. When he reached forward and placed the base of the fork on top of the coin, there was a shiver in the air, and the sound of the engine seemed more muted than before.

"There," Ignotus said, returning the fork and the coin to his pocket. "He can't hear us. We can speak freely now."

Daniel shook his head. He was no stranger to watching people perform magic, but when it was someone like him, who had no natural magic and was able to do it with only study and practice... there were no words, really.

"What is it?" Ignotus asked, noticing his reaction.

"It's just... I don't know," Daniel said. "It never gets old. Seeing someone who's not an adept do something like that."

Ignotus made a dismissive noise, though it seemed to Daniel that he was pleased. "Magic is too romanticized. People want to make it into something big and mysterious, for good or ill, but it has order. It has rules. And if something has rules, and you learn them, you can master it. Therein lies the beauty." He shifted in his seat, so he was turned more toward Daniel. "But I doubt you came here to discuss magical theory. How can I help you this evening?"

"I suppose you heard about the murder of Dr. Fairchild," Daniel said.

"Hmm, yes," Ignotus said flatly. "Tragic."

"What do you know about him?" Daniel said. "Had any information about him been circulating recently?"

"As a matter of fact, yes," Ignotus said. "There were some rather interesting murmurings as of late, but I hadn't put any real stock in them. There didn't seem to be anything about him that set him apart from all the other charlatans out there prattling on about their harmonic nonsense. But his untimely death gave everything a bit more credence."

"What were the murmurings? Anything related to the RPC?"

"No specific mention of them, no, but it wouldn't surprise me if they were caught up in the middle of this. Details were scant, you understand, because he hadn't published anything yet, but the word was that he had isolated the part of the brain that is responsible for generating and controlling magic in adepts."

Daniel stared at him. "He what?"

Ignotus gave a long-suffering sigh. "I *said* he—"

"I heard you," Daniel snapped. "But if he understood the mechanism that controls magic, doesn't that mean he could—I don't know—turn it off? That he could *cure* magic?"

"Indeed," Ignotus said, pursing his lips in distaste. "It's still a bit hard for me to believe. I've spent the last few days reading his work, and it's rather pedestrian. His theory was rudimentary, his methodology banal, but I suppose even a broken clock is right twice a day."

"I don't care about his methodology," Daniel said through gritted teeth. "What would a discovery like that *mean*? In practical terms?"

"It would mean open season on adepts," Ignotus replied, adjusting his glasses. "Nobody has been able to eradicate natural magic completely, even with RPC money and influence behind them. But if this is true..." He spread his hands in front of him, framing a scene. "Imagine it. The RPC calls a press conference. There's bunting, New Avalonian flags everywhere, winsome orphans standing around looking grateful."

"Orphans?" Daniel repeated.

"A band plays a patriotic tune," Ignotus went on, as if Daniel hadn't spoken. "There are inspiring opening remarks, then the illustrious Colonel Teasley steps up to the microphone. And what does he have to say? That New Avalonians no longer have to live in fear. That scientific breakthroughs and homegrown ingenuity have finally given us the tools to stamp out the scourge of magic once and for all. Families with adept children won't have to worry about controlling their little ones' powers anymore. They won't have the specter of containment hanging over their heads. One quick procedure, and just like that"—he snapped his fingers—"the children will be free. No more constant vigilance. No more shame. No more neighbors whispering behind the parents' backs at religious services, saying, 'Oh, yes, they seem nice enough, but you know how *those* people turn out.'"

Daniel thought of Cecily, and his heart clenched.

Ignotus continued, caught up in painting his scenario. "Criminals with magical ability could be medically rehabilitated before rejoining society. Civil servants and candidates for office could provide credentials ensuring that they'd either been born without magic, or they'd undergone a normalizing procedure to ensure their trustworthiness. The dawn of a newly enlightened society. Orderly. Pure." He turned his head to face Daniel. "It's a doozy of a campaign promise, don't you think? Opposition to the RPC wouldn't stand a chance."

Daniel bit his lip, turning Ignotus's words over and over in his mind. "We've been working on a theory that Fairchild was targeted in an effort to sow discord within the RPC. It seems like there might be something to that, if he was so central to their plans."

"Tell me more," Ignotus said, so Daniel did. When he finished, Ignotus sighed in exasperation.

"Was Oliver behind this theory? It seems like the kind of labyrinthine, overcomplicated thing he would come up with."

"You think there's another explanation?"

Ignotus shrugged. "Hard to say. It could be that Fairchild was an RPC believer and it got him killed. But maybe he had his own plans for his discovery. If he were on his own, he'd have become famous overnight, hailed as savior, rich beyond all imagining. Perhaps he didn't fancy being under anybody's thumb."

"So you're saying it was an inside job?"

"I think that is more likely than machinations by a vast conspiracy whose motives and identities are matters of pure speculation, yes."

Daniel nodded. "Does that mean they have his research? Surely, they wouldn't slaughter the goose until they had the golden eggs."

"It's possible," Ignotus said. "But even if they don't, it's only a matter of time before it resurfaces." He shifted, tapping a finger absentmindedly against his leg. "If there really is a physiological locus for magic, someone else is going to find it. Even in situations with much lower stakes, if there is knowledge out there that is deemed valuable, people won't let it stay buried forever. That is one thing those fetishists of modernity have right. The truth will out. Even if you find Fairchild's work, this is not going away."

Daniel considered that as Ignotus pulled out the tuning fork, twirling it lazily between his fingers. He seemed strangely calm about this grim revelation, but then, that was his way. Plus, as a conjuror, this didn't change things much for him. Not like it did for the adepts.

"I'll pass all this on to Esme. She'll likely have some more questions for you no matter where it leads us," Daniel said.

Ignotus nodded and repeated the process with the fork and the coin. "Our business is concluded, Douglas. You may return Mr. Sullivan to his vehicle."

"Yes, sir."

Ignotus returned his focus to Daniel. "Keep me apprised of any further developments."

"We will," Daniel said.

"Oh," Ignotus said offhandedly. "And do give Oliver my best. It's been far too long since I've experienced the pleasure of his company."

Daniel had to fight to keep from banging his head against the window. When they weren't picking at each other like schoolchildren, Ignotus and Oliver maintained an ongoing flirtation, and neither was above carrying it out by proxy, with Daniel as the go-between. None of it was new, but especially after their worrisome conversation, he was not in the mood.

"I'm not your matchmaker," he grumbled as the car slowed to a stop not far from where he'd left his own car.

"A blessing all around, to be sure," Ignotus said.

Daniel rolled his eyes as he opened the car door and stepped out. He thought he was free and clear, but then he heard Ignotus's voice again.

"Oh, and Daniel!"

With a sigh, Daniel leaned down and poked his head back into the car. Ignotus's face was a faint outline in the darkness, eyes obscured by the light reflected in his glasses.

"Good hunting," he said.

Daniel nodded, oddly touched by the sentiment. Then he swung the door closed, stepped away, and watched as the taillights disappeared into the night.

CHAPTER 16

CECILY

Cecily and Paloma were sitting in the staff dining room the next morning when Daniel poked his head around the door.

"Good morning," he said, smiling, and Cecily was relieved.

They had left things on a fairly positive note the previous afternoon, but considering how tense their conversation had gotten, she'd been a little worried about how he would respond to her upon their next meeting. That smile, however, let her know he wasn't holding a grudge. Her stomach swooped, relief rushing in.

"What are the two of you up to?"

"Cecily is introducing me to *macarons*," Paloma said, pronouncing the word with a flourish, "which are pretty much the greatest thing I have ever tasted in my life." She popped half of a raspberry one into her mouth for emphasis.

The two of them were still in their pants and boots, having worked in a brief practice session on the roof. When they were finished, Cecily had insisted on bringing Paloma with her to track down whatever was left of Alphonse's triumph after two dinner services, and they had been sitting there chatting as they sipped their warming drinks—tea for Cecily, strong black coffee with cinnamon for Paloma—as they gorged on treats.

Daniel gave Cecily an accusing look. "You've created a monster. I hope you realize that."

Cecily shrugged, sipping her tea.

Daniel shook his head, face turning serious. "We're meeting in Esme's office in a few minutes to go over some new information. She wants you to be there."

"All right." Cecily wiped her mouth with a napkin and began gathering her dishes.

"Paloma, you should probably come, too," Daniel went on, "since you're involved with Cecily's training,"

Paloma paused, coffee cup halfway to her mouth. "You want me to come?"

Daniel's eyes narrowed. "Yes. Why do you sound surprised?"

"It's just that most of us don't usually get invited to the super-secret boss meetings."

Daniel stared at her. "There are not," he said finally, voice flat, "any super-secret boss meetings."

Paloma still looked unconvinced. "If you say so."

She picked up her cup and saucer and followed Cecily to the kitchen where they handed off their dirty dishes before making their way down the hall. When they were about halfway to Esme's office, Paloma veered off and opened a door Cecily had never used before, gesturing for Cecily to follow. Perplexed, Cecily did, only to find herself... in Esme's office. Turning around, she saw Daniel come in, too, and when he closed the door, it practically disappeared into the paneling in the corner of the room behind the chaise.

She looked at Paloma, dumbfounded. "I had no idea that was even there."

Paloma shrugged. "The main door is designed to create a good first impression for guests, but that one is more convenient a lot of the time, since it's closer to the kitchen and the wings." She glanced at Daniel. "Where should we sit?"

"Wherever you want." Daniel waved a hand at the room.

Cecily circled around to perch on the edge of the chaise, just as she had the last time they'd gathered here. Paloma sat down beside her, while Daniel took one of the club chairs.

Claudia had just finished setting out tea and coffee as they settled in. She was edging past them toward the corner door when Paloma reached out and grabbed her arm.

"Hang on," Paloma said. "Is that my blouse?"

Claudia scowled, the first significant emotion that Cecily had seen from her in their brief acquaintance. "I needed one to wear with this skirt today, and mine still has that stain from dinner the other night."

"And how is that my problem?" Paloma asked. "What have I told you about taking things without asking?"

Claudia sighed deeply and rolled her eyes, yanking her arm from Paloma's grip. Without another word, she stomped out the door, not quite slamming it, but closing it with more force than was strictly necessary.

Paloma muttered something under her breath in what sounded like Iberian, then looked at Cecily. "Do you have any younger siblings?"

"No," Cecily said. "Just an older brother. Though to be honest, he does usually *act* like a younger sibling."

Paloma sighed, and Cecily could see the family resemblance clearly.

"Sisterhood is a heavy burden to bear."

"All right, everybody," Esme said, exuding an air of purpose as she swept into the room with Oliver and Leo on her heels. "Let's get down to business. Leo, why don't you lead off and tell us what you were able to put together?" She took a seat at her desk, while Leo propped himself against it, flipping open a notebook.

"So, yesterday, I went down to the tax office to see if I could find out more about this Center for a Flourishing Humanity that Fairchild was working with... for... whatever. Anyway, it has a filing in place as a state-recognized charity, but it was pretty bare bones—nothing there about what they actually do beyond, you know, promoting the general welfare and improving life for New Avalonians. What the filing did have was an address, up on the northern coast of Seaboard, near the strait. So I went to the map room at the library and got a road atlas of the area.

"When I looked up the address, I found that it was for an Ocean Serenity Sanitarium. Did a little more digging in the periodicals room and found out that it's a popular place among muckety-muck hypochondriacs. They're best known for promoting the rest cure to treat a wide variety of ailments, including, though not limited to, the affliction of magic." He paused for everyone in the room to roll their eyes. "And the primary investor is none other than Member of the National Congress and Reason and Prosperity Coalition flunky Carlton Turner-Hoff."

There were murmurs of surprise around the room.

"Well, that is an interesting turn of events," Esme said.

"It pretty much seals the deal that Fairchild and the RPC were in cahoots," Oliver said. "But do we have any idea of what they are trying to accomplish?"

"There were a few medical journals in the periodicals room, so I looked to see if Fairchild's work was featured in any of them. There wasn't much, but I took notes on what I could find." He waggled the notebook in his hand for emphasis.

"Mind if I take a look at that?" Daniel asked.

Leo shrugged, holding it out, and Daniel stood and crossed to the desk. He took it and leaned against the desk himself, opening to a marked page.

"What about you, Daniel?" Esme said as he scanned the pages. "What did Ignotus have to say?"

Daniel didn't respond right away, focused instead on finishing his perusal of Leo's notes, but then, with a sigh, he closed the notebook and set it on the desk. "Before I start, I want to emphasize that this is all hearsay so far—Ignotus didn't have any hard proof for what he told me."

Oliver raised an eyebrow. "Well, that doesn't make for a particularly auspicious opening. What did he have to say?"

Daniel crossed his arms over his chest. "That there have been rumors Fairchild isolated the part of the brain gives adepts their powers. That he basically found the source of natural magic."

Everyone stared at him.

"That can't be right," Oliver said.

"What would that even mean?" Paloma asked, her eyes wide.

"It would mean we'd be at the mercy of anyone who had that knowledge and the means to do something about it," Esme said grimly. "Did Ignotus say if he thought the RPC had Fairchild's research on hand?"

Daniel shook his head. "He didn't know. But he said that if one person had figured it out, it was inevitable that someone else would, too."

"Did you tell him what we'd worked out so far about the killer?" said Esme. "Did he think we were on the right track."

"I did, and he did not," Daniel said. He glanced at Oliver. "He said your theory was labyrinthine and overcomplicated."

Oliver squawked in indignation.

"Ignotus thinks it's more likely that Fairchild was inside job," Daniel continued. "That someone was worried they'd lose control of Fairchild once he realized the potential of what he'd learned."

The room fell quiet, permeated by a new sense of urgency that was almost tangible. Cecily's hands curled into fists, nails digging into her palms.

"Well," Oliver said finally, "sitting here worrying isn't helping anyone. What are we going to do?"

"I could drive up to the sanatorium and do some investigating," Leo said. "I can go tomorrow, or I can wait a couple of days and go when the club is dark."

"No," Esme said. "I think time is of the essence here. We can get Gerald to sub in for you with the band."

"What kind of investigating are you planning to do?" Oliver asked.

"Oh, you know," Leo said, "take a look around the property. Find whoever is in charge of admissions and give them a sob story about how my precious daughter has been struggling with her 'affliction,' and we've tried everything we can to help her, but nothing has worked, and we're at our wits' end, and is there anything, anything at all they can do to help us?"

He looked rather pleased with this little bit of skullduggery.

Oliver appeared less impressed. "Mm-hmm, and what's this precious daughter's name again?"

"It's, uh..." Leo's eyes swept frantically around the room until they settled on the sideboard behind Esme's desk. "Credenza."

Oliver pursed his lips, expression despairing. "Yeah, you might want to work on that a little before trying it for real."

"Fair," Leo said.

"There's also this," Esme said, tapping a newspaper on her desk. "Teasley is having some kind of fundraiser tomorrow night at the Ambassador Hotel. That means a lot of RPC types and their associates in one place at one time." She looked at Oliver. "If there is anything to what Ignotus is saying, it would probably be good to go see what you can find out."

The very thought made Cecily's chest go tight, and she wasn't even the one being asked to attend.

Oliver only nodded, looking thoughtful. "Anyone particular you think I should focus on?"

"Teasley, obviously," Esme said. "Though he may be difficult to get close to since he's the main attraction. Turner-Hoff, for sure, if he's there."

"Don't forget Bradshaw," Leo said.

As the others went on concocting plans, rattling off names and tactics, Cecily felt the tightness in her chest go tauter and tauter, squeezing her lungs and making it difficult to breathe. She knew this was the kind of thing that she had signed up for, but the notion of it being the RPC that they were up against changed everything. The prospect of a shadowy killer hadn't been nearly as frightening. Teasley and the other RPC members had loomed so large in her mind since her powers had manifested, becoming the stuff of her nightmares, that even saying their names felt fraught with danger. And if Oliver's efforts failed, if Leo couldn't find what he needed, the success of the plan could come down to her ability to draw their quarry out.

Possibly to confront them face-to-face. Probably to let them see her powers in action.

The room suddenly felt too close, too warm. She needed air. Yes, if she could just get some air, she would be fine.

As she got to her feet, Cecily could feel Paloma's eyes on her, but nobody else seemed to notice as she moved to the corner and slipped out the secret door.

.

CHAPTER 17

DANIEL

Once everyone was satisfied with their plans for the next day or two, Daniel looked over at the chaise to check on Cecily, only to discover she was no longer there. Puzzled, he glanced around the office, but there was still no sign of her.

"Try the roof," Paloma said.

Daniel turned to where she still sat on the chaise, bent over so she could retie her bootlace. "What?"

Paloma gave him a knowing smirk. "You're looking for Cecily, right?" she said, sitting back up. "Try the roof. That's where we've been doing most of our training. She seems to like it up there."

"In the cold?"

Paloma shrugged, spreading her hands and getting to her feet. "Maybe all that energy inside her helps keep her warm. I don't know."

Daniel frowned. "I didn't even notice her leaving."

Paloma opened her mouth to say something, then apparently thought better of it. Instead, she heaved a despairing sigh and left the room.

Determined to ignore her, Daniel retrieved his coat and mounted the stairs to the roof. As he went, he remembered he'd stuffed his gloves into one of the pockets and tugged them on. The more he thought about Cecily's disappearing act, the more irritated at himself he became. He'd known his news wouldn't be easy for Cecily to hear. He'd asked to see Leo's notes in some vain hope that something in them would disprove Ignotus's theory. Still, he'd underestimated the impact on her. Now, he could only wait to see by how much.

A gust of cold hit him square in the face as he pushed open the door to the roof. The heavy clouds that had been lingering for days seemed to have only gotten more oppressive in the time he'd been inside the building; they made it feel more like dusk than midday, turning the sky the color of slate. He didn't see Cecily at first and nearly turned around to go back inside, but then he caught a glimpse of bright green off to the side, under the tarps. Her borrowed scarf.

She was sitting on one of the metal benches, arms wrapped around herself, lost in thought. She jumped a little when she heard his footsteps, turning toward the sound. Her cheeks were pink with the cold, making her look almost childlike, but her eyes were guarded. Once she realized it was him, though, her face transformed in a way that made his breath catch, all relief and welcome. He swallowed, trying to maintain his composure as he reached the bench and sat down next to her. "Hey."

"Hey," she replied, sounding a little shy.

"I looked up when we were finished talking, and you were gone."

"I know," she said. "I'm sorry. It just... got a little overwhelmed."

"Hey, no need to apologize." He nudged her shoulder with his. "Are you okay now?"

"Yeah," she said, though she didn't sound entirely convinced. "I'm fine."

After a beat of silence, Daniel said, "Want to talk about it?"

Cecily sighed. "I meant what I said about wanting to help. That's why Paloma and I have spent so much time working up here. But hearing everyone talking about contending with RPC members, and thinking about using my powers—I mean, *really* using them, on purpose..." She shook her head. "I've spent so many years trying my hardest not to draw attention to myself. And now, I'm not only supposed to do that, but I may have to seek out the very people I've been trying to hide from… It's just a lot."

"You're doing really well, though," Daniel said tentatively. "Your power didn't spark, even though you were under stress."

Cecily shrugged. "I'm not sure that would have happened anyway. That was the type of conversation that lends itself more to all-consuming panic."

Daniel cocked his head, curious. "What's the difference?"

Cecily's brow furrowed in concentration. "The power comes to the surface when I feel… disregarded, I guess? Like people don't take me seriously. Like I'm not worth their consideration. It's as if the electricity can't stay inside because it wants people to *notice* something. With the 'fretfulness'"—she gave the word an acerbic twist, recalling the way her mother always referred to her distress, and Daniel felt a spike of pure loathing for Melanie Dearborn—"it's kind of the opposite. It happens when I feel threatened. Scared. When I just want to disappear inside of myself and hide from the rest of the world." She smirked, a look that didn't sit right on her, and let her eyes slide to the floor. "Which is most of the time."

"You're too hard on yourself," Daniel murmured.

Cecily shrugged again. "Maybe. Although now that I think about it, I haven't felt either of those things waiting to pounce in the last couple of days." She looked up again, a bit of the light back in her eyes. "That's got to be a good thing, right?"

"Yeah," Daniel said. "I think it does." She held his gaze for a long moment before looking away, self-conscious.

"This must all sound laughable to you. You do scary, dangerous stuff all the time."

"I'm not laughing," Daniel said.

"What was it like?" she asked. "When you first started? I'm guessing they didn't tell you everything right away."

Daniel chuckled. "No, they did not. I didn't even know that they were adepts at first—that Oliver caught me because he could sense my intention to pick his pocket before he actually saw me. All I knew was that they were willing to feed me and give me a warm place to sleep, and that was enough. In fact, it seemed like more than enough. Too good to be true. Esme did some hinting about me going to school, but when I told her I didn't do that anymore, she let it go. I was hardly the only dropout in the neighborhood. Plus, since I had more security, I felt better about checking out books from the library where I'd spent so much time. So that's what I did. I read, and I did odd jobs around the building—running errands, helping with renovation whenever it was time to upgrade something. And I waited for the other shoe to drop."

"Did it?" Cecily asked.

He shrugged. "I thought so at the time. We were all sitting in Esme's office—Esme, Oliver, and me—and the news came on the wireless. I was sketching and not paying a whole lot of attention, but then they started talking about Forge County."

Cecily's stomach went tight. He didn't explain what he meant, but he didn't have to. It had been a huge controversy. Coal miners in Cumberland had been campaigning for better working conditions and higher wages, and they had been met with fierce opposition from the mine owners and other businessmen attached to the industry. A group of miners in a place called Forge County had gone on strike, picketing outside the mine and refusing to work until their demands were met. The owners had tried to bring in scabs, but the community was united, and it hadn't worked. Then they'd brought in the army. The miners were given twenty-four hours to vacate the property and call off the strike. When they didn't comply, the soldiers opened fire, killing twenty-five miners and family members, including women and children. The incident had been in the papers for weeks, inspiring calls for mining regulation and hearings in the National Congress. And the company that owned the mine was the Cumberland Coal Corporation—a subsidiary of Dearborn Consolidated.

"The story made me angrier and angrier as it went," Daniel continued. "And when I heard that Dearborn Consolidated was involved... I kind of lost my head. I threw my sketchbook across the room and stomped around, ranting and swearing." He gave a crooked smile. "Esme said it was the most she'd heard me say at once since she'd met me. Eventually, they got me calmed down, and I explained why I was so upset—my history with your family.

"I saw them give each other a look, and thought, 'Well, this is it— I've gone and ruined everything.' But Esme just said some comforting things to me and told me to go get some rest. The next day, though...

"Esme called me into her office. I wondered if I was in trouble after all, but that wasn't it. Instead, she asked me what I thought they did there, besides just telling fortunes, and I was honest and said I didn't know. So, she told me.

"I wasn't sure what to think at first. I loved the idea of sticking it to the authorities and the RPC and anyone else who made life for people like us difficult, but I wasn't sure what I could contribute since I didn't have any magic of my own. Esme assured me that there was a place for me and that she'd tell me more soon.

"A few days went by, and I started to wonder if anything was ever going to happen when suddenly, it did. Oliver took me aside and said I'd be going with him on a job that night. There was a family with a little girl who was an adept, maybe four or five years old, and their neighbor had seen her doing magic and reported them. They'd been on probation, but then the girl had been spotted again, and they were terrified they were going to be split up and sent to the centers."

Cecily closed her eyes, feeling a sharp rush of panic at the mere thought. Under the Embargo, anyone who was reported as using magic was charged and put on "probation," which was essentially twenty-four-hour surveillance for as long as the courts determined appropriate. Agents could pop up anywhere, watching adepts as they went to work, school, religious services—anything that put them out in the community. Conjurors had it even worse, since they were doing magic by choice, not natural disposition. If agents saw any other use of magic, or if the adept was reported again, they were sent to so-called containment centers. In the case of a child, any guardian who was legally responsible for them went, too.

Nobody knew for sure what happened inside the containment centers. The government refused to give out any information about them, citing national security concerns, and very few people who went in ever came out. But rumors had always circulated—that adepts were kept sedated so they couldn't access their powers, that some who were judged especially dangerous were put into dedicated solitary cells designed to counteract their unique powers. And that was the adults. Children had their own centers, and those were even more secretive.

"We were going to be taking the family to contacts that would help smuggle them south to Costa Primera. I remember that drive so clearly. That family was so scared, so desperate. My job was to act as lookout while Oliver made the transfer to the courier, and I was absolutely terrified that I was going to screw it up. That if I let me attention waver, even for a second, the whole thing would fall apart. I didn't think I could live with myself if my failure led to them getting taken away.

"The rendezvous point was in the middle of nowhere, but that just made me more vigilant. I was aware of every gust of wind through the trees, every snapped twig. I felt like I was about to jump out of my skin. But nothing happened. Nobody came after us. The whole thing went off without a hitch, and the family got away. And that was it. I was hooked. I knew what I wanted to do with my life."

"I think I feel a little of that, too," Cecily said. "But I don't really know what use I can be. All of this"—she fluttered her hands in front of her chest, alluding to her power—"still seems like such an uphill climb."

"Paloma told Esme that you're progressing well," Daniel said.

Cecily snorted. "Not as well as I'd like."

Daniel considered her for a moment, determination building inside him. Then he slapped his hands on his knees and stood up.

"Show me."

Cecily's head whipped up to meet his gaze. "What?"

"Give me a demonstration." He held a hand out to her. "Let me see what you can do."

"Oh, I don't know, Daniel." She looked more than a little alarmed, and Daniel felt a twinge in his heart that she still doubted herself so thoroughly.

"Come on," he said, voice softer than before. "Please."

Cecily stared at his hand for another long moment, then took it and got to her feet. She let him lead her out from underneath the tarps to the open space near the back of the building. When they were close to the center, she stopped, letting go of his hand.

"Okay," she said. "You probably want to back up a little. I'm never quite sure how this is going to go."

Daniel obligingly took a few steps backward. Cecily, meanwhile, took a deep breath and cupped her hands in front of her, concentrating. After a moment, sparks flared in the cradle of her palms. Slowly, they began to swirl around each other, forming filaments that gradually shaped themselves into a sphere. The structure was fragile, a delicate filigree of light. As she drew her hands apart, the sphere expanded, growing to roughly the size of a basketball. Cecily looked up at Daniel, eyes bright, as if to say, "Are you seeing this, too?"

"Beautiful," he breathed.

Just then, the wind kicked up, lifting the sphere into the air. Cecily made a sound of protest and reached out to catch it, but she was too late. As she and Daniel watched, the gossamer threads of electricity unraveled, riding an updraft into the low-hanging clouds, where they disappeared into the smudges of gray. A moment later, lightning rolled through the cloud cover in flickering bursts. The thunder that followed was more a gentle rumble than a dramatic boom, and for a moment, nothing else happened. But then, Daniel felt a feather-light touch of deeper cold on his skin, then another and another. He reached out a gloved hand, and as they both watched, snowflakes settled on the navy-blue wool.

"You talked to the sky," he said, his tone awed. He looked up to find Cecily wide-eyed with the same astonishment he was feeling.

Her cheeks flushed. "It was an accident. I didn't know it was going to happen."

"But you did it." Daniel dropped his hand, looking up to the clouds again. "We've all been waiting for the snow, and when you spoke to them, the clouds answered."

"It must have sounded like gibberish," Cecily said. "I'm only just learning the language."

"You have to start somewhere," Daniel said. "I mean, you probably sounded terrible when you were first learning Belleterran, and now, it's like music when you speak it. With time, you'll master this, too."

Cecily gazed at him, her expression full of some unreadable emotion. Then she surged forward and pressed her mouth to his.

To say that he was caught off guard was an understatement, but after a first shocked moment, the reality of *Cecily kissing him* fully registered, and his instincts kicked in. He wrapped one arm around her waist, pulling her close, while his other hand drifted up to cup the back of her neck. She responded by twining her hands into his scarf and pressing up into him, giving herself more leverage. Her lips were cold, but the inside of her mouth was hot, and the contrast made his toes curl in his boots.

Eventually, they had to come up for air, but they didn't move away from each other. Their breaths misted together in the space between them as they both tried to wrap their minds around what had just transpired between them.

"I hope that was all right," Cecily said, voice a bit shaky.

Daniel reached up and tucked a piece of hair behind her ear. "More than all right. It was probably a long time coming, honestly."

She looked at him shyly and smiled. "Yeah. I think maybe it was."

Tentatively, he leaned in and kissed her again. It was gentler this time, an exploration rather than a freefall. He realized he wanted to experience every kind of kiss with her and that, incredibly, he might be able to. He barely dared to let himself believe it.

"Come on," he said finally, pulling away touching his forehead to hers. "Let's get you inside where it's warm."

CHAPTER 18

CECILY

It didn't take long for Cecily to realize that she was in over her head when it came to Daniel.

She'd had crushes, of course—what teenage girl hadn't? But even apart from the chokehold her mother had kept on her social life, nobody in her set had seemed interested in pursuing her, the disastrous incident with Tommy Featherstone notwithstanding. There had been the standard schemes and gossip among Ad Astra's society matrons, attempting to contrive the most advantageous matches for precious sons, but those hadn't come to much. Everyone wanted to be seen with the Snowflake, but nobody, it seemed, wanted to embrace her.

It wasn't until she'd gotten to Belleterre that she'd had a proper suitor. Guillaume had been handsome, sophisticated, kind in the uniquely Belleterran way that came from acting on genuine feeling rather than social expectation. He had also been a skilled and passionate lover, which had made their time together... instructive for Cecily. She had been sad to see him go when he had been called home to his country estate when his father fell ill, but once he'd left, her life hadn't changed all that much. She'd missed him, but she'd also just gotten on with things. She hadn't bemoaned his absence. She hadn't pined.

And wasn't that what you were supposed to feel when you were separated from someone who was important to you? Weren't you supposed to ache for them, long for them? Wish more than anything that you could be together again?

She realized now that some part of her had always longed for Daniel. Somewhere, in the dark recesses of her heart, she had pined for him. And now, against all odds, they were together again.

The day before, after they'd come in from the roof—after they'd *kissed*—they'd spent most of the afternoon in the Lounge, talking about nothing and everything. Paloma had come up for a while to join them, but mostly, it had just been the two of them. Then they'd had something approaching a proper dinner in the staff dining room with Esme, Leo, and Oliver before the first dinner service started and watched both of Paloma's performances from the wings, passing a plate of Alphonse's profiteroles back and forth.

What she felt now that they were... whatever they were was an almost feral thing, raw and terrifying. But it was also intoxicating, wondrous, and even strangely peaceful. Like a missing piece of her had finally snapped into place.

If this was what being in over her head was like, then let her drown.

Now, she was curled up in the corner of one of the sofas in the Lounge, wrapped in a quilt and reading a book. She was also doing her best not to feel ridiculous, which was a challenge, because she was rather spoiled for choice when it came to reasons for feeling ridiculous.

One was the way she had to keep fighting to keep from checking the small tabletop clock she could see through the doorway of Daniel's nook. He was supposed to be arriving from the boarding house at any time, but the hands seemed to be dragging or even, though she knew this was extremely unlikely, going backward.

Another reason was the quilt. She had devoted more thought than was probably reasonable to choosing an outfit for the day from her limited options. Eventually, she'd settled on a soft green dress with blue-and-purple detailing and elbow-length sleeves. It was a bit more bohemian than what she typically wore and rather ill-suited to the current weather, but she'd told herself it wasn't as if they were going anywhere. She'd liked the way it set off her eyes and revealed just the right amount of collarbone, which she'd hoped Daniel would like, too. And now she here she was, huddled under a quilt that obscured the dress altogether, because the Lounge was freezing. She could have changed, she supposed, but she didn't. She wanted to feel pretty, even if no one could actually see anything.

And finally, she was reading—and enjoying—a story about pirates joining forces with a pod of mermaids to defeat a ghost ship crewed by the undead. *For the love of all things holy*, she thought, *I am a* grown woman. It had been years since she had last opened a book like this one. But what good had that ended up doing her in the long run? Giving up one pleasure because she was too old for it, too mature, hadn't made way for any others to take its place. Why had she done that to herself? Just because it was what others expected?

"Hey," a voice said, pulling her out of her thoughts.

When she looked up, Daniel was leaning, quite fetchingly, in the doorway, watching her.

"Hi," she said from her blanket cocoon, feeling new warmth bloom inside her.

"Can I come in?"

She felt her cheeks color. "It's not like you have to ask. You do live here."

He shrugged a shoulder. "Still seemed polite." He nodded in her direction. "Why are you wrapped up like a birthday present?"

"Um, because it's cold in here?"

"Ah, yes. That radiator can be finicky."

He pushed off the doorframe and began unbuttoning his coat as he came into the room. He shucked the coat off, tossed it onto the sofa across from Cecily, then walked over to the recalcitrant radiator. Without hesitation, he picked up a large wrench lying on a nearby pile of wood and began banging the radiator with it. At first, nothing happened, but after a few good whacks, the radiator let out a groan, then a hiss. Daniel nodded in satisfaction and returned the wrench to its resting place.

"Silly me," Cecily said. "I thought you were going to use the wrench as, you know, a wrench, not a bludgeon."

"You have to speak the radiator's language to get it to respect you," he said. "A little tip for when you're living in your house train."

"Noted."

There was pause then, just a little bit of awkwardness. That happened every so often now, when Cecily and Daniel recognized things had changed but were uncertain about what they had changed into.

After a beat, Daniel came over and sat down on the sofa with Cecily, close but not touching. "What are you reading?"

In response, Cecily held up the book, displaying the cover that read *Swashbuckling Tales for Children of All Ages* above an illustration of a pirate ship on a storm-tossed sea.

Daniel's face turned serious, and his eyes slid away.

"If I'm not mistaken," Cecily said softly, "we had this book in the library at Dearborn House. Back when we were kids."

"You did," Daniel replied, just as quietly.

"Is it a coincidence that you have it here now?"

Daniel swallowed. "I found it in a second-hand bookshop, years ago. I picked it up and started flipping through it, and suddenly I was back in the library with you, with the rain beating on the window and a fire in the hearth. I had to have it." He took the book from her and ran his hand over the cover. "Then I brought it back here and never looked at it again."

"Why?"

He shrugged. "It brought up a lot of different feelings. Some good, but some not. I could never bring myself to face those again. I guess it was enough for me to know that the book was there. If I ever needed it."

Cecily nodded wordlessly. She thought she understood. He meant if he ever needed *her*.

Daniel leaned over and placed the book on the trunk between the sofas. "Did you specifically pick that one to read because it was familiar?"

"No," Cecily said. "I mean, yes, I did once I recognized the cover. But the pickings on your bookshelf were pretty slim. I didn't have many options, except your sketchbooks, and I couldn't read those."

Daniel shifted, his body going tense.

Cecily braced herself, unsure of what she'd done to illicit that reaction.

"You haven't looked at the sketchbooks at all?"

She shook her head. "No."

"You've been here for days. You weren't curious?"

Cecily squirmed under his scrutiny. He looked confused, but also maybe a little hurt.

"It wasn't that," she said. "I just wanted to be asked... to look. It felt like I should wait for you to offer." She felt her cheeks flush again, as if that was just something that would constantly happen around him now. "Sorry, that must seem ridiculous—"

"No," Daniel cut in. "It doesn't. It's... nice."

"So, are you going to?"

"What?"

"Ask me to look."

Daniel smiled, a slow, crooked, wonderful thing prompted by her forwardness, but his eyes still looked uncertain. Cecily waited, giving him an opportunity to brush the question off with a quip if he chose to. Instead, he got up and moved to where he'd dropped his coat. He picked it up and pulled something out of the pocket—a sketchbook, one of the smaller ones.

When he sat back down on her sofa, Cecily shifted so that she was sitting next to him with her feet on the floor, still wrapped in the blanket, though it now draped more loosely around her shoulders. He held the book out without looking at her, but she didn't take it until he turned his head and met her eyes, giving her a nod.

Cecily felt that she was handling a precious artifact, and she handled it accordingly—deliberately and with great care. She turned

the pages slowly, perusing a sketch of the street outside the Hierophant and some loose movement drawings of Paloma practicing.
Then she paused.

She'd stopped on a sketch Daniel had done of his father, Declan. In
the drawing, Declan stood in the garden at Dearborn House, tending
to one of the flowering trees. He wore overalls with his usual flat cap,
and a caddy of garden tools rested at his feet. He was turned partially
away from the viewer, but Daniel had still captured some of the most
striking details Cecily remembered about the groundskeeper. His
look of quiet determination. The deft movements of his capable
hands.

She glanced over at Daniel. He was gazing at the drawing with an
indecipherable expression. His face was impassive, but his eyes were
damp and filled with something like longing.

"You must miss him," Cecily murmured.

Daniel cleared his throat. "Every day," he said, but he didn't meet
her eyes.

She decided that was a bruise too deep to prod and resumed
turning the pages.

There were a few more landscapes, then a sketch of Aaron wiping
down glasses behind the bar. The second sketch of the Dearborns'
garden caught her by surprise. At first, she couldn't figure out why
he'd even done it, but then she noticed the two small children huddled
in the hedge's shadow. Without thinking, she reached out and touched
the spot where they sat, remembering what it had felt like when he
took her hand, thinking of how much she'd missed him. She could tell
he was watching her closely, gauging her reaction, but she was
worried that she might be the one to cry if they lingered on this one
too long, so she moved on without comment.

She passed a sketch of Oliver stretched out on the chaise in Esme's
office, reading the paper and smoking a cigarette. She smiled over
another of Esme in her fortune-telling getup. The next one, however,
drew her up short.

It was her, up on the roof. She was wearing her hand-me-down
coat and scarf and holding her hands out to catch the snowflakes that

had just begun to fall. He had caught her midlaugh, and she was positively beaming, her face lit up with wonder and joy. The garden sketch had caught her off guard, but this was something else entirely. She felt her eyes well with tears.

Daniel leaned toward her. "Did I upset you? I'm sorry—"

"No," Cecily said, voice thick. "No, I'm fine. It just took me by surprise." She stared at the image, trying to see herself in the joyful, carefree figure Daniel had drawn, but she couldn't. She turned to him, brow furrowed. "Is this how you see me?"

"Yes," he said. "Always."

She had to shut the book then, closing her eyes so that she wasn't overwhelmed with what she was feeling. As she focused on breathing, Daniel gently took the book from her hands, and she heard him set it down on the chest. When she opened her eyes again, he was gazing at her without profound tenderness.

"Listen closely, because I want to make sure you hear this. You are remarkable, Cecily Dearborn. You make me feel things…" He paused, unable to find the words. "You make me feel."

Overcome, Cecily leaned forward and pressed her lips to Daniel's —the softest, lightest touch. When she pulled away, it was only to put enough space between them for her to speak.

"I'm whole when I'm with you," she said. "I feel safe and cared for in a way that I never have, anywhere."

Daniel reached up and cupped her face with one hand, kissing her with more urgency this time. As the intensity between them grew, he shifted his body so that he was lying on the sofa, pulling her down with him, on top of him. The quilt fell to the floor, but Cecily didn't need it now. She could feel the solid warmth of him along the full length of her body and where his hands touched her through the thin fabric of her dress, one sliding up her back to tangle in her hair, the other drifting down to rest on the curve of her hip. And for a while, there was only heat and touch and Daniel.

Sometime later, they lay together on the sofa, their hunger for each other tempered for the moment. Cecily's head rested on Daniel's chest, and she could feel the soft, dull thrum of his heart under her cheek. She pressed her nose into the crisp cotton shirt, breathing in the warm scent of him.

"What are you thinking?" he murmured, stroking her arm.

Cecily turned her head so that she was looking up at his face, chin resting on her hands so the point wasn't digging into his chest.

"With your drawings," she said slowly. "You have a way to keep a piece of me with you all the time. But I don't have a way to keep a piece of *you* with *me*."

"So, what should I do?" Daniel asked, amused. "Sit for a portrait for you to keep in your locket?"

Cecily shook her head. "No," she said derisively. "That's not the same." Suddenly, her eyes lit up. "Ooh, I know!"

She rolled off Daniel, immediately lamenting the loss of his warmth, and settled onto the strip of floor between the sofa and the chest. She picked up the sketchbook and turned to a blank page in the back. She glanced at Daniel, seeking permission, and he nodded. Sifting through the clutter atop the chest, she found a pencil, then, without further ado, began to draw.

Daniel, taken aback, leaned forward to get a better look at the page, but Cecily held up her free hand to block his view.

"No peeking!" she said. "You will hamper my creative process."

Daniel sighed, settling back into the sofa to wait.

Before long, Cecily dropped the pencil with a flourish and held up the drawing for his inspection. "Behold!"

In the corner of the page, two stick figures stood in a cascade of tiny snowflakes. The figures had big round lollipop heads on their skinny bodies, topped with looping curlicues. Their eyes and noses were dots, their smiles upturned semicircles.

Cecily beamed at him over the top of her work. "What do you think?"

Daniel furrowed his brow, pensive. "So... that's us."

"Yes."

"Um, which one is supposed to be me?"

"This one!" Cecily said, feigning indignation as she pointed at the squiggles on one figure's head. "See, those are your curls. And this one"—she shifted her finger to squiggles on the other figure—"has finger waves, so it's obviously me."

"Mm-hm," Daniel said, still looking skeptical.

Cecily gave an expansive sigh. "I'm the one in the skirt."

"Oh, of course!" Daniel said, smacking his forehead. "I can absolutely see it now." He leaned closer. "Excellent likeness. The resemblance is uncanny."

Cecily swatted his arm, then set about carefully tearing the corner off the page. Once it was free, she folded it into a tiny square.

"See?" she said, opening the locket and tucking the square inside. "Now I can always have a little bit of you with me, too."

Daniel reached out to stroke her hair, then let his hand slide down to cup her cheek. "There's some time left before I have to go get ready," he said, eyes gleaming. "Why don't we put it to good use while you still have all of me with you?"

She didn't argue.

CHAPTER 19

DANIEL

"Aaaah," Oliver said, stretching luxuriantly and draping his arms along the back seat of the club's nicest auto. "I could get used to this, being ferried around by a loyal underling."

In the front seat, Daniel ground his teeth. It wasn't that he minded driving on jobs. In fact, he typically preferred it, appreciating the sense of control it afforded. But he had not enjoyed any of the handful of times he'd had to pose as an actual chauffeur, and Oliver wasn't making this one any better.

"And I could get used to punching your stupid face," he grumbled, turning a corner.

"Shh," Oliver said, lifting an imperious hand as he let his head fall backward against the seat, eyes closed. "You are imposing upon my tranquility. I need quiet to complete my mental preparation for the mission."

Daniel had a few choice words about what it really was that Oliver needed, but he kept them to himself, focusing instead on navigating the streets around the Ambassador Hotel, which were bustling with bar and restaurant patrons. The fundraiser had been scheduled to begin at seven o'clock, and it was now almost eight—a strategic move on their part. By arriving fashionably late, when the event was well underway and the staff were busy and distracted, Oliver stood a much better chance of slipping in unnoticed. While his power gave him the insight he needed to fast-talk his way both into and out of most situations, it wasn't as precise as what Aaron or Ebony could do in terms of bending people's impulses to their purposes. In fact, the twins would have been far better choices for this job —if anyone had known for sure what it was they were looking for. Which they did not. Oliver was the only one who could pick up an unexpected point of interest in the crowd, so here he and Daniel were.

Daniel pulled the auto to a stop at the curb in front of the hotel and shifted into park. Then he hopped out, straightening the lapels on the godsforsaken livery jacket he'd thought he'd seen the last of, and rounded the back of the car to open Oliver's door. Oliver emerged, looking particularly dapper in his coal-black tailcoat, a pristine silk scarf draped around his neck.

He turned to Daniel with a rakish air. "Very good, Jeeves. Could be some time here." He tapped Daniel on the shoulder with his cane and continued in a sing-song tone. "Don't wait up!"

"One hour," Daniel said through clenched teeth, but Oliver's only acknowledgement was a bright grin. Then he was disappearing through the gilt and glass front doors.

Daniel hopped back into the car and eased it around to the parking area at the rear of the hotel. Thanks to their late arrival, the space was already crowded. However, Daniel managed to find a spot off to the side that gave him a good view of the lot, as well as the covered area on the back side of the building; it looked to be some kind of loading bay, when it wasn't full of limousines and the like. It was quiet back there, compared to the street. Off to one side, he saw a few silhouettes of other liveried drivers headed toward the back of the lot—ostensibly to the outlet that would take them to the next street over, where they could grab a bite at the café while they waited for their employers to finish rubbing shoulders with the great and powerful. Daniel wasn't planning to be there for that long, so he just pulled his jacket more tightly around himself and settled in to wait.

He found, however, that waiting was exceedingly difficult, which was not a problem he'd had much before. Usually, if he wasn't actively running surveillance, he kept his mind occupied by daydreaming or making plans for his next drawing. Sometimes, he even dozed off. Plus, his afternoon with Cecily had given him more than enough pleasant memories to dwell on. Even so, he was jumpy and restless, anxious to find out what was happening inside the hotel.

As he sat there brooding, a door opened at the top of a short flight of stairs, and a slight figure came out, carrying a large metal bin. The figure rushed to the far end of the covered bay to dump the contents of the bin—food scraps, as far as Daniel could tell—into a larger bin, then, eager to get out of the cold, darted back up the stairs and through the door. To the kitchen, Daniel realized. The kitchen that would presumably have access to wherever the event was underway.

A moment later, Daniel was out of the car and making his way across the lot, glancing over his shoulder to make sure no one was watching. He took the stairs in two quick leaps and slipped into the kitchen, pausing for a moment to find an interior door. Once he spotted it, he maneuvered through the busy space, careful to steer clear of hot, heavy pans and the knives that workers wielded at blinding speeds. A few people seemed to notice him, but they must have decided that he wasn't intent on any mischief, because they quickly turned back to their work.

Daniel stopped at the door in the far corner of the kitchen, peeking out through the small round window set at eye level. Then he eased it open and slid through.

He was in the back of a grand ballroom. In his footman's livery, he could pass for one of the similarly attired waiters if necessary, but nobody seemed to pay him any mind. Before him, tables dressed with white linen, crystal, and silver filled the room, each surrounded by some of Ad Astra's best and brightest—businessmen, lawyers, philanthropists, and socialites, all present and accounted for. He squinted, trying to pick Oliver out of the crowd, but he wasn't able to. The lights in the massive chandeliers had been turned down low, directing everybody's attention to the dais at the far end of the room. It was decked out in green-and-gold bunting, with giant sprays of flowers in coordinating colors trailing off the edges of the dais onto the parquet floor. A giant banner proclaiming "REASON—PROSPERITY—UNITY" hung in the center of all of it, only a few feet above a central podium flanked by tables of presumably important officials. Barring the winsome orphans, it was more or less the exact scene Ignotus had described in the car.

As Daniel watched, a small, fastidious man with a thin mustache stepped up to the podium, and the room quieted.

"Ladies and gentlemen," the man said. "Thank you for coming tonight and for your support in the ongoing fight for the heart of our country. Your resources allow our representatives to pursue and promote our most cherished values of"—he gestured to the banner above him—"reason, prosperity, and unity."

A few of the guests recited the words with him, as if they were a religious incantation, and a shiver ran down Daniel's spine.

"Our guest of honor needs no introduction," the man continued. "But I would be remiss if we did not recognize all the work he has done and the success he has achieved on behalf of us all. Please give a round of applause and a very warm welcome to Member of the National Congress Colonel Emerson Teasley."

The room erupted in cheers—subdued, moneyed cheers, but cheers nonetheless—as Teasley rose from his seat at one of the tables on the dais and made his way to the podium. He exchanged a warm handshake with the fastidious man, then took his place behind the microphone as the noise subsided.

"Thank you, thank you," he said in his trademark booming voice. He lifted a hand to his forehead, shading his eyes to see beyond the glare of the spotlights. "It is mighty good to see so many of you fine people here tonight, united in a common purpose. Some of my colleagues like to claim that there are no patriots in Ad Astra, but times like these remind me they are entirely wrong."

The audience clapped again, faces adoring, and not for the first time, Daniel was at a complete loss. He simply could not understand how so many people bought into Teasley's hardscrabble man-of-the-people routine. It was common knowledge that his family had made obscene amounts of money in shipping and that he'd been raised on an estate down the coast. His father's great passion had been horseracing, so Teasley had grown up riding and styled himself as something of a cowboy, but his life had been a far cry from those of the farmers and ranchers in the far south of the country whom he tried to emulate. Aaron had told them once that anyone from Cumberland could clock that accent as fake within three syllables.

"I know I don't need to tell you that our great nation is in a rough spot right now. We're facing economic challenges because other countries don't want to give us a fair shake on trade. Meanwhile, they can't see to their own needs well enough to keep their citizens within their own borders. Instead, those people come here seeking opportunity, but what about our homegrown people—the ones who started with nothing and became prosperous by the sweat of their brows? What about their opportunity? What about their dreams for the future?"

Daniel could feel the mood in the room shifting. Before, the general attitude had been one of polite, if enthusiastic, approval, but something more emotional and heated was emerging. People were clapping, nodding, and shouting agreement. He had a sudden awareness that he was seeing something not meant for his eyes. This was "polite society" when they thought no one else was watching.

"And perhaps foremost among our concerns," Teasley continued, "is the threat that magic still poses to our national character. The policies imposed by the Embargo were an excellent start, and we have made substantial progress in the years since they were enacted, but they are not enough! Just this week, in the heart of this great city, a terrible crime was perpetrated against a fine, upstanding member of the community by an unhinged adept."

The crowd booed and jeered until Teasley raised his hands, gesturing for quiet. "We lost a precious, irreplaceable life, but that is not the extent of the damage done. One of our great families is in turmoil right now because of how they've been dragged into the seedy workings of the magical underbelly, their home defiled, their beloved daughter missing. And yet, they have somehow mustered the resilience and courage to join us here tonight, because they still believe in goodness, in decency and responsibility, in the possibility of living free from fear. My friends, please share your graciousness and love with my dear, dear friends, AG and Melanie Dearborn."

Daniel stared in shocked horror as two figures seated at the round table closest to the dais stood and mounted the steps, joining Teasley at the podium to the sound of more applause. Mr. Dearborn looked solemn and tired, while Mrs. Dearborn looked as immaculate as ever in a somber deep-blue dress and matching hate, its attached veil partially obscuring her eyes. Not black, Daniel noted cynically. Not as long as they could keep milking Cecily's disappearance for sympathy without tipping all the way over into victimhood. Any suggestion that they believed Cecily was dead would make them objects of pity, and they couldn't have that. Resilient dignity made much better copy.

"Thank you all for your support," Mr. Dearborn said. "This has been a very trying time, and your goodwill means the world to Melanie and me."

Mr. Dearborn placed a hand at his wife's back, demonstrating more feeling than Daniel had even seen in their home, as she dabbed at her eyes. Daniel felt ill.

"As Colonel Teasley has said, our lives have been turned upside down by the practitioners' agenda of sowing chaos and unrest among New Avalonians. While we have always supported the Embargo, I am sad to say that it took this tragedy for us to fully grasp the threat magic still presents across the land. We need more than well-meaning policies at this point. We need bold action. We need to ensure that those with uncontrolled—and perhaps uncontrollable—power are not allowed to place our children in danger any longer. For too long, we have been held back by those promoting the rights of practitioners, as if they were regular, everyday citizens. But I'm here to tell you they are not regular citizens. They are something else. And the time has come for all of us to recognize that."

He paused for a moment, and Daniel could just imagine Mrs. Dearborn coaching him at home. There was no way he'd come up with all of this on his own.

"It's too late for us. While we hope and pray that we will be reunited with Cecily soon, our lives will never be the same. I wouldn't wish this pain upon my worst enemy. We must work together to make sure it doesn't happen to any other families in New Avalon."

He stepped back from the microphone and nodded in acknowledgment as the crowd cheered again. He began leading Mrs. Dearborn back off the stage, but she paused as she passed the microphone, then leaned in to speak.

"Magic has taken our daughter," she said, voice cracking on the last word, and Daniel couldn't help but think she'd missed her calling on the stage. "We just want her returned safely."

The applause became louder as the Dearborns reclaimed their seats and Teasley stepped back up to the podium.

"This is why we fight, friends. So that no one else must suffer as the Dearborns have. So that broken families can be reunited, as we hope theirs will be when their darling Cecily is recovered. And to that end, I am making an important announcement tonight. Ladies and gentlemen, right here, right now, I am beginning my campaign to be your next president of New Avalon."

The response was deafening. Daniel reeled, disgust roiling in his gut. The room felt suddenly too close, oppressive, and without thinking, he started backing toward the kitchen door. He turned when he was just a few feet away and shoved his way through, abandoning his efforts at stealth. The kitchen workers looked up, more alarmed than they had been on his first trip through, but he ignored them, desperate to get outside.

As he pushed through the exterior door, he welcomed the rush of cold, fresh air in his face. Once he was down the stairs, he staggered to his auto, braced his hands on the hood, and took in deep, calming breaths. On the one hand, the fanaticism and self-righteousness on display in that room hadn't been anything new, and Teasley making a big move like running for president was hardly surprising. But Daniel couldn't get the image of the Dearborns standing on the stage out of his head.

It was one thing for them to attend an event like this, even while their daughter was missing; their political allegiance was well-established, and turning personal tragedy to their advantage was not out of character. But what he'd just seen went beyond lending their name and prestige to a distasteful cause. They were advocating for the violent persecution of adepts like their own child.

All the pieces he and the others had uncovered were coming together with a terrible sort of clarity. Fairchild's explosive work alone represented a tantalizing hypothetical to anyone with the RPC's goals in mind, but Turner-Hoff's involvement with the sanatorium suggested it was more than that. There were specific plans in motion for the RPC to move against magic users, and for all that Esme thought some coalition partners were trying to pretty up that endeavor for the public, the display tonight illustrated that Teasley, for one, felt no compunction about proceeding full throttle. And Cecily's parents were along for the ride.

Daniel knew enough of them to understand that they wouldn't see it that way. In their minds, Cecily wasn't included in these machinations. If she did turn up again—and he doubted they were as torn up over her disappearance as they were making out, or at least not for the reason they wanted people to think—he knew they would take measures to ensure that her name was cleared of the taint of magic. Consequently, she would never be subject to the trials the rest of the magical world would experience; the rich and the powerful never were. And that just made the whole thing more evil.

He was still trying to collect himself when he heard the door open and close behind him. He glanced over his shoulder, almost as an afterthought, expecting to see another member of the kitchen staff. Instead, to his surprise, he saw two men in evening dress standing at the bottom of the stairs, and when he squinted, he was even more surprised to see that they were Members of the National Congress Turner-Hoff and Vandermark. The two of them were talking, Turner-Hoff gesturing animatedly, but Daniel couldn't hear them. Moving slowly and soundlessly, praying he didn't attract their attention, Daniel crept over to a nearby auto. Ducking down to hide behind its bulk, he strained his ears, trying to make out what they were saying.

"—told me someone was poking around at the hospital today," Turner-Hoff said. "Claimed he was looking for a place to send his daughter, but she said he got cagey when she asked for specifics."

"Cagey, how?" Vandermark asked.

"She didn't go into details." Turner-Hoff ran a hand over his thinning hair. "I think just being evasive. But I tell you, I don't like it, old boy. Do you think he could be press?"

"Why would the press be interested in the sanitarium?" Turner-Hoff let out a sigh that Daniel saw more than heard.

"You know how they are. Always trying to make us out to be demagogues or some such nonsense. It's why I tried to keep my name away from it—to protect it from any kind of unpleasantness. But maybe someone made the connection anyway?" He puffed on his cigar. "And another thing—what are we going to do without Fairchild? We made all these promises based on our plan to implement Partners in Progress, and now that program is dead in the water."

"I've told you, we'll be able to make up at least some of that loss," Vandermark said. "Don't despair just yet."

Turner-Hoff snorted. "Easy for you to say," he grumbled. "You're not the one who has to answer to the hospital board. And I don't want to catch Teasley's attention either. The last thing I need is him sniffing around and meddling in the day-to-day operations. He doesn't understand the light touch required in that type of work the way we do."

"Teasley has bigger fish to fry at the moment," Vandermark said, gesturing back toward the crowded ballroom. "As we all knew he would. He's taken all the necessary steps to make sure things run smoothly while he focuses on the campaign." He put a comforting hand on Turner-Hoff's shoulder. "He has his role in the Coalition's plans, and so do we. He trusts us to play them well."

Turner-Hoff visibly relaxed. "You're right. There's just so many things in motion right now. It's making me jumpy."

"Understandable," Vandermark said. "But could we continue this conversation inside like civilized people? It's freezing out here."

Turner-Hoff still looked dubious, but he nodded, and the two of them went back through the kitchen door. Daniel waited a beat to make sure they were gone, then walked back to the auto and let himself in. He sat there thinking of what he'd just heard, unable to make heads or tails of it. Turner-Hoff, who had always been seen as a hardline RPC loyalist, seemed to be having misgivings about the Coalition's agenda, while Vandermark, who was considered a moderate or even a traitor to the cause, was toeing the party line. It felt like that should be significant, but Daniel couldn't put his finger on *why*.

Suddenly, there was a knock at the front-passenger window. Daniel jumped, ready to either bluff or fight his way out of an altercation with a security guard, but it was only Oliver.

Oliver gave him a derisive look and opened the door. "For someone who was harping on the time, you don't seem aware of how much has passed."

Daniel rolled his eyes, and Oliver slid into the passenger seat, all pretense of being a man of leisure apparently forgotten. He pulled the door shut, but rather than diving into an account of what had happened, as Daniel expected, he sat staring out the windshield, lip caught between his teeth.

"Well?" Daniel asked.

"Ignotus was wrong," Oliver said, rolling his cane between his palms.

Normally, a pronouncement like this would be accompanied by loud and gleeful satisfaction. The fact that this satisfaction was not in evidence only increased Daniel's unease.

He frowned. "What do you mean? What happened?"

"Well, Teasley announced he's running for president."

"I know," Daniel said.

Oliver raised his eyebrows. "You do?"

Daniel ducked his head sheepishly. "I got tired of waiting and went inside to see what was happening myself."

Oliver rolled his eyes. "Of course you did. Anyway, everyone was over the moon about the big announcement, and he was pretty mobbed there for a while after he finished his speech, so I wandered around chatting with people to see if I could pick up on anything interesting. Which I didn't. But I was able to sample some excellent champagne, and these delicious little canapes—I'm not sure who was doing the catering, but we should look into having them do events at the club."

"Focus, please," Daniel said.

"Right, sorry. Anyway, the crowd around him seemed to disperse a little, so I made my way over to the edge of the circle and worked on getting close to him. I made up some rubbish about being in the same fraternity he rushed in school to get him talking, and soon, he was acting like we were old friends. When I asked him what he thought of the Dr. Fairchild situation, he got more serious—very conspiratorial, railing against practitioners as threats to our security. He was appalled that the authorities hadn't caught Cecily yet. Said he was considering quietly funding a reward for information leading to her capture."

Daniel scowled. "So much for reclaiming the beloved daughter to heal a broken family."

"Right? But the point is"—Oliver turned to face Daniel—"he genuinely thinks she did it."

"Which means…" Daniel said, unable to continue the thought.

"Yeah," Oliver said. "I know."

It meant this was a dead end. If Teasley believed Cecily was guilty, it meant the RPC was not behind the murder after all.

So they were right back to where they'd started, with no solid leads to follow. And now the clock was ticking.

CHAPTER 20

DANIEL

They went straight to the club, arriving just as the first dinner service was winding down. Daniel waited in Esme's office while Oliver went to find her. She'd told them she had clients scheduled for the night, but they knew she would want to hear what they had to say as soon as possible. After a few minutes, mother and son came hurrying into the office, Esme still in her fortune telling garb. Her already-serious face turned even more solemn when she saw Daniel.

"What happened?" she asked, sinking into her desk chair.

They told her everything they had seen and heard at the fundraiser —Daniel first, then Oliver. She listened attentively, as was her wont, digesting their words without interruption. When Oliver was done, she sat quietly, staring into the middle distance. Then she got up and began to pace the area behind her desk.

Daniel wanted to shout at her, demand some kind of a reaction, but he knew from experience that she couldn't be rushed.

Finally, she stopped, hands resting on the back of the chair she'd just vacated. "This doesn't make any sense."

"I don't disagree," Oliver said. "But it's what we have to work with."

"We've got to be missing something." She looked to Daniel. "Is there anything you can think of that we haven't considered yet? Something that you saw in the house that day?"

Daniel screwed his face up in concentration. He ran through the morning of the murder in his head, poking at the memories, scrambling to pinpoint something that might have been relevant.

Then he remembered. "The phone," he said slowly.

Esme and Oliver exchanged a look.

"What?" Oliver asked.

"Dearborn was on the phone—the one on the international line, down near the kitchen. He'd had to leave Fairchild alone in his study to answer it. The timing of it seemed suspicious to me."

The incident seemed an obvious clue now, since it was one of the things that had tipped him off that something was wrong in the first place, but with everything that had happened over the last few days, it had slipped his mind.

Esme looked at Oliver. "Was there anything about that in the papers?"

Oliver shook his head. "Leo is better at keeping track of all those details than I am, but I don't remember seeing anything."

Esme took a deep breath. "All right, it's not a lot to go on, but it's a start." She glanced at the grandfather clock in the corner. "I have another client in five minutes, so I need to get back in there. For now, the two of you should get some rest, but first thing in the morning, head down to AALE headquarters and see what you can find out."

Daniel and Oliver nodded.

Esme started making her way to the door, only to pause, worrying at her lip. "Keep this development quiet for now. I want to know more before we tell Cecily about it."

They nodded again.

Then Daniel cleared his throat. "What about her parents? Should I tell her that part?"

Esme gave him a look of such compassion that he had to turn away, eyes focused on the scorched table nobody had bothered to move yet.

"I think you have the best sense of what to do there out of all of us," Esme said, her voice gentle. Daniel could only nod as she slipped out, pulling the door shut behind her.

Daniel got very little sleep that night. He kept playing out variations of the conversation he might have with Cecily the next day—being cool and matter-of-fact, doing his best to cushion the blow—but none of them ended up anywhere he wanted to be. The prospect of being back under her parents' thumb would have been awful before, but now it was going to break her heart, which was going to break his heart, and that was just far more heartbreak than he could deal with right then.

Just after sunrise, he gave up, got out of bed, and dressed in his regular clothes, grateful that it wasn't that cursed livery. As soon as he dared, he used the boarding house phone to call the club so Oliver would be waiting for him at the curb. When he pulled up, Oliver looked fairly sedate, wearing one of his plainest suits and leaving behind his watch chain and carnation. Daniel knew that must have pained him grievously, but this was one of those instances where they wanted to keep a low profile.

"Why are we doing this so godsdamned early?" Oliver asked with a yawn as he got in the car.

"Esme said first thing," Daniel replied. "Also, it's almost ten, which most people consider a perfectly reasonable time to get up. Decadent, even."

Oliver made a noncommittal sound of acknowledgement as he pulled an elegant pair of dark glasses out of his vest pocket and put them on. "Any particular reason you didn't want to come inside?"

"No," Daniel grunted as they lurched away from the curb, but Oliver just gave him a knowing look.

Did it make him a coward that he hadn't wanted to run into Cecily? Yes. But he still hadn't decided exactly what he was going to tell her about the fundraiser, so he was willing to take every bit of extra time he could manage.

They went downtown, where the imposing edifice of Ad Astra Law Enforcement headquarters loomed above the surrounding buildings. Daniel parked a few blocks away to keep from attracting any unwanted attention. As Oliver sauntered down the sidewalk to see what he would uncover, Daniel popped into a nearby diner and ordered a cup of coffee.

Halfway through the cup, Daniel began to feel a pit perkier, casting off some of the mental cobwebs of his long night. Unfortunately, the burst of energy didn't do much for his mood. Here he was, hiding for all practical purposes, while Oliver did the work of getting actionable information. Yes, waiting in the shadows had proven helpful the night before, what with him stumbling onto the conversation between Turner-Hoff and Vandermark, but he didn't want to make it a habit. He wanted to *do* something.

It was indisputable that Oliver was the right person for this job. Even discounting his power, he was better at handling people than Daniel was. Daniel knew that. But he still hated being at loose ends. With a clarity that made him cringe, he realized he had cast himself as Cecily's champion over the last few days, the knight in shining armor charging to the rescue of the damsel in distress. But he hadn't actually done any rescuing, had he? Despite his best efforts, there was still someone out there with a vested interest in tracking her down, someone who had proven they were willing to kill. Because nobody had been able to figure out who that was, Daniel didn't know how to protect her. And protection was basically the only thing he had to offer.

Oliver slid into the chair across from Daniel, snapping him out of his musings. He looked annoyed.

"How'd it go?" Daniel said, trying to push away some of his gloom as Oliver signaled for the waitress to bring him a coffee. "Did you find out anything useful?"

"No." Oliver paused to flash the waitress a dazzling smile as she put a cup in front of him and poured. "Thank you, sweetheart."

The waitress gave him a circumspect smile of her own, but he waited until she was out of earshot to continue, his face falling back into a near scowl. "Apparently, AG did tell them he'd left Fairchild alone in the study because he was called away for a phone call, but our intrepid public servants didn't think to ask him who it was he was talking to." He took a sip of coffee and sighed with pleasure, some of the tension leaving him. "Oh, that's good. So, anyway, I think was another blind alley."

Daniel sighed, fighting the urge to just put his head down on the table and stay there for a while. At a nearby booth, another customer got up, buttoning his suit jacket and picking up his briefcase. But when he walked to the door, his newspaper remained on the table with the front page facing up. Unsurprisingly, the top story was Teasley's announcement at the fundraiser. The story took up all the space above the fold, including a picture of the Dearborns at the microphone, with Teasley off to the side, radiating strength and concern. Daniel couldn't tear his eyes away. It wasn't just a picture to him. It was an accusation. That whatever he was doing for Cecily, it wasn't enough.

He leapt to his feet so abruptly, he almost knocked over his chair.

"Let's go," he growled and tossed a few bucks on the table. Oliver watched him intently but said nothing as they made their way to the car.

The drive was likewise quiet, and when they arrived at the club, Oliver immediately went off to find his mother, leaving Daniel to his own devices. And as much as it pained him to admit it, that meant talking to Cecily. Drawing the situation out further wouldn't do any good. At this point, the anticipation was probably worse than the actual conversation. It would be best for both of them to just get it over with.

As it happened, he didn't have to venture very far to find her. He was approaching the stairs to go check the roof or the Lounge when Paloma and Cecily came down them. They were wearing their pants and boots, disheveled and flushed from the cold, but in high spirits. Cecily was laughing at something Paloma had said when she caught sight of him, and somehow, her face lit up even more when their eyes met.

Daniel was flooded with a strange combination of elation, to see her looking so happy, and dread, because he knew it probably wasn't going to last much longer.

"Hey," Cecily said, a little breathlessly, pausing at the foot of the stairs.

"Hi," Daniel said, taking a few steps forward, hesitant to close distance between them with someone else nearby.

Paloma glanced from one of them to the other, realization dawning, and Daniel was grateful that for all her flaws, she was a romantic at heart.

"So, yeah. I'm just going to go this way and, um..." She didn't even bother finishing the sentence, just headed toward the kitchen, leaving them alone.

"Hey," Cecily said again once she was gone, walking toward him slowly.

"You already said that."

Cecily shrugged as she stopped in front of him, reaching out to take his hand and twine their fingers together. "What can I say? You make me a little absentminded."

This was agony. How was he supposed to disappoint her after that? He cleared his throat, trying to boost his resolve.

"How'd it go up there today?" he asked.

"Really well!" she said, beaming. "When this is all over and I'm home, it is going to be so satisfying to show my mother how much better I am at controlling it now." Her smile turned a little vicious. "I can't wait to see the look on her face."

Normally, Daniel would have been delighted by this note of wickedness at Mrs. Dearborn's expense, but something else Cecily had said caught his attention.

"You're still planning to go back, then? To Dearborn House?"

"Well, yes," Cecily said, brows furrowed in puzzlement. "It's my home. Why wouldn't I go back there?"

And that was a fair question. Why wouldn't she go back to all that security and privilege? Yes, she wanted her freedom, but what had he thought—that she would be content living in a glorified attic? Devoting herself to someone who could barely take care of himself, let alone anyone else? She'd stayed with him because he'd promised to keep her safe, and he couldn't even do that right. They'd been running around on a wild-goose chase while the killer was free to hunt her down even as they stood there.

He wasn't being fair, he knew. He hadn't yet told her what he'd seen the night before, but a small, nasty voice in the back of his head whispered that he shouldn't have to. The Dearborns had always been ruthless and transactional when it came to their daughter. He had never understood why Cecily didn't recognize it, why she valued their approval so much. But he could see now that was never going to change.

"No reason," he said darkly and turned to walk down the hall. "There's no reason at all for you not to go back."

He'd hoped this surliness would be enough to dissuade her from pursuing the matter, but that proved to be in vain.

She was immediately on his heels. "What's wrong?"

"Nothing."

"No," she said. "Something is definitely wrong. What is it?"

He came to an abrupt halt and rounded on her. She took a surprised step backward.

"How can you go back to them? After... everything."

Cecily furrowed her brow, looking uncertain. "They're my family."

"They're not. Or at least they don't deserve to be. They've done nothing your whole life but belittle you, try to fit you into some little socially accepted box. And you just take it."

"No, I—"

"You do," he said, momentum building with each word. "You never challenge them. You never stand up for yourself. The worst you do is run and hide, and what good does that do at the end of the day? Nothing."

His voice rang in the quiet of the hall as he fell silent. Cecily didn't speak for a long moment.

"It's complicated," she said finally. Her voice was small, and her face was doing something he didn't like.

He felt disconnected from himself, though, caught up in the riptide of his fury. "It's really not. Every day, you get to decide how to respond to them, and every day, you take the easy way out. They don't

189

have any real reason to treat you better. You're giving them permission to hurt you."

He knew instantly that he'd gone too far. He saw anger flare in her eyes and wondered if her powers would spark, but they didn't. Instead, when she finally responded, her voice was cold and controlled, which was almost worse.

"How can you, of all people, say that to me?" she asked. "When you know what I've been through? When you know what it took just for me to make it through the day, even before I had my powers?"

"I—"

"It's big talk from someone who isn't feared and hated because of his magic," she went on, undeterred. "Who doesn't have a murder charge hanging over his head. Whose father didn't make him feel like a burden who had to earn the right to even exist."

The rage he'd been trying to douse came roaring back to life. "My father is dead because of your family," he said, the words sharp on his tongue. "So don't play that sympathy card with me. Even without your magic, you have more power than I could even dream of, and you always have. It's not my fault if you choose not to use it."

Cecily recoiled, her expression filled with hurt and condemnation. For a moment, nothing happened, but then she narrowed her eyes at him, looking him up and down. Taking his measure.

"You are not the man I thought you were," she said, and she turned on her heel and left.

CHAPTER 21

CECILY

One thought circulated in Cecily's head as she stormed off. One thought over and over.

How dare he talk to her like that? How *dare* he?

She was so caught up in her fuming that it took her a moment to realize she had no idea where she was going. Her initial impulse had just been to get away from Daniel, and her feet had carried her most of the way to the backstage dressing rooms. Now, though, she had to figure out what to do with herself. She did a quick mental inventory of all the spots she had to choose from in the club and decided none of them seemed quite right. The mere thought of them gave her a constricted, almost claustrophobic feeling. On top of that, there was a good chance Daniel would track her down in whatever place she chose, and she did not want to talk to him right now.

Well, that clinched it. She would just have to leave. Not forever. That would be both stupid and ungrateful. But for a little while, just to clear her head.

That decided, she retrieved her coat and hat, then she headed down the back stairs to the exit at the rear of the stage. A tiny voice in her head began whispering that this was a bad idea, but she did her best to muffle it. She had her charm. Nobody knew she was in this part of the city. She would be fine. Really.

The dry, brittle air was bracing as she stepped out into the alley, and she inhaled deeply. The chill helped bring her out of herself a little, allowing her to take stock of precisely how she was feeling after her fight with Daniel. And she realized she felt… good?

That couldn't be right. She was angry. Furiously, incandescently angry. But when had she last felt something like that? Had she ever? She'd spent years tamping down her feelings, pushing them into a small quiet place within herself so that she could remain calm and poised. She'd had to, to protect herself and others. But even when she slipped and lost control, succumbing either to the panic or her powers or both, she felt other things—weakness, helplessness, despair. Not this all-consuming rage

She found she much preferred this—because Daniel had been wrong. Deeply, horribly wrong. He, more than anyone, knew what it had been like for her, even before her powers had manifested. How trapped she'd been. How powerless. She remembered what Daniel had said about Oliver letting his guard down around the people he knew would forgive him his moods. He allowed them to see all of him because he knew it was safe. Well, she'd done with Daniel over the previous days, and how had he responded? He'd thrown it right back in her face.

At least with her mother, she knew what she was going to get. And that was the thought that brought her up short. Melanie's judgment, that cold, resigned disappointment never surprised Cecily; she knew it far too well. But she realized that, on some level, she'd still been hoping that this might be the thing that turned everything around. That the prospect of losing Cecily might be enough to change Mrs. Dearborn's perspective. That she might even be proud that Cecily had finally learned to control her powers. And now Cecily knew, suddenly and with absolute certainty, that none of that was going to happen. That's what Daniel had been trying to tell her. Nothing was going to change.

Her steps slowed as this realization coalesced in her head. She was still furious, and furious was a reasonable way to feel in her situation. But it had been directed at the wrong person.

Daniel had said some terrible things to her. She had a right to be upset about that. But she'd said some awful things, too, and no matter what cutting words either of them had thrown at the other, the fact remained that he was not the reason Cecily had been made to feel small and broken and wrong for so many years. In fact, there had been many times when he'd been the only thing keeping her from disappearing entirely.

With a sigh, she turned around and started back toward the club. As she walked, she began rehearsing what she would say to Daniel when she returned. She knew she should probably wait a little while, to give both of them a chance to calm down, but then what? A stubborn part of her still didn't want to apologize if he wasn't going to reciprocate, so she wouldn't lead with that. Instead, she would ease into it, feel him out a little. Maybe ask about the fundraiser. He'd been in a much better mood before he and Oliver had gone to that—perhaps something had happened there. If they could work through that together, maybe he would be more willing to open up about why he'd blown up at her. It was worth a try.

While the analytical part of Cecily's brain turned all this over, another part was still engaged in observing her surroundings—and that part detected movement down the alley. For all the time she'd spent traipsing around alleys since her ordeal had begun, she hadn't seen many other people in them, so when she sharpened her focus enough to identify two large, male figures walking toward her, alarm bells sounded in her head. She pulled her coat tighter, trying to reassure herself that there could be a perfectly innocent reason for their presence, but on some level, she knew that wasn't the case.

So what to do? The back door of the Hierophant was so close that she could reach it in seconds. Meanwhile, she didn't know the rest of the neighborhood, so even if she tried to run, she wasn't sure where she would go. *All right then*, she thought, squaring her shoulders. *Let's brazen this out.*

She kept her pace steady and her eyes straight ahead, acting as if the men weren't even there. She watched the distance between her and the club get shorter and shorter, while her presumed assailants came closer. Then they were within an arm's reach of each other. For one blessed fraction of a second, she thought everything was going to be okay, that she was going to pass them and disappear into the safety of the club, where she would chide herself or being so paranoid and go fix things with Daniel. But that fraction of a second passed, and then their hands were on her.

She fought with a strength born of panic, drawing on long-buried memories of fighting with Herbert when she was so much smaller and so afraid. She kicked out as one of them grabbed her, knocking over some of the nearby trash cans, and swung her elbow into the other's face. He swore and stepped back, pressing a hand to his bloodied nose, and Cecily felt a flash of hope. But there were two of them, and they were bigger than her. It wasn't long before the one holding her had her arms pinned to her sides, while the other shoved a damp cloth over her nose and mouth. She continued the thrash, but the fumes from the cloth—something sharp and chemical, but also strangely floral—quickly took hold. She struggled to remain conscious, but darkness began encroaching on the edges of her vision, and soon, it consumed her entirely.

Cecily came back to herself slowly, then abruptly wished she hadn't. The first thing she noticed was the bitter cold in the air around her. The next was the burning pain in her mouth and throat. Where had that come from? Was she ill? In a flash, she remembered the cloth against her face, its cloying sweetness. She blinked, expecting her eyes to adjust to the dark room, then realized the blackness seemed so total because her head was swaddled in cloth. She could feel the coarse grain of it brushing her skin and the trapped moisture of her breath against her nose and chin. After that, she noticed other things. She was in a hard chair. She couldn't move her arms or legs. She was, as far as she could tell, alone.

Her chest tightened with each realization. She could sense the beginnings of panic stirring, feeling the first agonizing coils clawing their way up her throat. The paralyzing onslaught was on the way, and she couldn't afford it right now. Desperately, she tried to quiet her mind enough to find calm, to find peace, to find something to hold on to before she was lost.

What she found was one word—first in Daniel's voice, then in Paloma's, then both together.

Breathe.

So she did. It was difficult to get enough air to fill her lungs completely through the cloth, but she managed, narrowing her focus to the rise and fall of her chest, the expansion and contraction of her diaphragm. As she regained control of herself, details began seeping into her awareness, giving her further impressions of this place that she couldn't see. Besides being cold, the air was still, which suggested that she was indoors rather than outside. It was notably quiet, but the sounds she did hear seemed to echo, so the space was probably quite large. She rocked back and forth to see if the chair would move at all; it did not. There was a strange smell, too. Something about it seemed familiar, but she couldn't quite place it.

Suddenly, there was a new sound. After a moment, she identified it as footsteps. She suppressed the urge to hold the breath she had just worked so hard to steady, but she tried to make it shallower and quieter, so she could concentrate on the gait of the person who had joined her. The steps were heavy and dull—likely a man in sturdy shoes. They came closer and closer, until they stopped right in front of her. Her heart was pounding in her ears as she felt hands scrabbling at the cloth over her face.

Then the cloth was gone, leaving her head exposed. The light in the vast space was not bright, but she still recoiled from it, her eyes unprepared after the complete darkness. At the same time, the smell sharpened in her nose, and she could finally identify it: blood. With a sense of dread, she cracked an eye open and saw a line of irregular, grotesque shapes dangling from hooks along a far wall. At first, they only inspired a deep, wordless feeling of horror, but after a second or two, she was able to discern that they were sides of beef.

Meat. She was in a meatpacking warehouse. Well, that was revolting.

The figure who had freed her stood mere feet away, still holding what she could now see was a canvas bag. He wore workman's clothes and a hat that shadowed his face in the dim light. Cecily couldn't have said who he was, but just like the smell, he was maddeningly familiar. It took the sound of his voice to make the penny drop.

"Hello, Cecily."

CHAPTER 22

DANIEL

Daniel stared after Cecily's retreating back, fuming. But once she disappeared around the corner, it was like someone stuck a pin in him, letting out all the fury and leaving only sick regret behind.

Hells, what had he done?

He could try telling himself he hadn't meant any of it, but that wasn't entirely true. Some of those resentments had festered deep within him for a long time. Still, he'd never meant to hurt Cecily with them. Many of the same things that made him feel powerless and trapped affected her, too.

He needed to go someplace quiet. He needed to think.

The roof and the Lounge were out, as the odds of running into Cecily in those places were very high. Esme's office wasn't a great option either. After a bit of further consideration, he headed to the main dining room.

The vast space was hushed when he walked in. On most days, it wouldn't have stayed that way; before long, staff members would trickle in to start prepping the room for the first dinner service. But since it was the club's dark night, it would remain still and quiet for the foreseeable future. The lights on the stage were on, but they had been turned down to give off only a warm glow. While some illumination trickled in from various doorways, most of the room lay in shadow. Daniel made his way carefully to the bar and snagged a matchbook from the crystal bowl that was set out for customers. Then he walked over to the corner booth he had a particular liking for, lit the candle sitting in the middle of the table, and sat staring at the flame.

He thought of that stupid pirate book up in his room. How he'd had to have it, then couldn't bear to open it. There were memories like that, too—ones that he clung to, but didn't like to think about, let alone discuss with other people. Most were related to his father.

Daniel sighed, resigning himself to rehashing the worst period in his life one more time. Everything he'd told Cecily about his father's death had been true—the dismissal, the sickness, all of it. But he'd left out one key part.

Declan had never commented on Daniel's friendship with Cecily, at least not directly. Every once in a while, Daniel would glimpse his father watching them with a wary expression, but then there were books to read and trees to climb, and he would go about his merry way. One day, though, as Daniel was recounting one of the adventures he and Cecily had gotten up to, Declan had stopped him.

"Son, I want you to be careful."

Daniel had furrowed his brow. "About what, Pop?"

"She's a good girl," Declan had said. "And I know she's been kind to you. But the likes of her don't mix with the likes of us. Your life will be much easier once you understand that."

Daniel had not taken this advice in the spirit it was intended. Instead, he had scowled and stormed away, stewing about how old-fashioned and cynical his father was. Of course he knew that he and Cecily were from different worlds—he saw every day how Cecily's family lived a life of ease while the people in his neighborhood struggled. How the Dearborns had every need seen to while those in his community, his own mother included, could get sick and die because they couldn't afford medical care. He didn't need his father to explain it.

But Cecily was his friend. His best friend. He didn't care if she had money, and she didn't care if he didn't. So why should either of them care what anyone else thought? They were better than that.

Two weeks later, his father had been fired.

Declan never blamed Daniel for that, which had only made the burden of his guilt worse. Patrick must have been forbidden from saying anything, either, but he made his feelings clear enough. Sometimes, Daniel would catch him staring, eyes cold and condemning, before he turned away. He'd talked about joining the merchant marine in passing a few times before that, but it was then that he got serious, unable or at least unwilling to stay and watch as their father deteriorated. Once he was gone, only Daniel was left to take care of Declan, each rasping cough a dagger to his heart. Then Declan was gone, too.

Daniel remembered vividly what it had been like, sitting in the front pew at the funeral. It seemed like very little time had passed since he'd been there for his mother, but at least then he'd had a brother and a father at his side. Now, he was alone. After that, he wasn't sure what to do. The neighbors had done what could for him, but they had their own troubles to worry about. Daniel tried to find work so he could keep up with the rent, but it wasn't long before he fell behind, and one day, he came home to find his belongings in a box on the stoop. That was the beginning of the bleak time before he came to the Hierophant.

It was during those long nights, sleeping in abandoned buildings or sheltered places in the park, that he had started building a wall around himself, each brick forged from his belief that good things weren't meant for the likes of him. It was already tall and solid by the time Esme took him in, and it had stood firm for all these years. Every once in a while, he would let somebody peek inside, but that was as close as he would allow them to get.

Cecily had taken a wrecking ball to that wall. She'd made him remember both what it was to want things and what those things could—what they had—cost him. And that visceral reminder had been too much, too fast. So he had taken a wrecking ball to her.

Daniel pressed his palms to his eyes, watching the ghost of the flame dance behind his lids. His initial impulse was to sift through the rubble and start building again, to pretend that the destruction had never happened in the first place. But he found that, down deep, he didn't want to. Now that he had room and air again, he wanted to keep them. He wanted to see more than bricks when he tried to picture a future.

If he had to take those things without Cecily, he would. But he hoped he wouldn't have to. He hoped he could convince her to forgive him, whether he deserved it or not. Maybe the likes of her could find a way back to him after all.

By then, the candle had burned down to little more than a puddle of wax at the bottom of the holder. Daniel blew out the flame and got to his feet to go find Cecily. As he stepped into the main hallway, eyes squinting against the light, he saw Paloma and Oliver talking down near the kitchen.

When Paloma caught sight of him, she narrowed her eyes and stormed in his direction. "*You!*" she growled, and when she reached him, she punched him in the shoulder. "What did you do?"

Ah. So she'd talked to Cecily.

"What did she tell you?" Daniel asked, reaching up to massage the spot where Paloma had hit him.

"Tell me? She hasn't told me anything. I haven't seen her for hours."

Daniel frowned. "Then why are you—"

"Because the last time I saw her, she was with you." Paloma threw a hand out in the general direction of the stairs. "And now she's *gone.*"

Something went cold and tight in Daniel's gut, his body responding to a notion his mind wasn't quite ready to examine yet. "Gone? What do you mean gone?"

Paloma crossed her arms as Oliver joined them. "I *mean* that nobody can find her anywhere. She's not on the roof. She's not in the Lounge. I can't think of anywhere else to look."

Daniel stared down at her, a considered dread settling over him in the wake of his knee-jerk alarm.

"We—" His voice cracked. He cleared his throat and tried again. "We had a fight."

Oliver's eyebrows shot up. "A fight? But it was just yesterday that you two were all googoo eyes and flirty giggles. It was disgusting. What happened?"

Daniel opened his mouth to answer but thought better of it. Instead, he closed his eyes and scrubbed a hand over his face.

Oliver gave a resigned sigh. "Ah," he said, not unkindly. "You happened. That's what you're telling us, isn't it?"

Daniel stared at the floor, cursing himself inwardly.

Oliver clapped him on the shoulder. "Come on. Let's figure out where she went."

They searched every inch of the club. It seemed unlikely that they could have misplaced a whole person in the various nooks and crannies of the building, but they checked anyway. In desperation, Daniel got one of the autos and drove up and down the nearby streets, hoping both that he would find her and that he wouldn't. That she hadn't been so upset she'd taken her chances on her own. He even went to the boarding house to see if she had reclaimed her room. He'd known that was a long shot, but he'd felt a bone deep need to explore any possibility. He couldn't yet face the reality of what it would mean if they didn't stumble across her soon.

After returning to the Hierophant, he parked and headed toward the back entrance, bracing himself for whatever he would find inside. But it turned out he didn't have to wait that long. As he approached the door, he saw Oliver, Paloma, and Aaron standing in a huddle, looking down at something in Oliver's hand. As he got closer, he could see overturned trash cans and—*oh, gods*—what looked like splatters of blood on the ground nearby. Paloma glanced up then, perhaps alerted by the sound of his footsteps, and she murmured something to the others that made them turn.

He took a deep breath and tried to conjure up a semblance of composure. "Any news?" he asked as he reached them.

Paloma and Aaron glanced away, but Oliver held his gaze.

"We found this," he said, his tone mild but also matter-of-fact, the way it always was when he broke bad news. "Here in the alley." He held out his hand, and Cecily's charmed locket lay in his palm, the chain snapped in two.

The distant sounds of activity from the street faded away, replaced by a roaring in Daniel's ears. Slowly, he reached out and took the locket from Oliver's hand, running his thumb over the *J* engraved on the front. Daniel still wasn't sure what the engraving meant, but he did know that this locket was a token of Esme's past that she had given up to help make sure Cecily had a future. That made it precious.

After a moment, he found the tiny catch on the side with his fingernail and flicked it open. The scrap of paper from the day before was still there, safe and dry. He couldn't resist opening it and looking down at those tiny, clumsy figures, their stick arms joined in a V where their hands should be. Then he refolded it, returned it to its snug little compartment, and closed the locket, tightening his fist around it and squeezing until the hinge dug painfully into his skin.

"I'm going to find her," he said, staring at nothing, his breath curling in the air in front of him. "I'm going to get her back."

CHAPTER 23

CECILY

"Herbert!" Cecily said, staring at her brother in wide-eyed astonishment. "What are you doing here? Father said you were in Costa Primera!"

"Well, I was, but I came back when I heard about the trouble you got into." He took a step forward. "Are you all right?"

"No, I'm not all right!" Cecily shouted. "I am *tied to a chair!*"

"Yes, well, I didn't know they were going to do that," Herbert said, looking abashed.

Cecily's stomach sank, a feeling that was familiar from years of dealing with her brother's harebrained schemes. "You didn't know *who* was going to do that?"

Herbert swallowed. "My, um… my benefactor. Or rather, his people."

Cecily narrowed her eyes. "Herbert, our family has more money than some small countries. Why would you possibly need a benefactor?"

Herbert drew himself up, as if she had somehow undermined his dignity. She braced herself, preparing for him to rant about why such an arrangement made perfect sense and berate her for deigning to question him, but when his words came, bursting out in a flood, his tone was wheedling and petulant. "You know how Mother and Father are! It's always 'Grow up, Herbert!' this and 'Be responsible!' that. No matter what I do, I can never make them happy."

Cecily gaped at him. "*You* can't make them happy? You're the golden child! They cater to your every whim! Meanwhile, I've been walking on eggshells around Mother for a decade. She can barely stand the sight of me!"

Herbert scowled. "Oh, stop being so dramatic."

"See! You sound just like her!"

Herbert took a deep breath and let it out through his nose. "My point is, I wanted to do something to prove myself to them. To make them proud. And my benefactor offered me that chance."

"Uh-huh," Cecily said. "And how does you proving yourself equate to me being snatched off the street?"

"He took an interest in your predicament. Said he wanted to talk to you about what really happened." Herbert grimaced. "This isn't exactly what I thought he meant."

"You absolute dunderhead," Cecily seethed. "I am *wanted* for *murder*! Did you ever stop to think that someone concerned with my whereabouts might not have my best interest at heart?"

"But he said he did!" Herbert said plaintively. "He said he could fix you. Make you better."

That drew Cecily up short. She stared at him, her dim, blustering ox of a brother. He was a boor and a bully, but it seemed deep down, he did have some reservoir of fondness for her. It was clumsy, rooted in the fear and loathing he'd spent years soaking up from their parents, but still—he genuinely seemed to think he was helping her, which made the whole thing that much worse.

"I don't need fixing," she said in a low voice.

Herbert rocked back on his heels. "But you just said it was hard getting along with Mother. If you—"

"All of that is because of her own insecurities, not anything to do with me. I know that now."

Herbert's face twisted into a sneer, less accommodating now that his aid was being rebuffed. "Oh, you know that, do you? What else do you know? Do you know the authorities have been at the house every day since you've disappeared? Do you know that our stock is in the tank right now? Mother's been having migraines for the first time in years, and she and Father still made a point of going to Colonel Teasley's fundraiser the other night. They had to prove to everyone that they hadn't been harboring a murderer this whole time. They had to speak out against practitioners so no one thought we were a family of sympathizers."

Something inside Cecily went cold. Her parents had done that? Well, that explained some of Daniel's righteous anger. She was feeling it herself now.

"All that's on you, little sister," Herbert continued. "That's what I know."

"Herbert," said a voice from the shadows. "Is that any way to talk to our guest?"

Herbert turned toward the voice, looking cowed, and with a jolt, Cecily recognized the figure striding toward them as MNC Vandermark.

It wasn't a particularly striking figure. If Teasley had swelled to ghoulish significance in Cecily's mind, Vandermark had remained overlooked and, apparently, underestimated. He was slightly built and on the short side, narrow faced and thin lipped, with small round tortoise-shell glasses. The only outward sign of his power and influence was his clothing—a beautiful tweed suit with sleek black wingtips accessorized with a sharp silk tie and matching pocket square. Her mother would have approved.

Herbert dragged over another chair, and Vandermark sat down opposite Cecily, crossing his legs. He languidly shot his cuffs and settled his hands on his knee.

"Herbert, make yourself useful and go see to the car," he said. "You sister and I have a lot to talk about."

Herbert wavered on his feet, looking uncertain. Cecily felt a small flare of hope that he would stay with her and help her get out of this mess, but with one last regretful look, he turned and left the warehouse. His cowardice wasn't exactly surprising, but it still stung. She was really on her own.

"I must apologize for him," Vandermark said, as if Herbert were a part of his own family rather than Cecily's. "He's a good kid at heart, but a little rough around the edges."

"What is he doing here?" Cecily asked. "What have you promised him?"

"The thing about Herbert," Vandermark said, "is that he just wants to feel important. So when I asked him, for the good of the country, for the good of the Dearborn name, to keep an eye on you and told him it could help him make a name for himself in our circles, he happily agreed. He's kept me up to speed on all your doings for these last few years. When we heard you were coming back from Ville du Soleil after your unfortunate episode in the library, I summoned him home from Costa Primera to ensure that we had the most up-to-date information available as the situation developed. And it paid off. It was thanks to Herbert that we had access to the house, thanks to Herbert that we knew just when to arrange a phone call that would get your father out of the study."

Cecily stared. So Ignotus had been right. It *had* been an inside job.

"But my parents didn't even know Herbert was in town," Cecily said, trying to put the pieces together. "He wasn't there when they made the appointment with Dr. Fairchild."

"No, he wasn't. But if there is one thing your brother excels at, it's delegating. He gave multiple servants incentives to keep their ears to the ground and report back to him. And they did their jobs admirably."

Cecily frowned. "The servants hate Herbert."

"Perhaps," Vandermark said. "I think, however, that they may hate your parents more. And money talks, as they say."

Cecily wondered who it had been, hoping it wasn't anybody she'd grown up with. But then, could she blame them? It was true that her parents had never done much of anything to inspire loyalty.

"He's been extremely useful, your brother," Vandermark said. "But it's become very apparent to me that you are the more astute sibling. You take after your mother that way."

It was perhaps the first time in Cecily's life that she had ever been compared favorably to her mother, and she found she did not like it at all.

"You've given us a run for our money these past few days. I'm actually rather impressed, for all that it was an inconvenience. Of course, none of us had the foresight to account for Mr... Sullivan, is it?" He raised an eyebrow but didn't wait for a response. "Spiriting you out from under our noses.

"I was vexed about the whole thing at first, but when we got word that Sullivan had disappeared, and then Herbert told us about your childhood friendship..." He spread his hands. "It was only a matter of time. We've had eyes on the Hierophant since last night. Our men were ready to settle in for the long term, since your friends there never seemed to let you out of their sight. But then you decided to take a walk this afternoon. A great stroke of luck on our part." He cocked his head. "What prompted you to do that, I wonder?"

Cecily swallowed, determined not to take the bait. "I'm surprised you were willing to wait," she said rather than answering, relieved her voice came out steady. "Instead of just barging in and ransacking the place."

Vandermark shrugged. "I suppose I could have ordered my men to charge in with guns blazing. But that spectacle wouldn't have served my purpose. Too much unwelcome attention."

Cecily gave a disbelieving laugh. "And Dr. Fairchild didn't attract attention?!"

He gave her a bland "What can you do?" sort of smile. "Fairchild was a unique case. There were multiple variables at play with him. He was being most uncooperative—'too big for his britches,' I believe is the expression. So when the opportunity arose to not only put an end to that but also bring in a high-profile adept, of course, I took it. I admit that I didn't mean for it to blow up in the papers the way it has, though."

He looked bemused, almost sheepish. "I figured your mother

would use her considerable influence to keep the business hushed up. She's a very resourceful woman, Melanie." He smiled, and Cecily wondered, not for the first time, if their relationship really had been entirely platonic. "But after your vanishing act, I was left with little choice but to reach out to my contacts in the press. It was imperative that we track you down.

"We've wandered off topic, though. My point is, I have no complaint with your little underworld chums. I've heard about the performances at the Hierophant—Mrs. Fullerton is said to put on an excellent show. It would have been a shame to spoil that with unnecessary violence."

"What was it that Fairchild did that made you so mad, anyway?" Cecily asked, more than happy to steer the conversation away from her friends at the club. "We know about his discovery. Did he have his own plans for the cure that conflicted with yours?"

A tiny smirk played at the corner of his lips. "You could say that."

"What was it? Were you reluctant to share the wealth? Did you want to take all the credit for saving New Avalon from its infestation of magic?"

"Not at all," Vandermark said. "I think eradicating magic from the populace at large is a fool's errand."

Cecily paused, struggling to keep up with each new revelation. "So, wait—you aren't working with the rest of the RPC to cure magic? What about the sanatorium? Turner-Hoff and Sutterfield and Teasley?"

Vandermark sighed. "Fools. All of them. They believe that if they close their eyes and wish very hard, they can reshape the world the way they think it should be." His lip curled, voice full of derision. "It's a child's way of dealing with life."

None of this was making sense. Daniel had told her about a note from Dr. Fairchild's office that mentioned T. If T wasn't Teasley or Turner-Hoff, who was—

Then it hit her.

T for Thaddeus. Thaddeus Vandermark.

He'd been the one engineering this the entire time. And not on behalf of the RPC. He apparently had his own hand to play. But what was it?

She was still reeling, but Vandermark continued undaunted, as if he'd been waiting to share these details with someone for a long time.

"The others have no vision, no sense of innovation. Being able to turn off magical abilities at will has the potential to be very useful, yes. But it's not the real prize. If we understand how the brain manifests those abilities, we have an opportunity to enhance them. Or even, eventually, to instill them in brains that are not naturally predisposed. That is true progress." He looked beatific at the prospect.

"But... why?" Cecily asked.

"If we had time, I could tell you a story. The story of the War Beyond Worlds. But we don't have that time. Suffice to say, we are all players in a struggle which, though largely invisible, has the power to determine the fate of our very souls." Absentmindedly, he turned a heavy gold signet ring on his right hand. The ring had a rough green jewel in it, and with a start, Cecily recognized it as the same type of stone she'd seen encased in Esme's crystal ball.

"Magic gives us the advantage in that struggle. Teasley. Turner-Hoff, all of them—their aspirations are too small. They don't understand what we could really achieve if we try. With the proper tools at our disposal, we wouldn't have to be satisfied with ruling New Avalon, or even all of Domamundi. There are virtually no limits to what we stand to gain in the service of the Ascended Ones."

Cecily stared at him. Esme had been right. She'd been *right*. Or she and Vandermark were suffering from the same delusion, which seemed unlikely at best. Cecily mentally shook herself. *Keep him talking,* she thought. *Gather data. Find out what you can.*

"So, is all this about gaining powers for yourself?" she asked.

Vandermark shook his head, looking almost wistful. "No. That is not my part to play in the grand scheme of things. While the prospect of gaining abilities is enticing, my role is more... administrative. I am the catalyst that will set the plan in motion."

"Does that mean you have Dr. Fairchild's research? Seems like it would be shortsighted to get rid of him without it."

For the first time in the conversation, Vandermark showed a glimmer of something besides calm self-assurance. "He was more savvy on that particular point than I would have liked. He kept the bulk of his work to himself, only gave me notes. But I have scientists going through those with a fine-tooth comb, looking for a way forward. It won't be long until they're able to replicate his data. And there's still a chance that Fairchild's personal records might turn up. Nobody's been able to account for them yet." Some of his placid equanimity returned. "Either way, his death will only be a temporary setback."

"So what does any of this have to do with me?"

"Ah, yes, I can see why that might still be confusing. Thanks to Fairchild's regrettable but necessary demise, I could never get my hands on a full assessment of your ability. But anecdotally, I have been led to understand that you are quite powerful as adepts go. Do my sources have that right?"

Cecily didn't answer, deeply suspicious of where the conversation was headed.

Vandermark looked almost amused. "Neither confirm nor deny. A judicious course of action. But I think they're correct. And I would like a demonstration of what it is you can do."

"Why?" Cecily asked, her sense of disquiet growing.

"To determine how useful you could be in our fight. I understand that your power is raw, untested. But I suspect that under the right circumstances, you would just *blossom*." He held up a hand and splayed his fingers, mimicking an opening flower.

Cecily reminded herself to breathe. "I'd never do anything useful for you."

Vandermark's face fell. "I thought you might say that." He turned and called out over his shoulder, "Mr. Stone!"

Another man emerged from the shadows, and Cecily had to fight back a gasp. He was intimidatingly large, well over six feet, with broad shoulders and blocky jaw. His nose was crooked, as if it had been broken and reset poorly, and his knuckles were scarred. This was a man well acquainted with physical violence. But the most frightening thing about him was the dull, cold look in his eyes. Like he was empty.

Vandermark pulled something out of an inner jacket pocket and held it out to Mr. Stone without looking. Cecily recognized it as a pearl-handled folding knife, and some of her panic came rushing back. But when he spoke, his words surprised her.

"Remove Miss Dearborn's bindings, please," Vandermark said.

Cecily tensed as the big man moved forward, positive it was a trick, but sure enough, all he did was bend down and, almost gently, cut the ropes holding her arms and legs. She could see now that there were also ropes tied to a ring in the floor, securing the chair, but he left those in place. When he was finished, he returned to this spot at Vandermark's side and handed back the knife.

Cecily remained in her chair, rubbing feeling back into her wrists. She watched Vandermark warily.

"See, Mr. Stone here"—Vandermark gestured to the man—"has an ability very similar to your own. As these things go, the caliber of his power is on the low side of average, but with proper guidance and discipline, he has been able to achieve great success. Even without the benefit of Fairchild's research, the advancement of Mr. Stone's powers was what allowed us to cast suspicion on you for Fairchild's death."

So this was Fairchild's true murderer. Cecily felt on odd sense of betrayal at the news, even though she had never seen Mr. Stone before in her life. It seemed wrong that he could use the power they shared in that way.

"I brought Mr. Stone with me tonight because I suspected you might be reluctant to cooperate," Vandermark said. "So here's what's going to happen next: he's going to attack you."

"What?!" Cecily yelped, leaping from her chair and taking a few steps back to put its meager protection between herself and the big man. She almost tripped on another of the rings that she could now see were scattered throughout the room.

"He has more training than you do," Vandermark went on, "but if you really are the more powerful, it should be an even contest. If you fight back, I'll be able to see just what kind of power you have. If not…" He spread his hands in a shrug.

Cecily swallowed. "He could kill me."

"He could," Vandermark confirmed. "He probably will."

"But I thought you wanted me to be part of your holy war. How can I do that if I'm dead?"

"What we have here is a win-win situation," Vandermark said. "If you fight Mr. Stone, I'll get valuable data, then I'll call him off, and we can all leave together. If you don't, and he kills you, you'll no longer be my problem."

"Wait—" Cecily began, but Vandermark was not waiting.

"Mr. Stone, if you please."

Mr. Stone lunged.

CHAPTER 24

DANIEL

Everyone swung into action immediately. The Hierophant was, by design, located in an area that kept nosy neighbors to a bare minimum, but Paloma, Aaron, and Ebony spread out to ask the few nearby residents and business owners if they had seen Cecily earlier that day.

Esme cleared off the table in her fortune-telling room and used a city map to scry for Cecily's location. The technique, which she had learned from Ignotus, involved inducing a vision rather than just accepting one as it came, and she rarely performed it, as it was enormously taxing and could leave her bedridden for days. She hadn't even hesitated, though, when she thought it might help Cecily, and Daniel could have kissed her for it.

"Okay," Leo said, bustling into Esme's office, where Daniel and Oliver were waiting. He spread a map out on the desk, displaying a circle drawn in grease pencil around a portion of the warehouse district near the docks. "Esme said we're looking for a meatpacking warehouse, but this was as specific as she could get in terms of a location. She said she was sorry that she couldn't pinpoint it more closely."

"No," Daniel said, picking up the map. "No, this is so helpful. Please tell her thank you. I know how hard it is for her."

"How is she?" Oliver asked in a hushed voice.

Leo turned and gave him a gentle smile, placing a hand on his shoulder. "She's tired, but she's fine. I have her tucked up on the sofa in her dressing room with a cold cloth on her head. I'll head back in there to sit with her in a minute, but she wanted me to bring this out to you and tell you to go get our girl."

Oliver nodded, and Daniel and Leo both pretended not to notice his shaky, relieved exhalation. Then he squared his shoulders and took a deep breath. "Let's do this."

As Leo returned to Esme, Oliver and Daniel began cross-referencing the target area on the map against phone directory listings for meatpacking firms. That provided them with a list of five locations. Daniel stared at the names and addresses he'd recorded on a sheet of Esme's letterhead. On the one hand, five was a miniscule number compared to the options they'd had before. Still, five seemed like so many when the seconds were ticking by, each one fraught with the possibility that Cecily was in more and more danger.

About this time, Paloma, Aaron, and Ebony returned, perhaps inevitably, but still regrettably, empty handed. They listened as Daniel explained what they knew.

"Well, there you go," Paloma said. "We'll split the locations and go out in two groups. Divide and conquer."

"Oh, yes, excellent plan," Oliver said. "We have no idea what we are walking into. We could be facing a literal army, and if a party of five is inadequate for the task at hand, two even smaller parties will definitely make the situation better."

Paloma scowled. "It would let us cover more ground more quickly."

"And what happens if—*when*"—he glanced at Daniel—"we find her, hmm? The winning team barges in and takes on a potential horde of guards with a can-do attitude? Or drops everything to go track the other group down? These are not stellar options, Paloma."

Paloma looked like she was gearing up for an explosive argument, but before she had a chance, Daniel turned to Ebony.

"Could you make a charm that would help us? Something like the one you made for Cecily?"

Ebony snorted. "For all the good that did her."

"Eb," Daniel said. "Can you just try? Please?"

After a beat, Ebony nodded. She crossed her arms, twisting her mouth to the in thought, then looked from Aaron to Oliver and back. "Okay," she said. "I think I have an idea. Aaron, Oliver, give me your watches."

Aaron looked bewildered but complied without argument.

Oliver, meanwhile, paused after he'd pulled out his watch and unhooked the fob. "You know, this is a limited edition. It was quite expensive, so if you—"

"Your watch will be fine," Ebony said, rolling her eyes. "Just hand it over."

Oliver did so reluctantly.

Ebony held one watch in each hand, scrutinizing them. "So, what I think I could do is infuse a little of your powers into each watch. That way, they'll both be able to send"—she gestured to Aaron—"and receive"—she gestured to Oliver—"an emotional impression of, say, urgency if one group finds her and needs the other to come."

"But that still doesn't address the issue of how we find each other," Oliver said.

"If what I'm thinking pans out, you can take Aaron's watch, and he can take yours. Then they'll act like something of a beacon. Each one will draw the owner back to it."

They were all quiet for a moment.

Aaron raised his eyebrows. "Is this what you've been learning from those conjurors you've been spending so much time with?"

Ebony dipped her chin a little, flustered by the scrutiny. "Yeah, pretty much."

"Well, it's damn impressive," he said. "Why don't more adepts take advantage of it?"

"I'm still not one hundred percent sure it will work," Ebony replied. "And it will only be temporary. But we can try."

Daniel and Oliver glanced at each other.

Oliver nodded. "Okay. What do we do?"

"I need some paper and a pen."

"Here." Oliver gestured to the desk, which already had both sitting on top. "Have a seat."

She did and immediately set out about writing as the others watched. After a moment, she looked back up at them. "Y'all can't keep just staring at me like that. It's creepy, and I can't think."

"Well, what else are we supposed to do?" Aaron said. "Just stare at the wall?"

"Yes!" Ebony said, bending her head over her paper again. "If that's what you need to do. I don't care. Just stop looking."

The other four glanced at each other, turned around, and basically did just stare at the wall, listening to the pen scratch across the paper as Ebony wrote.

After a few minutes, she put down the pen. "All right. I think this is the best it's going to get."

She got up and came out from behind the desk.

"So, the way this works is all three of us are going to touch the watches at the same time, and I'm going to recite an incantation. Then we test them to see if the infusion worked."

"Why do you need an incantation?" Paloma asked, eyes wide with interest. "I don't know much about all this, but isn't it a physical transition of power? How does talking help?"

"The words don't actually do anything themselves," Ebony explained. "But they help the conjuror focus their intention. The stronger the intent, the more deeply the energy of the magic can meld with the matter of whatever is taking the charm, in this case, the watches."

Oliver's face pinched. "And you're sure my watch is going to be okay?"

"Oh, for the love of—" Ebony exploded, then cut herself off. "Take these!" She put the watches in Aaron's hands. "Now, hold them up in front of you."

Aaron did, lifting them to chest level.

Ebony nodded to Oliver. "Put your hands on his."

Oliver did so, if somewhat hesitantly, and the two of them looked at her expectantly.

"Okay, now I need to, oh—Paloma, can you hold this up so I can read it?"

Paloma stepped forward to take the paper.

Ebony settled her hands on top of Aaron's, taking a deep breath. "All right. Here goes nothing."

Paloma held up the incantation, and Ebony read it aloud. Oliver and Aaron looked from her to each other and back, wondering if something in particular should be happening and what that might be. When Ebony finished reading, she paused for a moment, as if listening to something none of the rest of them could hear.

Apparently satisfied, she lifted her hands. "Okay. There we go."

Aaron and Oliver dropped their hands, each taking a watch.

"That's it?" Oliver asked.

"That's it," Ebony replied.

Aaron shook Oliver's watch next to his ear. "How do we know if they work?"

"One of you go out in the hall," Ebony said, "and see if the one in here can pick anything up."

Aaron looked at Oliver, shrugged, and went into the hall, closing the door behind him. For a moment, nothing happened. But then...

"Gah!" Oliver jumped, looking startled, and scowled. "That isn't funny, wise guy!" he shouted toward the hall.

A moment later, Aaron came back in chuckling.

"What did you do?" Paloma asked.

"I shouted 'Boo!' at it," Aaron said, fighting back a grin.

Ebony sighed and closed her eyes for a moment, but she was quickly back in action. "Oliver, did you feel anything that let you know how to find him?"

"Yes," Oliver said, looking vaguely surprised. "It's hard to describe, but I could tell he was somewhere near the kitchen?" He looked over at Aaron, who nodded.

"All right," Paloma said. "Let's go. Aaron, are you driving our group?"

"I am," he said, and Oliver tossed him a set of keys. Aaron caught them, then looked over at Daniel. "For the record," he said, "this cloak-and-dagger business is bullshit."

The corner of Daniel's mouth quirked up, and Aaron clapped him on the shoulder as he walked past.

Once they were gone, Oliver cleared his throat and held something out to Daniel. "I brought you something."

Looking down, Daniel saw the pistol he took on dangerous jobs, tucked securely into its belted holster. Daniel stared at it for a moment. He didn't like using guns. He only carried a firearm when absolutely necessary. But Oliver was right; if there was a time when a gun was necessary, it was now. He took the belt and began buckling it around his waist. Oliver did the same for the piece he'd picked out for himself.

"We got ammo?" Daniel asked.

"Yup." Oliver held up a storage box.

"Then let's roll."

For the first few minutes, they drove in silence, each lost in his own thoughts. But as Daniel had suspected it would, Oliver's curiosity got the better of him.

"So, what did you two fight about?"

Daniel didn't answer at first, keeping his eyes on the road.

"She said she was going back to her parents," he said finally. "Once all this is over."

Oliver nodded, face pensive. "Okay. Was this before or after you told her you saw them at the fundraiser?"

"Um..." Daniel discovered he couldn't force himself to say the words aloud. It didn't matter. Even if Oliver hadn't known him so well, he figured his misery must have been going off like a klaxon in his friend's direction.

He wasn't wrong.

"Daniel..." Oliver said despairingly, face creasing in secondhand mortification.

"I was going to!" Daniel protested. "It was just... I couldn't find the right opportunity."

"Well, that seems like some admittedly clumsy miscommunication, but I wouldn't call it a fight." Oliver cut him a sideways look. "That's not all, though, is it?"

"No," Daniel admitted.

Oliver sighed. "What did you say?"

"I may have… implied that she deserved what she got from them because she wasn't willing to stand up for herself," he mumbled. "And that her family was responsible for killing my dad."

Oliver's horrified face whipped in Daniel's direction, slack-jawed. Daniel cringed.

"What in hells is wrong with you?" Oliver finally managed.

"Would you like an itemized list?"

"Daniel, that was *unconscionable*!"

"I know," Daniel said dejectedly. "Do you not remember the list that I just mentioned?"

Tension hung between them in the quiet as Daniel stopped for a red light, then pulled through the intersection once it switched to green.

"Look," Oliver said. "We established a long time ago that I respect your dive-right-in, ask-questions-later approach to life. I know it's important to you to handle your problems yourself. But, pal, in the long run, that is only going to carry you so far."

Daniel just sat there stewing, so Oliver went on.

"If you don't stop pushing people away, you're going to end up somewhere you don't want to be. Sad and alone, like one of those old washed-up boxers we see hanging around the gym. Mumbling about your glory days. Drinking cheap hooch out of a paper bag." He shuddered, as if the cheap hooch was the worst part of all that.

"I don't push people away," Daniel grumbled.

"You do."

"Well, you never seem to go anywhere."

"I'm tenacious," said Oliver. "Other people might not have my fortitude."

Daniel bit the inside of his cheek. Oliver wasn't really saying anything he didn't already know. But he thought he'd had time with Cecily.

"If I don't get a chance to make things right with her..." he began, but he couldn't finish.

"You will," Oliver said, adamant. "Because we're going to find her, and then I'm going to take deep satisfaction in watching as she makes you grovel."

Daniel sighed. "I truly hope so."

"We'll find her," Oliver said again, all trace of levity gone. "I promise."

Daniel sat back in his seat and hoped with everything in him that Oliver was right.

CHAPTER 25

DANIEL

The first warehouse Daniel and Oliver tried was a bust, as was the second. Driving to the third spot on the list, Daniel had to fight down the stirrings of panic. Since they hadn't yet received a signal from the other group, this was looking like their last hope of locating Cecily and getting her back before things got really dire. Unless they were already dire. Unless he was too late.

Taking a deep breath, he tightened his grip on the steering wheel. He couldn't let himself get swept up in wild conjectures about something that may not have even happened—"borrowing trouble," his father had called it. He had to stay sharp, stay observant.

That was how he noticed the lone auto parked in a narrow side street as they approached the last warehouse—and recognized the figure getting out of it as Herbert Dearborn.

"This is the place," he said, his entire body going on alert.

Oliver stiffened as well, as he absorbed some of Daniel's tension. "How do you know?"

"That was Cecily's brother back there with the auto."

Oliver's eyes went wide as Daniel pulled their own auto over to the curb.

"Use the watch," Daniel said. "I'm going for Herbert."

"Daniel, wait—"

Daniel cut him off by slamming the door shut, leaving his friend to swear futilely behind him. He unholstered his gun as he walked, gripping it with both hands and keeping it pointed at the ground. He did his best to keep his steps quiet and light, so he was almost right on top of Herbert before he was spotted. Herbert was taking a drag on his cigarette when his eyes went wide in recognition. He fumbled with the butt of his smoke, almost burning himself as he tossed it to the ground, then made a move toward the auto, but Daniel was too quick for him.

"Ah, ah, ah…" He lifted the gun so it was pointed at Herbert's chest. "Don't move. Hands where I can see them."

Herbert complied but fumed quietly. Daniel took a few more steps toward the auto and leaned forward to look in the window. A pearl-handled revolver lay on the passenger seat in plain sight. Daniel recognized it as the type popularized by Cale "The Terminator" Bowker, a notorious bank robber who had wreaked havoc up and down the west coast in Calafia before going down in a blaze of glory exchanging gunfire with law enforcement. Daniel snorted. That just figured. The Dearborn men had gone hunting occasionally, for wild turkey and ducks, so Herbert knew his way around a shotgun. There was no good reason, however, for anyone with his kind of cushy, pampered life to carry around that sort of firepower. It was a prop in some drama Herbert had built up in his mind. A rich kid's toy.

Keeping an eye on Herbert, Daniel sidled over and plucked the revolver out of the auto through the open window, using one hand to tuck it into the back of his waistband. Then he steadied his own weapon again and took another step toward Herbert.

"Now, where is your sister?"

Herbert swallowed. "I… I don't know what you're talking about. How should I know where she is?"

Hells, he did not have the patience for this. "Herbert, I know you know where she is. You know that I know. Why don't you save us both a lot of time and trouble and just tell me?"

Herbert's lip had curled ever so slightly at the use of his name, and

Daniel knew—he *knew*—that it was on the tip of Herbert's tongue to correct him. To say that Daniel should refer to him as "Mr. Dearborn." But while that tiny part of him was indignant, most of him was still terrified, so he didn't say anything cocky. In fact, he didn't say anything at all.

That silence was the last straw for Daniel. He closed the remaining distance between them and pressed the muzzle of the gun to Herbert's forehead. Herbert immediately began to tremble, fighting back tears. Daniel found this reaction immensely satisfying, which probably should have disturbed him but didn't. He had no real intention of shooting Herbert, but Herbert didn't need to know that.

"Last chance," he said. "Where is Cecily?"

"Inside," Herbert blubbered. "In the big room at the center of the building."

"Who else? Who's with her?"

"Just Vandermark and one other guy."

Vandermark. That was interesting. Daniel quirked an eyebrow. "Only the two of them?"

"Yeah, yeah, that other guy is huge, and I think he's also an adept." He let out a sob. "Please don't shoot me."

Just then, Oliver hurried up, out of breath. He looked startled when he saw the tableau Daniel and Oliver made.

"Daniel—" he said, seemingly intent deescalating the situation, but Daniel had already stepped away from Herbert, lowering the gun.

Herbert sagged to the pavement, weak with relief.

Daniel retrieved the pearl handled revolver and held it out to Oliver, who took it, wide-eyed.

"He says there's only two people inside with her," Daniel said. "Stay here and wait for the others. I'm going in to take a look."

Oliver didn't even try to protest this time, just sighed deeply as Daniel rounded the auto and pushed his way into the warehouse. Daniel did hear him call out, "Do not take them on by yourself—hold off until our backup arrives!"

Then the door swung shut, and he was alone.

Daniel made his way down a shadowy corridor, all of his senses primed for signs of danger. When he reached the end of the hall, he peeked around the corner, not putting it past Herbert to lie about the number of people in the building. But he didn't see any armed thugs in the empty space.

He only saw two bodies sprawled on the floor, one a tall, heavily built man, and the other a young woman in a borrowed coat and boots.

Daniel felt a sharp pang in his chest, and he leaped forward, completely disregarding Oliver's request. The room smelled of the meat hanging nearby, ozone, and something like burnt hair. Daniel didn't quite know what to make of that, but he figured it couldn't be anything good. Keeping his gun up, he made his way toward Cecily, pausing for the briefest of moments to assess the man's situation.

He was entirely still in the way only the dead could be. A dark pool of blood had spread out from the base of his skull, where it rested on one of the rings set into the floor; the best Daniel could tell, he had fallen on it, and the impact had been enough to sever his spine.

Good riddance, Daniel thought. He didn't know what this man had done yet, but he was pretty certain the guy had deserved what he'd gotten.

When he reached Cecily, he shoved the gun into its holster and fell to his knees, heaving an enormous sigh of relief when he saw that her chest was still rising and falling. Her face was deathly pale, though, under the fresh bruises that were rising, and her hair and clothes looked scorched.

"Cecily," he said in a stage whisper, torn between worry and the recognition that Vandermark was still unaccounted for. "Cecily, wake up."

He shook her gently but got no response. He glanced around the room, checking for threats, then tried again. "Cecily, we have to get out of here, so I need you to open your eyes. Please, sweetheart, come back to me."

Interminable seconds ticked by, but then, miraculously, her eyes fluttered open. He let out a shaky, grateful breath.

"Daniel?" she said, blinking as if she couldn't quite get her eyes to focus. "What are you doing here?"

He smiled down at her, struck by affection and tenderness so profound they hurt. "I came for you, silly."

"Oh," she said. "Okay."

Daniel sobered. "Can you sit up?"

"I think so." With his help, she pushed herself upright, lifting a hand to the back of her head with a hiss. Looking closer, Daniel could see that a goose egg was already forming where she'd hit the floor.

"We'll give it a minute to see how you do before we try standing," he said. "But we need to be leaving sooner rather than later."

"Yeah, okay."

He reached up and tucked a lock of hair behind her ear. "What happened?"

"Vandermark wanted to see my power. See what I could do. I told him no, and he got this other adept—" Her eyes went wide with alarm. "Mr. Stone! Have you seen him? He may be hiding—"

"He's dead," Daniel rushed to say. "He can't hurt you anymore."

He'd meant to reassure her, but something heavy and sad crossed her face. "Did I... Was it me?"

"No," Daniel said soothingly. "At least not directly. He cracked his head open on one of those rings in the floor."

"Ah." She nodded then took a deep breath. "Anyway, when I refused, Vandermark had him attack me to force me to fight back."

Daniel swore.

Cecily's mouth, though, quirked up in a grim half smile. "It didn't go the way he'd planned. I think he expected me to try a little, then beg for mercy. It never occurred to him that I'd have some idea what I was doing—I'll never be able to repay Paloma for that. So Mr. Stone and I went back and forth a bit, then we each released a big burst of energy at once, and they kind of... bounced off each other." She demonstrated with her hands by bringing them together, then flinging them apart. "I remember flying through the air, and then I must have blacked out."

Daniel nodded, glancing around again. "I don't mean to rush you, but do you think you can stand?"

Cecily nodded. "I think so, yeah."

Again, Daniel helped her rise. He held onto her as she swayed a little on her feet, but she steadied soon enough.

"Good?" he asked her.

"Good."

He drew his gun and turned toward the door. He was about to give the signal to move when he heard her voice again.

"Daniel... about what I said..."

"Hey, no," he told her. "I was way out of line. I'm willing to take responsibility for that whole awful conversation. But we need to go now, before Vandermark comes back."

As if on a cue, a voice rang out from across the room. "Well, well, well—isn't this sweet?"

Daniel spun around, lifting his gun and using his other hand to push Cecily behind him. Across the room, Vandermark was pointing his own gun at the two of them. His hand did not shake.

"Good of you to join us, Mr. Sullivan."

CHAPTER 26

CECILY

"I apologize for not being here when you arrived," Vandermark continued. "I had to go call my, ah, cleaning crew to come take care of Mr. Stone there. I had anticipated that he would be walking out with us, but well, *c'est la vie.*" He shrugged. "I just can't afford to leave evidence lying around."

He took a few steps forward. Daniel raised his free hand to steady his own gun.

"I'm going to need you to put down your weapon," Vandermark said.

"I don't think so," Daniel said.

Vandermark's eyes narrowed. "It wasn't a request."

"We have people on the way, too," Daniel said. "This situation has the potential to get very ugly. Or you could just let us go."

Cecily wasn't sure what to make of this. She supposed it was possible he had mustered a large group of Esme's contacts to help rescue her, but somehow, she doubted that. It seemed far more likely that Daniel and anyone else who had volunteered to help were winging it. And they may have had some experience circumventing the law, but they were not hardened criminals. Not the way Vandermark's underlings apparently were.

"I find it interesting—a little charming, even—that you somehow see us as equals." Vandermark took another step toward them. "The future I am working toward is beyond what you could even imagine. Miss Dearborn's power could help turn the tide for us. I can see you have feelings for her, but I have worked too hard and too long to get here only to be derailed by youthful infatuation."

"Well, it seems we're at an impasse," Daniel said. "Because I am not letting you take her."

Vandermark's eyes narrowed. "There is no way that I am letting her go."

Cecily watched this playing out in increasing dismay. Things were spiraling out of control, and there didn't seem to be anything she could do about it. Neither of them was going to back down; at this point, it was essentially a crap shoot as to which of them would end up shooting first. On the one hand, Vandermark was a complete wild card. She had no idea what kind of cost-risk analysis was playing out in his head. Shooting Daniel, shooting her, shooting Daniel then her— there was no way to predict what he would choose. On the other, Daniel, was an immovable object. Whatever had transpired between them before she'd been taken, it was behind him now. He was going to protect her or die trying.

Dread, heavy and familiar, coiled through her insides, its grasping fingers reaching for her triggers: the one that rendered her immobile or the one that made her lose control. But with great effort, she pushed the heaviness back. She was not just an observer here. She was a participant – *the* participant, really, the reason all of this had happened in the first place. And if there was any chance at all that she could avert a crisis, by the gods, she was going to participate.

"I'll go with you!" she burst out, meeting Vandermark's eyes. "All right? I'll go with you if you leave him be."

Vandermark's eyebrows shot up in surprise. "You will?"

"Yes," Cecily said, raising her hands and beginning to move slowly toward him, though she was careful to stay out of his line of fire. "But we have to go now, and you have to leave him unharmed."

"Cecily," Daniel growled, "what are you doing?"

She chanced a glance at him.

"I know you," she said, infusing each word with as much feeling as she could. "You're not going to give in, so he is very likely going to shoot you, and I can't stand here and watch you die." She shook her head. "I *can't*. We have to find a solution that gets both of us out of here."

"I'd listen to her, Sullivan," Vandermark said, edging nearer to her, but keeping the gun pointed at Daniel's chest. "She seems to have a handle on the situation."

"Shut up," Daniel snarled at him, then turned as much of his attention as he dared to Cecily, eyes pleading. "Don't do this. There's got to be another way."

"But what if there isn't?" she said.

Daniel didn't answer, but she saw his jaw clench. Vandermark was mere inches away now. If Daniel was going to do anything to keep the two of them from leaving, he was running out of time. Cecily prayed he wouldn't. Didn't he see? One wrong move now could end in catastrophe, but if she could just get all of them out of the building alive, they'd have chance. Daniel could regroup. He could get the others to help him find her and get her ba-

Vandermark grabbed her by the waist. pulling her flush to his body, her back to his front. He jabbed the gun into her side, and it was then that she realized what a huge miscalculation she'd made. If she had devoted any real thought to what leaving with Vandermark would look like, which, admittedly, she had not, she might have guessed he would just let her walk out in front of him, maybe that he would take her arm and drag her with him. But now, she was a human shield, swinging the entire situation to Vandermark's advantage.

"Yes, this arrangement suits me just fine," Vandermark said. "Sullivan, drop your weapon."

"What's to stop you from shooting either of us if I do?"

"Nothing," Vandermark said, almost cheerfully. "Better hope you stay on my good side."

It was true. By allowing Vandermark to grab her, Cecily had effectively cut off any chance Daniel had to defend either himself or her.

Daniel snarled at Vandermark, but he lowered his arms slowly, then crouched down to lay his gun on the floor. His posture was tense as he straightened, holding his hands out to his sides.

Cecily burned with self-recrimination. What had she been thinking? She had always been so afraid of hurting someone by losing control of her powers, but how was this any different? Daniel, Esme, Paloma – they'd all been encouraging her to take charge of her life rather than bowing to others' expectations. But if taking charge ended like this, why should she even bother?

"Now then, how are we going to do this?" Daniel asked.

"Well," Vandermark said slyly, toying with them, "let me just think on that for a moment. It seems I have more leverage in this negotiation now. I'm not sure it's necessary any longer for me to honor Miss Dearborn's demands."

Of course Vandermark wasn't going to abide by her condition. Why would he? She had to face the fact that he was better at this than she was. He'd had time to develop this scheme, lots of it. He had cunning. He had so many resources at his dispos-

Wait.

She looked around. If he really did have access to all those resources, why were they in this godforsaken warehouse? Why had he only brought along her boneheaded brother and Mr. Stone? Yes, he was in deep with the RPC, and yes, he may yet have the wherewithal to muster his magical army. But not yet. For the moment, he'd gone rogue, turning his back on the RPC's most deeply cherished values in service of his own ambition. In a way, he was an outlier, just as she always had been.

An insight hit her with startling clarity. Whatever he'd had to say about her clash with Mr. Stone, however much he threatened them now, Vandermark didn't want to harm her. She was too valuable to him. She was the linchpin for putting his plan into action. And it wasn't because of her powers, or at least not just because of that. She was a trophy, representing his rarified vision of the future.

He'd said it himself—she was a "high-profile adept" from a good family in the ruling class. That's what would impress his cronies and bring them around to his way of thinking, in a way someone like Paloma or Oliver never could. It was a terrible reversal of her mother's obsession with respectability, in which her value was determined by the same factors, just from opposite directions.

And she was tired of it.

"Stop," she said. Her voice didn't come out as strong as she she'd have liked, but the fact that it came out at all seemed like a success.

Vandermark pressed the gun further into her ribs. "What?"

Cecily took a deep breath. She knew she had to play this very carefully.

"Stop it. What are you hoping to achieve here? Your 'cleaners' can come in and take care of Mr. Stone's body, maybe Daniel's, too." Her stomach churned at the thought. "But what about me?"

"What about you?"

"You're not going to shoot me." Her voice sounded stronger now, but she was still acutely aware of how risky this was.

"Oh, I'm not?"

"No. I'm worth too much to you. There are a lot of different ways you could benefit if I'm alive. You could be a hero by bringing a violent practitioner like me to justice. You could concoct some story about what really happened to Fairchild and get all the glory for clearing the name of an innocent girl. The choice is yours. But all of those things go away if I'm dead, and it will be hard to make up the ground you've lost on your mission."

He didn't respond right away. A tiny hope kindled inside Cecily. Maybe she was getting through to him. Maybe she could still salvage this.

"Perhaps you're right," he said slowly. "It would simplify things if we dispensed with pretense altogether."

Then he moved. Cecily knew in an instant what he was doing. It happened quickly, maybe even too quickly for conscious thought, but her body understood. And as the gun swung in Daniel's direction, her body chose what to do.

Electricity flared out not just from her hands, but from her entire body, surrounding her in a crackling halo of light. Vandermark screamed, arching his back and turning his head to protect his face. Cecily grabbed the hand that still held her pinned to his chest, and when his other arm fell to his side, dropping the gun, she grabbed that one, too, completing the circuit and sending power arcing through him. His body spasmed, the scream turning into more of a choking whine, and after a terrible moment, he went limp. It was only then that Cecily let go, allowing his lifeless body to tumble to the floor.

The only problem was, without him there to support her anymore, she followed suit almost immediately. Her head felt strangely muffled as she lay there on the floor, almost like she was underwater. She heard Daniel's footsteps as he ran to her and his voice calling her name, but he sounded very far away. Even when his face came into her line of vision, he seemed oddly distant, though his eyes were full of fear.

"Cecily! Cecily, can you hear me? Oh, hells." He looked up. "Oliver! Help!"

Cecily wanted to comfort him, reassure him that she was fine, but she couldn't find her words. The effort was making her so tired, and she closed her eyes, just for a moment.

"No, no, no," Daniel's voice said. "Cece, baby, stay with me. Come on, help is almost here."

She managed to crack her eyes open again. Since her words had wandered off, she tried to reach up and touch Daniel's cheek. To let him know everything was going to be okay. But her hand only made it up a few inches before it fell back against her chest. Why was everything so hard?

She really was exhausted. Maybe if she just slept a little, things would get easier. Yes, that was it. Just a quick rest would set it right. She let her eyes slide shut again.

"Cecily, no! Cecily!"

She went away for a while after that.

CHAPTER 27

CECILY

When Cecily drifted back toward awareness, everything was dark. She had a distant memory of doing something like this recently, but she'd been afraid then. This darkness wasn't frightening. It was warm and comforting, putting her in mind of being tucked up in bed on a stormy night, knowing she was snug and dry while a tempest raged outside. In fact, she was tempted to sink back into the dark for a while, but then she noticed the voices.

"How long did he say this was going to take?"

"Just be patient. Her body needs time to recover."

"I just want to know if too much time has passed. How will we know if it's working or not?"

Someone sighed. "Have you ever heard that a watched pot never boils?"

"Cecily is not a pot!"

"Oh, by the gods, Daniel, give it a rest."

Cecily wanted to laugh, wanted to join in the teasing, but she wasn't quite close enough yet. With effort, she reached for the voices, trying to will herself to where they were.

"Paloma! I think she's waking up!"

With some effort, Cecily opened her eyes. Daniel was sitting in a chair by the bed, beaming down at her. The bed... Looking around, she realized she was in his nook, dressed in the borrowed nightgown she'd been using. Paloma's head popped up over Daniel's shoulder, and she smiled.

"Welcome back," she said.

"What... What happened?" Cecily asked. But then she remembered. "Wait—Herbert, Vandermark—"

"We'll get to that," Daniel said. "How do you feel?"

"Tired," she said, considering. "Weak. But okay, I think." She shifted, trying to get more comfortable. "How long was I out?"

"It's been about thirty-six hours."

Her eyes went wide. "Really?"

He nodded. "After... well, afterwards, we couldn't get you to wake up, no matter what we did. Scared the bleeding hells out of me, if I'm honest. So we called one of our conjuror friends, Ignotus. He told us this type of thing happens sometimes when an adept overextends their power. He gave us the recipe for an elixir to help restore your energy."

"An elixir? Made of what?"

"Oh, it was a big list of plants and herbs and things," he said. "I handed it off to Paloma, and she took care of it."

Cecily looked over Daniel's shoulder, and Paloma nodded.

"I know a few traditional remedies my mother taught me before she passed, but this was like nothing I've ever seen. It's fascinating, what the science and the magic can do together." She put a hand on Daniel's arm. "I'm going to go let the others know she woke up."

Daniel nodded, and she left. Cecily tried to push herself up on her elbows, but Daniel put a gentle hand on her chest.

"Don't push yourself. Just rest."

Cecily scowled but settled down into the pillows. "I feel like I've already rested for a long time."

"There's no rush," Daniel said. "You don't have to run anymore."

That simple statement caught her off guard, but she realized it was true. They had solved the mystery. They knew what had happened to

Dr. Fairchild. And the person who'd been responsible was dead. He was dead because Cecily had killed him.

The momentary, tentative bit of hope and relief she'd felt at being free morphed into something shameful and hard. She wanted to make herself small and hide, the way she had when her powers first manifested, when she'd felt she might literally explode and rain down destruction.

But she couldn't seem to muster the energy to get out of the bed, so she did the next best thing and curled into a ball, tugging the blanket up around her chin.

"Hey," Daniel said. "What's wrong?"

"Vandermark," she said, and when she couldn't bring herself to elaborate, it didn't matter. Daniel understood.

"You shouldn't blame yourself," he said. "You did what you had to do."

"Did I, though? Did I have to do it?"

Daniel was silent, letting her words hang in the air, but his eyes were wide and soft. That encouraged her to go on.

"I didn't want to die. And I couldn't let him hurt you. I *couldn't*."

He reached up and gently took her hand.

"But was that my only option? I've spent a big part of my life convinced that I was going to lose control of my power and hurt someone and hating myself for it. And then I did. And now he's dead."

"You didn't lose control," Daniel said. "You were in absolute command of your powers. I could see it, and it was beautiful."

Cecily frowned. "You're missing the point."

"I don't think I am." He scooted his chair a little closer to the bed. "I've never had to do something like that—not up close and personal. But there was this one time where a supply drop went bad, and Oliver and I had to get out fast. Law enforcement chased us, and I had to do some inadvisable stuff to try and lose them. It was dark, and when I took a particularly sharp corner, the LE car couldn't compensate. They spun out and crashed into the trees at the side of the road. There was an item in the paper about it the next morning. Both officers were announced dead at the scene.

"It bothered me a lot. I kept thinking that even if we were on opposite sides, those guys had families, friends. And it could just as easily have been me and Oliver. We had luck on our side. That's all."

"But that was an accident," Cecily said. "You didn't choose to make that happen."

"Didn't we?" Daniel said. "We ran. If we'd given up and let them catch us, they wouldn't have crashed. But then we would have been in jail instead of helping families who needed us. And what if it was the officers' own fault for chasing us? Or the National Congress's fault for putting all of us in the position to begin with? Why does it have to be one and not all three?" He stroked her knuckles with his thumb.

She sighed. "There aren't any easy answers to that, are there?"

He smiled at her sadly. "No."

"So, how do you decide what's the right thing to do?"

"You try your best," he said. "And realize that some people don't, and that you're not responsible for them. I mean, Vandermark knew what you could do."

Cecily pursed her lips. "I'm not sure he did, though."

"Okay, maybe not the full extent of it. But he knew. And he did those things anyway. Then he paid the price for them. Don't take the burden of his choices on yourself."

Cecily nodded, which sent a wave of dizziness rolling over her. She pressed her eyes closed and clutched the blanket.

"What is it now?" Daniel asked, leaning forward.

Cecily took a deep breath and opened her eyes. "Nothing. I'm fine. Just got a little woozy."

"Uh- huh. What did I tell you? You still need rest."

Cecily narrowed her eyes, but she didn't argue.

"Go back to sleep," he said.

"But you'll worry."

"I won't worry as much now that I know you're okay." He stood and smoothed the blanket for her before leaning down to kiss her forehead. "And I'll be here when you wake up." He slid something into her hand before he turned away and pulled the curtain shut behind him, leaving her alone.

In the last moments before she drifted off, Cecily opened her hand to see what Daniel had given her. It was a tiny wooden train.

If Dr. Fairchild's death had been a scandal, Vandermark's was an absolute free-for-all. As it turned out, while Daniel was watching over Cecily, Oliver had been putting the fear of the gods into Herbert and more or less bullying him into helping them create a cover story. The day after the incident in the warehouse, a contrite and legitimately anguished Herbert walked into AALE headquarters and confessed to his involvement in a secret conspiracy. He had, he told the astonished officers, been recruited by MNC Vandermark, who had told him that any resistance on his part would result in the grievous injury or death to his family. Vandermark had then used Herbert to gain access to Dearborn House, where Mr. Stone had murdered Dr. Fairchild in an attempt to drive a wedge between Mr. Dearborn and other members of the RPC by insinuating that the Dearborns had a dangerous magic user under their very own roof. Herbert claimed this was motivated by Vandermark's desire to sabotage Dearborn Consolidated's infrastructure bill contracts, as well as some purely personal grievances on Vandermark's part.

"You really were attached to that 'driving a wedge' theory, weren't you?" Cecily asked Oliver as he told her this story.

Oliver just grinned.

Herbert had taken the authorities to the warehouse, which still contained Vandermark and Mr. Stone's bodies, and explained that the two of them had fought when Vandermark reneged on the sizable compensation he'd promised Mr. Stone for the Fairchild job. Why this confrontation had occurred in a random meatpacking warehouse near the docks was not addressed in any detail.

"So, they just bought his story?" Cecily asked Oliver. "Just like that?"

"They had eyewitness testimony from one of the city's, nay, the country's leading families and no viable alternatives for an explanation, so yeah, pretty much."

Cecily shook her head. "That's rather depressing."

Oliver shrugged.

"We've established that they are frequently not good at their jobs."

When the story had hit the papers, the reporters had focused not so much on the details of the crime itself, but on the questions of why Vandermark, an anti-practitioner, had been consorting with adepts in the first place and how he had done it right under the RPC's nose without anyone noticing, the latter of which, Cecily thought, was a perfectly legitimate question. And there was one more detail that needed to be resolved: why had Cecily disappeared after the murder, and where had she gone?

"I know you're going to hate this part," Oliver said. "But we need an inspirational reunion with your family to finish this thing out."

Cecily sighed. "I figured."

And that was how she found herself on the steps in front of Dearborn House with her parents, facing more or less the same group of reporters who had greeted her on her first night back in Ad Astra, albeit with a few new faces in the mix. As her eyes drifted over the crowd, she was surprised to see a woman standing next to Stewart Mills, her bright red hair peeking out from beneath a lovely aubergine cloche. The woman looked like she was only a few years older than Cecily, but thanks to her sharp-eyed gaze and confident posture, she fit right in among the male reporters. *Good for her*, Cecily thought as the woman turned her head to say something into Stewart's ear. Admittedly, Cecily's relationship with the press was complicated, but it warmed her to see someone else making their own way in the world, regardless of what others might say about it.

Then the press conference began. As Mrs. Dearborn stood there with an arm wrapped firmly around Cecily's shoulders, Mr. Dearborn explained that Cecily had been the first to discover Dr. Fairchild's body. Knowing how quickly rumors could spiral out of control, she realized she would be a prime suspect in the case, so she'd fled to stay with a friend until she could figure out what to do next. Who this friend was and why Cecily hadn't tried to contact her family to let them know she was safe were details that, like those related to the warehouse, were conveniently glossed over.

"And so," Mr. Dearborn said, coming to the end of his speech, "Melanie and I are unutterably grateful that Cecily has returned to us safe and sound and that we can now put this terrible business behind us. I'm sure all of you understand what a difficult time this has been, and we ask that you respect our privacy as we rebuild our lives in the aftermath. We will not be taking questions at this time."

The gathered journalists didn't seem at all interested in respecting the family's privacy and erupted in shouts and questions as soon as the last word was out of Mr. Dearborn's mouth. Mrs. Dearborn steered Cecily inside, leaving her husband to deal with the commotion. She took Cecily to the ground-floor sitting room to wait until the scrum had dispersed. Cecily sank gratefully into one of the silk-upholstered armchairs near the fireplace as Mrs. Dearborn went to the sideboard to fix a drink.

"What a relief to have that over with," she said as she poured out a finger of whiskey, and Cecily couldn't help nodding in agreement. Drink now in hand, Mrs. Dearborn walked over and sat in the other chair, though she didn't slump into hers the way Cecily had. She sat up straight and alert. Ready for business.

"I've already been thinking about which social events we should use to begin restoring your reputation," she said. "The one silver lining in this whole terrible business is that everyone in society is *dying* of curiosity about what happened to you, so we'll have no shortage of opportunities."

Cecily gaped at her mother. She had no intention of attending any society get-togethers, now or ever again. She'd said as much to her parents during their excruciatingly awkward meeting with Herbert, during which Herbert and Cecily had explained what had actually happened with Vandermark. It had, in fact, been one of the conditions for her participation in today's charade for the press.

"Mother," Cecily said. "I told you. I only came back here for the day. I'm leaving again this afternoon."

Mrs. Dearborn waved a dismissive hand. "Don't be absurd, Cecily. That makes no sense. What are you going to do? Go back to that, that nightclub where you were hiding? Live like a chorus girl?" She shook her head. "There's nothing for you there. You're back where you belong now."

Cecily was speechless. But rather than search for words, she got to her feet and began making her way upstairs.

"Cecily?" her mother called after her. "Cecily, where are you going? Come here this instant!"

But Cecily didn't so much as look back.

Her first stop was the infamous study. Just entering the room sent a chill down her spine, but it had the most accessible phone, which she used to call the club and let them know she was ready to leave. Then she went to her room. As she walked in, she paused, thinking of the life she had lived here. She wanted to hug the younger version of herself, the one who had lain in the bed and dreamed of escape. She wanted to tell that girl she would make it one day. But she couldn't. So she went to the closet, pulled out a large carpet bag, and began to pack.

There wasn't much she wanted to take with her—just a handful of mementos from Belleterre, a few pieces of jewelry, and some books. And also her good coat. She may have been starting fresh, but it would have been foolish to let that go to waste.

As she worked, her mother came in looking as frazzled as Cecily had seen her in recent memory. She was actually *panting* from her rush up the stairs.

"What are you doing?" she asked, holding the bedpost as she caught her breath.

"I'm packing," Cecily said evenly.

"Cecily, I demand you stop this foolishness! I thought you'd put these childish outbursts behind you, but here you are again, acting hysterical to garner attention."

"I am not hysterical," Cecily said, adding another book to the bag. "Which you'd be able to see if you were actually paying attention.

What I am is resolved to carry out the course of action I shared with you yesterday."

"You cannot be serious about going back to that place."

"I can, and I am."

"This is outrageous. I forbid it! Do you hear me? I will not stand for this sort of impudence after things have just started getting back to normal."

Cecily closed and fastened the carpetbag.

Mrs. Dearborn's hands clenched into fists at her sides. "We can report those people to the authorities," she snapped, getting desperate. "Say they kidnapped you. Send someone to go get you and bring you back."

Cecily paused, looking her mother straight in the eye. Then she raised one hand in front of her, letting sparks dance along the tips of her fingers. "You can try."

She knew it was a petty move, showy and self-indulgent, but it was also effective. Her mother's face went positively white.

With a grim sense of satisfaction, Cecily shrugged into her coat, lifted the carpetbag, and made her way toward the ground floor. Mrs. Dearborn trailed after her.

"But what are we going to tell people?" she demanded as they descended the stairs.

"That is not my problem."

"Selfish girl!" Mrs. Dearborn spat. "You're not even considering what this will do to the family, are you?" They were at the rear of the house now, near the small back driveway that was often used for deliveries because Mrs. Dearborn didn't want tradesmen sullying her pristine marble entrance. When Cecily opened the back door, her mother stopped, as if crossing the threshold, leaving the prestige of the house, was a bridge too far for her. But she had one last salvo to throw Cecily's way.

"This is not the way we raised you!" she shouted, and Cecily almost had to laugh.

"You're right. Goodbye, Mother." And she walked out to where Daniel was waiting for her at the curb.

The next morning, Cecily stood at the boarding house window, wrapped in a quilt, and watched the sun rise. Her feet were cold on the floorboards, nothing like the plush carpet in her room at Dearborn House, but she didn't care. This was a new day in a new life, and it was hers.

Over on the bed, Daniel stirred, looking for her as he came fully awake. Spotting her at the window, he rolled to his feet and tugged on a pair of pajama bottoms before joining her. He wrapped his arms around her, tugging her close, and pressed a kiss to the bare skin of her shoulder.

"What are you doing?" he murmured.

"Just watching the sun come up," she said. "The colors are pretty spectacular this morning."

"Hmm," he hummed in conformation, nuzzling into the space behind her ear before hooking his chin over her shoulder.

"I know it's not a train window," he said. "But it's still pretty good."

"The train doesn't have to be an actual train. It's more a state of mind."

"Ah," he said. "I see."

She turned in his arms so that she was facing him. "Good morning."

"Good morning," he replied.

"We get to do this all the time now," she continued, as if the idea had just occurred to her.

He smiled at her fondly. "We do."

"What shall we do with our day?"

In answer, Daniel leaned in and kissed her, slow and thorough. Cecily felt herself melt in his embrace, a feeling still as thrilling and wonderful as it had been that first time on the roof. But then the melting went deeper, turning into something that was becoming familiar in its own special way. Since the day they'd met, the two of them had been connected, and that connection had endured through everything – through the difference in their classes, through separation, through perceived betrayals, through all of it. But this – *this* – was true union. Not just physically, but in all the ways that counted. They didn't feel the need to prove themselves anymore. Cecily had chosen Daniel. Daniel had chosen Cecily. They had admitted that they were each other's, and that was all they needed to be.

Cecily thought back to the night she had returned to Ad Astra and longed for the quiet at the top of the skyscrapers. She had been miserable then, and lonely, and deeply, deeply afraid. So much had changed in such a brief period of time. Things weren't perfect, but she was happier than she'd ever been in her life. And if there were still dangers and challenges to face, she and Daniel would face them together.

She didn't need a refuge made of metal and glass anymore. Now, she had the stars.

"Come back to bed," Daniel said against her mouth, taking her hand and pulling her along with him.

So she did.

EPILOGUE

IMOGEN

Imogen stepped out into the bitter cold of the alley, letting the stage door bang shut behind her. She paused to light a cigarette, pulled in a deep drag, and let it go with a long, relieved exhale. She allowed herself to just stand there smoking for a minute, not rushing herself to get on her way. It had been a long night, and she was tired, though she knew from experience that it could be much, much worse. The Shooting Star wasn't as posh as the charm schools downtown like the Hierophant and the Casablanca, but it was a sight better than a lot of the other clubs up on the north side of the harbor. Mick, the owner, wouldn't hesitate to toss anyone who groped the waitresses or the talent, and unlike many of the bosses, he didn't have Frankie turn new immigrants away at the door. So if he was a bit stingy with their tips, she was willing to let it slide.

She was gazing up at the few stars that were visible above the city lights when she heard footsteps off to her left. She turned her attention to the dark recesses of the alley just as a deep voice said, "Imogen Parker?"

Imogen dropped her cigarette and crushed it with the toe of her shoe, pulling her handbag closer to her body. It wasn't unheard of for customers to seek her out like this after a show, but they usually came in pairs or groups, young society swells lubricated by cocktails and their wonder at the feats they'd seen onstage. Sweet, really. Like puppies. Now, she could only make out one indistinct figure in the darkness. Tall and broad, in a wide-brimmed hat.

"Yeah, that's me," she said, straining to get a good look at him. "Can I help you?"

Faster than she would have thought possible, he was on her, wrenching her arm as he spun her and pulled her tight against his chest. She had barely even summoned the awareness to struggle before a moist cloth was pressed to her face and she sagged against her assailant. Her eyelids felt unbearably heavy, and though she fought to keep them open, it wasn't long until she succumbed.

The man in the hat gave a short, sharp whistle, and a second man, similarly attired, joined him. Together, they carried Imogen to the end of the alley, where an ambulance waited, engine running. The second man opened the back doors, and they eased her onto the gurney that waited within, strapping her down to keep her secure. When they finished, they separated, each moving around a different side of the auto to reach the front seat and slamming the doors with freshly painted lettering behind them:

Ocean Serenity Sanitarium
Where All Humanity May Flourish
A Partners in Progress Institution

As the final patrons spilled out of the Shooting Star's main entrance, the ambulance pulled into the flow of traffic on the street and disappeared into the night.

The End

The adepts of the Hierophant will return in 2024.

In the meantime, you can sign up for my newsletter to get information about new releases, cool extras, and other fun stuff at www.reneeedwardsauthor.com.

ACKNOWLEDGMENTS

Publishing a novel has been a lifelong dream of mine. The process that brought me here was long and challenging, but I was lucky enough to have the help of the generous, supportive indie author community along the way. To all the writers, podcasters, YouTubers, Facebook groups, and everyone else who shared their expertise, thank you!

I am also forever indebted to my first readers - Nicole Herron, Oakley Hall, and Bethany Hardwick. Thank you all for your time and valuable input! Additional suggestions for the text were provided by Red Adept Editing.

And finally, he already got a dedication, but he deserves a shoutout here, too. Jason has supported me so much through this whole process, even when I was annoying, even when I didn't think I was ever going to make this book happen. Thanks, husband. I love you!

ABOUT THE AUTHOR

Renee Edwards is a lifelong book person and trained librarian. Her favorite books to read are the kind with magic, adventure, and romance, so those are what she set out to write. She fiddles away on her laptop in Texas, where she lives with her husband and her cranky old lady cat.

Visit Renee at www.reneeedwardsauthor.com.